SPACE BALLS

HOUSTON, WE HAVE LIFTOFF

SARA L. HUDSON

Sara L. Hudson

STEAMY. FUNNY. ROMANCE.

ONE

#FUCKLOVE

Rose

FUCK LOVE.

I knock back the rest of my gin and tonic and lean forward over the artfully arranged table setting, propping my chin in my hand.

Fuck 'em.

Through the coral peonies, white hydrangea, and various heights of candles in the table centerpiece, I watch my brother twirl my best friend Jackie around on the dance floor. Flynn's talking to her while smiling widely, probably trying to distract Jackie from counting her steps. And by the dreamy look in my friend's eyes, he's doing a good job.

I take a deep breath, push my palms onto the tabletop, and straighten in my chair.

My brother is happy. My best friend is happy. This is the best possible outcome for two of my favorite people. This is good. No, it's *great*.

I throw up some jazz hands for effect. A couple passing by gives me the side-eye.

Whatever.

Reaching into my cleavage for my flask, all I find is my roll of fifties I keep for emergencies. I pout, remembering that my other bestie, Trish, said my metal flask ruined the line of my bridesmaid dress and made me leave it behind.

Ugh. Propping my chin again, I contemplate all the reasons I should be laughing and smiling with the rest of these yahoos.

I have awesome best friends and two lovable, if moronic older brothers. Who, even if they are in love with each other or someone else, still all love me.

I'm graduating college a whole semester early. With honors.

I have huge boobs, and I know how to use 'em.

Also, I'm ridiculously rich.

I *should* be poised to take on the world. And yet, I'm having a pathetic, chiffon-wrapped pity party for one at the bridal table.

Hashtag first-world problems. Hashtag drama llama. Hashtag get over yourself.

I catch Mike's eye, my brother's partner at the auto shop, and we both nod in greeting. He's sitting next to a pretty brunette two tables over. Of course he is.

I'm happy for them. For *all* of them. Really.

It's just that all this coupledom happened so *fast.* I finally found my ride or die girl posse on my twenty-first birthday. That was only six months ago. Six months and three friends. Then two bothers and a male interloper joined the party, and suddenly I'm the last woman standing.

I've always hated math.

Shimmying my breasts into place for optimal cleavage, I look around for a waiter to bribe into becoming my personal gin-

and-tonic errand boy. Or girl. I'm an equal opportunist to anyone who gets me a drink.

Eyeing the room, I slump back into my cleavage when all the waitstaff circling me are balancing full trays of hors d'oeuvres. No drinks.

This wedding needs to get its priorities straight.

Reaching across the table, I steal the glass of champagne from in front of Trish's place setting and down it in one go.

These glasses are for the bridal toast later. Whatever. Needs must be met and all that.

I steal Ian's champagne glass next, knocking it back, then line it up with the other empties in front of me.

"That's quite a line of dead soldiers you got there."

Blinking my professionally enhanced lashes at the man pulling out the chair next to me, I smile. He may not be offering me a gin and tonic, but if there's one thing that might get me out of my self-pity funk, it's a good-looking man. Especially if he's offering me a different sort of *cock*tail.

I pluck Jules' glass of champagne from in front of him and take a sip. "I was raised that if you're going to do anything, you should do it right. That includes getting drunk."

The man laughs, which does great things for his eyes. Brown eyes the color of that awful-tasting dark chocolate that health experts say is good for you.

He sits, crossing one leg over his knee, angling his body toward mine.

I take another sip, blatantly ogling the man. He has dark, silky hair and long lashes that, as he gives me a long once-over, sweep down toward high cheekbones. Lashes so lush you want to smack him for being born a man.

I cock my head to the side. "Who are you?"

His smile kicks up on one side. A look I'm sure is well-practiced, but nonetheless effective. "I'm Bodie."

I offer the hand not holding my drink. "Rose."

He nods, smile still in place. "I like that name."

I shrug, thankful he didn't say something lame like most men do when I introduce myself. Because let's face it, I'm not delicate like my namesake, and I sure as shit ain't sweet.

"So how do you know the happy couple?" His voice is lazy and low, but still clear over the din of music reverberating around the barn.

"Friend of the bride." I finish the glass. "You?"

"Same."

I frown. "Huh. Didn't think Jackie had that many friends." I raise one brow and look him over again. "Especially man friends."

He mimics my expression. "And why is that?"

Standing, I reach across him and grab Holt's glass, knowing I'm giving him a good showing of the girls in my deep-v bridesmaid dress. Settling back in my seat, I smirk when it takes Bodie a second to lift his eyes back to mine.

"One, because she was too much of a workaholic before she met me to make friends. And two, that man currently twirling her on the dance floor"—I tip my drink at my brother—"would be jealous as hell."

He acknowledges my words with another nod and a smile. His small actions tell me he's a laid-back type, a guy not easily flustered.

They're my favorite kind to mess with.

"I guess it would be more accurate to say that I'm more co-worker than friend." He leans back in his own chair, the fabric of his suit jacket grazing my bare arm. "Though now that Jackie and I are working together more, I'd say it's trending in the friend direction. Hence the wedding invite."

Ah. He's a NASA nerd. Which is surprising, seeing as he

looks more like a Ralph Lauren model than aerospace geek. "And what is it that you *do* at NASA, Bodie?"

It's subtle, but there is a shift in his shoulders, an additional veil of confidence that settles over him. "Astronaut."

I nod—"Cool"—then look over the table for another glass to steal.

In my peripheral vision, I see the veil drop. His once smirking mouth drops open.

I flare my nostrils to keep from laughing and turn toward him again, feigning confusion. "You expecting a bigger reaction?"

He shrugs, looking sheepish. It's cute.

I pluck Flynn's glass by the rim with my fingers and settle back in my seat. "Listen, Bodie." I cross the arm not holding the glass under my chest, squeezing in and up. His eyes drop to my plumped-up cleavage before meeting my eyes once more. I've always known how to work what I got to my full advantage. "Two of my best friends are astronauts. Jackie is a genius and Jules a perverted badass." I sip my stolen drink. "Plus, I just helped my other best friend, a best-selling author, no less, get out of jail." I let the base of the champagne glass rest in the valley of my boobs. "And that doesn't even include all of my impressive attributes, of which there are many." His eyes flicker to my chest again, and I tease him, leaning forward to give him a better view. "If you're aiming for a better reaction, you have to bring more to the table than a job title."

———

Vance

MY NIGHT just got a whole lot brighter.

I take another sip of my drink, but the voluptuous blonde's smile warms my insides much better than the whiskey in my glass. "Not so easily impressed, huh? I guess I'll just have to try harder."

"No need." She tilts her head back, exposing a long column of tanned neck, and swallows the contents.

Watching the muscles contract as she swallows is more fascinating than studying microcosms in microgravity.

Rose smacks her lips, scanning the table for another glass to steal, frowning when she realizes there are none. "Now, tell me. You the kind of guy willing to do what it takes to bring a girl to orgasm?"

My usually quick-witted mind blanks for a moment as I replay what she just said, my own glass halfway to my lips. Then I smile. "Care to find out?"

"No."

"No?" All good feelings leave.

"I don't want to *find out* and be disappointed." She points to her lap. "I'm asking you for an orgasm guaran*tee*."

The scotch I just sipped burns my nose as I laugh, morphing into a cough. "Well then"—I clear my throat, eyes watering—"consider yourself guaranteed."

"Awesome-sauce." She stands up, smoothing down her dress and patting the back of her updo. Quite a few people turn to look.

I have a feeling Rose is a lot like those asteroid showers I used to stay up late to watch when I was kid. From a distance, their paths light up the dark sky, their glow beautiful in contrast. But now that I'm thirty-six and an astronaut, I know the true destructive power of what just one of those burning rocks could do. And yet, all that knowledge doesn't make me any less enraptured by the woman before me.

"So." She places her hands on her hips and looks down at me. "We doing this or what?"

Rose's enticing allure is also making me break one of my hard and fast rules. Which is *never* hook up at weddings. The women attending these things are full of expectations. Turned on by the promise of happily ever after. For a determined single guy like me, hooking up with someone with happily ever after on the brain could be a bachelor death sentence.

So I don't do that.

But *this* girl—I watch her breasts bounce as she gives her neckline a tug—I could break my rules for this girl.

I stand, my head a few inches above hers. "Are the shuttles to the hotels even running yet?"

"Oh, we're not going to the hotel." She grabs my hand and tugs. "That'll take too long."

I stagger forward, easily led by this Southern siren. "Impatient, are we?" We weave through other tables, most empty as the dance floor gets more and more packed.

Rose grabs another champagne flute on her way. "You say I'm impatient, I say I'm an efficient facilitator." When we reach the wall of cream fabric hanging like a waterfall from the rafters, Rose drops my hand and gives me her stolen drink to hold.

I watch, amused, as she feels up the wall of fabrics and fairy lights like she's looking for something.

"Ah ha!" Looking proud as Moses, she parts the fabric, revealing a blocked-off section of barn.

"I'm pretty sure that's blocked off for a reason." I glance to both sides and behind me, but no one seems to be looking. "I don't think guests are allowed."

She rolls her eyes and scoffs before snagging her pilfered glass from my hand. "Didn't know you were such a goody-two-shoes."

That surprises a laugh out of me. "Never been called that before."

Her smile turns sly, and she uses her free hand to trace a finger down the side of my jaw. "I'm pretty sure if you hang with me long enough there will be a lot of never-befores."

Damn she's fun. "I don't doubt it."

The song changes to something slower, and she looks back toward the dance floor, watching as couples get closer, rocking together to the sway of the music. Instead of that dreamy look I'm used to seeing on women at weddings, her face darkens, her light brown brows pinching together.

"What's wrong?"

She starts at my question but recovers, squaring her shoulders to mine. "Nothing's wrong." Her frowning face is now one of determination.

"Your ex out there with someone new or something?" My voice is sharper than I meant, and I don't know why. It shouldn't bother me, the thought of Rose using me to get over someone. If anything, it should make my decision to hook up easier, as Rose won't be hopped up on fairy tales but rather searching for a quick Band-Aid over her heart.

"Please." She gestures to herself. "Like anyone would choose to leave this."

I chuckle, covering the sigh of relief that escapes me.

"All right, enough chit-chat, old man."

"Old man?"

She ignores me and finishes her drink, smacking her lips when she's done. "All you need to know is I'm getting off tonight." She drops her empty glass on the nearest table. "Whether I'm flying solo this mission, or you sack up and help a girl out, I *will* be enjoying the surge of orgasm endorphins." She raises a hand and waggles her fingers.

Once again, my mind stutters as I stare at her raised hand, my imagination running in a lot of dirty, depraved directions.

"Figure out which it's gonna be, old man." She finds the opening, parts the fabric once more, and disappears.

I feel oddly bereft at her sudden disappearance, like the lights just went out. There is something about this girl that draws you in. She's magnetic.

However, as drawn to her as I am, for that very reason, her ducking behind the curtain without me could be the course correction I need. I could wander back to my table, have a few more drinks. Toast the happy couple and leave, just as I planned from the outset. All I have to do is walk away. Play it safe.

I toss back the rest of my drink, set my glass down next to hers, then square up to the curtains.

As an astronaut, when have I ever played it safe? Besides, I'll just tell her I'm heading to Germany in two days for a space-walk debriefing. It's the truth. And hopefully that will stop any round two ideas in her head before they start.

Slipping through the fabric, it takes a minute for my eyes to adjust to the dimness. And then another for my brain to catch up with the sight before me.

There, against the wall, is Rose. A beam of light cuts across her body, illuminating her like a fairy in the moonlight.

A fairy with her hand between her legs.

The heavy fabric drapes swing into place behind me, cutting the noise of the wedding to a dull hum, allowing me to pick up on the whimpers and moans of the woman before me.

Her head is tilted back, her throat exposed once more as her breasts swell against her neckline, fighting their constraints. Her free hand holds her dress up to her hip, allowing her other to dip, swirl, and rub without impediment.

I've watched fiery flames of the sun's corona lick across the Earth only to be plunged into total darkness while flying over seventeen thousand miles an hour in space with only a tether to keep me from spiraling out into the star-scattered abyss of the unknown. But this... *this* is more beautiful than the glow of heat across our planet. And probably just as dangerous.

At her next whimper, I move forward. Her eyes flutter open at the scuff of my shoes across the floor.

A lazy smile lights her face before she closes her eyes once more. "You came." Her voice is breathy, the hand between her legs never stopping.

"I will." One of my hands cups her cheek, and I bend to touch my lips to hers, gentler and more loving than I meant. "But not before you."

And then I do what any man would do before such a fairy. A siren. A harbinger of destruction.

I drop to my knees.

TWO

ONE GIANT LEAP

Rose

I'm glad he waited until I managed to shimmy out of my Spanx before following me back here. 'Cause that would've just been awkward.

Focus. I settle back into the moment, concentrating on what my hand is doing to my clit. But my mindfulness falters when Bodie drops to his knees in front of me.

The light from the outside barn spotlight picks up on the satisfied gleam in his eyes and the flick of his tongue across his lips.

I nearly come.

"Show me." His eyes are focused on my damp hand circling my clit.

Part of me is disappointed. I've been hoping to see what he could do. Wondering if he was all good looks and no sack skills, or if he'd live up to his dreamy potential like so few of them do.

The other part of me mentally shrugs because this means less work for me. Because if he isn't gonna do any work, then I'm not gonna do any when I'm done. He's made his choice. He can just make do with his own hand.

I press three fingers over my clit and rub. Back and forth, stopping only to thrust inside every time I feel close. Enjoying Bodie's rapt attention. Wanting to prolong the moment. Bask in it.

Mr. Astronaut's heavy breathing tells me he's into what he sees. Though he isn't doing anything but holding my dress up higher.

Figures.

Whatever. *Concentrate.*

I rub faster, building the fire in me like the Girl Scout I never was.

So close, just a little more...

Bodie's breath blows over my clit, the cool tingle at odds with the heat building inside.

Bam.

My whole body arches and tightens, and warmth flows through my veins while light dances behind my eyelids. "Fuck fuck fuck fuck fuck."

I love this part, the nearly painful, mind-numbing pleasure. The electric current that shocks my system into a state of happiness I have yet to find anywhere else in my life.

Though Bodie's fingers dig deeper into my hips as I hump the air, my pleasure looking for something to latch on to, the rest of him stays still.

Too soon, the good feelings drift away, the details of my surroundings settling back down on me like a heavy dose of gravity.

The man before me has his eyes raised to mine now. God, they're soulful. He really is one of the most beautiful men I've ever seen.

Too bad he's lazy in bed.

"Okay, old man, you've had your show. Better get off your knees before you can't get back up—what the—!"

Bodie dives forward, sucking at my clit.

"Wait, wait." My fingers sift through his hair, pulling. "I just came!"

But he isn't listening, and neither is my body. Any other time I get greedy and try for a double hitter, my body screams at me.

Bodie has my body screaming in a different way.

I sink back against the wall and let him take control. He does something magical with his tongue that's a combination of a flick and a swish that steals my breath.

He throws one of my legs over his shoulder and thrusts two fingers inside me.

"Fuuuuuuck." My hips start riding his face, my hands, still speared through his hair, holding on for balance.

He growls. Whether it's from the pain of my hair grabbing or pleasure at me being so worked up, I don't know. And frankly, I don't care. Because I'm coming again, and it is ten times more glorious than the first.

If I took a selfie right now, it would probably look like I'm dying, no matter what filter I use.

Hashtag O face.

And I *am* dying. I swear I am. I can't breathe, I can't think. I can only *feel*. Feel his lips sucking my clit. His fingers inside me, curling and pressing over that sensitive spot. His other hand holding up my dress while grabbing hard on to the meat of my hip. Everything feels so. fucking. good.

When my body stops twitching and the leg holding me up starts to give out, Bodie rises, holding me to him, rubbing my back.

I wait for him to say something cocky. Something unnecessary to hammer home the point that he wasn't just all talk. That he made good on his guarantee.

You know, ruin the moment like I would if I were him.

He doesn't.

His silent victory over my lady parts makes him more impressive.

I push Bodie back, a sly smile fixed in place. "Your turn."

———

Vance

"Hmm, where shall we do it?" Rose steps out of my embrace and circles the room.

How she can act like she didn't almost collapse from pleasure is a mystery. *I* can barely move I'm so turned on, and it wasn't even my orgasm.

She slaps a saddle sitting on a sawhorse. "How 'bout it?"

My balls retract just looking at the hard, worn leather saddle. "How 'bout not?"

Rose nods, looking me, and then the saddle, over. "Yeah, that might be pushing it for a man of your age."

"Excu—"

"Honestly, I didn't think you had the cajones to come back here with me, so I didn't exactly think it through."

"I—"

"And I'm not about to lie down on the floor." She spins around. "I mean, I'm sure it's been swept, but I don't trust it." She lifts her eyes from the floor to the ceiling, contemplating.

I give up and just watch her pace. I'm obviously no help. One, I don't know this area like she seems to. And two, the lone stream of light through the window exposes the silhouette of

Rose's body through her bridesmaid gown, making my brain unable to function.

"Big House it is then." Rose stalks over to the curtain dividing us from the rest of the wedding, breaking my stare.

"Big house?" What the hell does a prison have to do with anything?

She continues to ignore me and finds the divide, peeping out into the reception. "We're in the clear. People are still dancing." She opens the curtains wider, scanning the room. "The other bridesmaids are with the groomsmen busy being couples in love, so no one will look for me for a while." From the tone of her voice, I'd bet money she's rolling her eyes. "I'll go first, then you follow after." She steps out, calling out over her shoulder, "Meet you on the porch."

"What porch?" But my words hit the curtains, which are falling back into place.

I've been left alone, in a barn, with a hard-on.

I adjust myself, sighing when no matter which leg hole I put it in, my dick still wants to jut out. Suit pants really aren't helping the situation. Shrugging out of my jacket, I drape it over my arm and walk with it held in front of me. The thought of walking into the wedding like this, like a pre-pubescent kid in high school, makes me want to rethink the saddle option.

Luckily, just as Rose said, no one is looking toward the back of the barn. Almost all the guests are on the dance floor doing the electric slide. Even Chief Astronaut Luke Bisbee, nearly seven feet tall, is rocking back and forth to the music, making everyone else look like his minions.

A flurry of coral fabric draws my eye to Rose at the door. She's waving her arm at a passing waiter.

Trying to look nonchalant so as not to draw attention to myself but walk fast enough to get out of here before someone spots me covering up my hard-on, I follow in Rose's wake.

Successfully flagging down the waiter, Rose scoffs and gestures to the bridal table. "Can you believe some asshole drank all the bridal table's champagne?"

The waiter, holding a tray of bacon wrapped asparagus, gawks at her. Probably because she's reaching into her cleavage as she speaks.

"I know, right." Rose rolls her eyes. "Some people." Her hand emerges, holding a roll of fifties. "But we can't let the bridal table go without champagne, can we?" She puts her non-money holding hand around the waiter, drawing him in like a close friend.

"Good man." She flutters her lashes. "I knew I could count on you." Pulling back, she pats him on the shoulder, and the poor kid nearly drops his asparagus. "Better just bring a whole bottle on ice for the table, huh?" Rose peels off two fifties, setting them down between hors d'oeuvres.

As soon as the fifties drop onto his tray, the waiter snaps to. "Yes, ma'am. I'll get right on it." And without waiting for a reply, he scurries away, nearly bowling over another waiter, this one with shrimp cocktails.

She turns to me with such force her skirt flares out, and I back up a step, worried she may damage my still hard junk. I thought my dick would've calmed down by now, but watching this girl walk, talk, take control, and hell, just go about her life has me just as hard as I was before.

"Have you ever heard of subterfuge, Bodie?"

"Excuse me?"

She rolls her eyes. "Good thing all the love birds are still distracted by classic eighties line dancing." She grabs my arm not holding my jacket in front of me and leads me out the door. "Might as well just go out together. But if someone sees me and I have to explain why I was walking to the Big House with you, I'm not going to be happy."

This is new. Someone who *doesn't* want to be seen with an astronaut.

I find that amusing rather than off-putting.

In fact, I'm so busy musing on how different this hook-up has gone in contrast to all my other hook-ups that I don't even register where we are going.

Until we reach the porch of the West mansion.

Rose leaps up the steps and hurries to the front door. I'd be impressed with the flawless landing in her high heels if I wasn't worried about where we are.

I pause on the step she jumped over. "You aren't serious, are you?"

She stops, screen door half open. "About what?"

"Do you seriously want to break into the West mansion to have sex?"

She opens her mouth, then closes it, a smile curling up her face. The spotlight out front highlights the dimple in her left cheek. "No, old man, *we're* breaking into the West mansion to have sex." And with that, she pushes open the front door, once more leaving me to follow.

I run a hand down my face, both amused and annoyed with myself. Because I know myself well enough to know that there is no way I'm not entering. Muttering, "One giant step for me, one giant leap for my dick," I enter the 'Big House.'

THREE

#SUCKERFORME

Rose

BREAKING INTO THE WEST MANSION. I snort, lifting my dress high so I don't trip over it as I climb the stairs. Although I introduced myself as Jackie's friend, I figured he'd know who I am. Or at least who I'm related to. But I guess it's payback for not caring he's an astronaut.

"Come on, old man," I call down the stairs when Bodie enters the house and closes the door behind him.

The first stair creaks under his weight.

"And be quiet. We don't want to get in trouble. I've already been arrested twice this year."

"What?" His expression, shadowed in the dark, is priceless.

This is fun. Now I can see why Flynn didn't tell Jackie about being a West at the start of their relationship.

"I'm kidding." I reach the top of the stairs and unzip the side of my dress. "Or *am* I?"

His response is cut off when I push the dress off my shoulders and let it drop, the chiffon pooling around my feet. Thanks to the discarded Spanx in the barn, I'm standing in only a nude lace bra and high heels. Since he doesn't comment on my lack of panties, there's no reason to tell him about the sweaty compression garment I left hanging on a nail in the tack room back in the barn. Let him think I went commando.

When he finishes picking his jaw up off the floor, he glances over his shoulder toward the door. "What if someone comes?"

"I guess we'll have to be quick then, huh?" I step out of my dress and saunter down the hallway to the guest room. No need to take him to my room, where something might tip him off to who I am. It's fun playing stranger danger.

My ass and boobs jiggle as I walk, but I've come to realize men appreciate the jiggle. I lean against the guest room door frame and look back.

Bodie's on tiptoe, carrying my dress.

I giggle.

He scowls. "This may be my first time breaking and entering, but I know you're not supposed to leave evidence at the scene of the crime."

I reach out to take it from him, but he holds it out of reach. "I don't actually want you to put it back on. I'm not stupid." He tosses it over his shoulder and walks toward me, backing me into the room.

I let him, knowing just how far in the bed is but pretending to be surprised when my legs bump into it, falling back onto my elbows a bit more dramatically than needed.

"Careful." He tosses the dress on the bench at the foot of the bed, along with his suit jacket, and leans over me.

I'm so sure he's going to kiss me I close my eyes. But he doesn't.

"Shit." The weight dips as he pushes off the mattress.

I open my eyes to see him closing and locking the door.

I tilt my head, enjoying the nervousness radiating off a man used to strapping himself on top of two million pounds of rocket fuel. "Are we safe now?"

"Who knows, but at least we won't be caught ass out if one of the Wests decides to retire early."

"Retire early?" I snort. "I was joking before, but seriously, how old *are* you?" I only called him old man because usually astronauts are in their thirties at the start of their career. Which isn't old, but it's definitely old*er* than me.

He pulls his tie free. "For God's sake, I'm not old." In a few short tugs, his buttons are undone and his shirt pulled from his trousers. And holy moly how did I not notice the elephant in the room until now?

And by elephant, I mean his dick.

'Cause it is pointing right at me, and even under the restriction of wool gabardine, it's impressive.

I lick my lips. "That for me?"

If a sigh, a grunt, and a growl had a baby, that would be the sound Bodie makes, his eyes lasered on my lips.

"Don't stop now." I nod toward his pants.

He shrugs the rest of the way out of his dress shirt, revealing tanned, toned abs and a gloriously dark happy trail that make me calling him old man comical. I bite my lip in anticipation of the main reveal as he toes out of his shoes and undoes his belt.

Did you ever have a sixth sense about something? Like you just knew something good or bad was about to happen? Like when you find yourself drunk in the backseat of a shitty Honda driven by a blonde with glasses and you just feel all will be right with the world? Or when your brother's ex-girlfriend shows up at the bar and you know shit is about to go down? And by go down, I mean getting handcuffed and having to call your lawyer. You know, a street-smart premonition power?

No? Well, whatever. I have that feeling now. Like, as soon as Mr. Astronaut reveals his dick, my life is going to be changed forever. I push up off my elbows and unhook my bra, wanting to be ready for whatever life-changing event is about to take place. My roll of fifties and a condom fall to the bedspread.

But instead of dropping trou, the damn man stands stock still, staring at my boobs.

I don't really get the power of boobs. I mean, I wield it, because, duh, who wouldn't? It's like a God-given female power play to balance out the patriarchy. But I still don't get it. Like, how are fat orbs that are milked to feed children a sex organ?

"Damn." It's Bodie's turn to lick his lips.

I widen my legs, beckoning him over. And thankfully he doesn't hesitate because these heels are heavy as hell, and I don't have the ab strength to hold them up very long.

He puts his hands under my arms and lifts me, dragging me farther onto the bed. He doesn't even grunt at my weight.

That's hot.

Head lying upon the pillows, I'm caged in, Bodie braced above me, our mouths inches apart.

It hits me that we haven't even kissed yet. At least not lip to lip on his part. And, for some reason, that makes me sad.

Taking charge, I reach up, running my hands though his hair, my nails raking over his scalp. He closes his eyes and moans.

Promising myself I'll pay more attention to core work in the future, I crunch up and kiss him.

My first thought is how thankful I am he kept his eyes shut and didn't see me struggle.

My second is how soft his lips are.

Quickly followed by third, which it isn't so much that his lips are soft, but rather the actual kiss is tender. Sweet. At odds with what I thought it was going to be—hard and dirty. I melt into it.

I send a prayer of thanks when he melts into it as well,

laying me back down and settling his weight between my legs and on top of me. Both my hoo-ha and weak abs thank him.

On a breath, he moans, or maybe I do. Our light movements, tongues, and delicate nips with teeth are so in sync that I can't even tell who's doing what. This kiss takes me out of my head, away from my constant refrain of frantic thoughts and self-doubt.

This kiss is so different from any other kiss, it might as well be my first.

I like it. But I also don't.

It's too... something.

Mentally, I pull back. Physically, I reach down and finish undoing his pants, cursing him when I have to lift my legs up again so I can use my heels to help push the waistband down over his butt.

Blindly, I reach out with my left hand and find the condom.

"In a hurry?" Bodie trails kisses down my neck, his movements still soft and tender.

I use my mouth to tear the corner of the package. "If you're not, I'm gonna get offended."

"Oh, I'm in a hurry, but I also want to enjoy every minute." He sucks on the peak of my breast, his tongue flicking over the nipple. Forgetting what I said about boobs being lame sex organs, I moan, almost dropping the condom.

An odd panic begins to build inside me. Like if I let myself lose control, get lost in his touch, I'll be allowing an intimacy to grow that I've never felt with another one-night stand—hell, that I've never felt ever.

I squeeze his dick hard.

"Jesus." His forehead drops to my collarbone, his shoulder muscles tensing like he's fisting the covers.

Taking the reprieve from his mouth, I slide the condom on.

It takes longer than usual, and just as I suspected, his dick is life-changing. Girthy.

I'm both disappointed and relieved I don't set eyes on it.

He takes my mouth with his again, this time more aggressive, as if I've pushed him to the edge. Instead of a sense of relief at the lack of tenderness, the panic continues to grow.

Planting my heels in the bed, I push up, thrusting his dick inside me.

Both of us freeze. Him surprised, me impaled.

Holy hard cock.

Bodie finds his voice first. "Did you just top me from the bottom?"

In answer, I practice my kegels.

"Fuuuuck." He rises up, pushing his weight into his forearms on the bed, the movement settling him even deeper inside me.

His cock might break me in two.

It would be a glorious death.

After a beat, Bodie begins to move, and I lower my heels, letting him take over.

But the slamming and pumping I expect doesn't come. He circles, presses, undulates. Sex with this guy is like riding a wave, the tide threatening to take me under.

The rise of a new orgasm pulses where his pelvis rubs against me. It is scary how badly I want that pleasure to take over me while we're connected. To just let him take control, to give myself over to it.

Hooking my right heel over his hip, I push off with my left, rolling him onto his back.

Once settled on top, I look down, surprised I don't have a six-pack from all my efforts or that his dick didn't rupture my cervix.

Instead I feel full in a very, very good way. And I'm in control. The way I like it.

And by the way Bodie's eyes focus on my ta-tas once more, I'd say he likes it too.

Bracing my hands on his shoulders, I fuck him. There really isn't any other word for it. Up, down, up, down.

Bodie's fingers pinch my nipples, grab my ass, rub my clit. While I fuck him he's doing ALL the things.

Damn it's good. So good.

My eyes roll back in my head, the pleasure about to erupt between us.

————

Vance

"Rose? Rose, are you up there?"

Both of our eyes fly to the bedroom door. Her seated position has my dick rubbing the front wall of her vagina, which clenches in surprise from the interruption.

"It's the wedding planner," Rose whispers, not looking all that concerned.

I would've thought the panic at being caught breaking and entering into someone's house to have sex would make me soft, but with Rose clenching down around me, plus her grabbing her own breasts, the weight of them spilling out the sides of her hands, I'm pushed over the edge.

I tense, all my muscles flexing as I buck beneath her. Her knowing smirk as she pinches her nipples only elongates my orgasm.

"Rose?" The voice gets closer.

Covering my mouth with her hand as my dick twitches

inside of her, Rose calls out toward the locked door, "Yeah, I'm here. What's up?"

"Oh thank God." From the echo in her voice it sounds like she's on the stairs in the foyer. "It's time for the toasts." The clack of heels tells me she's on the landing.

A drop of sweat beads at my temple.

"Okay, no worries." Rose scratches her nose. "I'll be right down."

"Great." More clacking, only this time the noise fades.

Rose gets up, my well-used dick sliding out of her.

"And, uh, could you get Trish too?" The wedding planner's voice echoes around the foyer. "She's, ah, in the trailer with Ian."

"Probably getting to finish what I didn't," Rose mutters, standing and snagging her bra from the bed. "Yeah, I'll take care of it," she yells.

My brain fires past the panic, thinking back play-by-play of what just happened. Embarrassment overcomes fear of being caught.

Rose didn't orgasm.

"I—"

"Well, old man." Rose snaps her bra clasp in front of her then spins it around her body, looping her arms in the straps. "It's toast time." She pulls it up, her boobs settling in the cups. "Time to go."

Worried the wedding planner is still in the house, I lift my hips, sliding up my pants that I never fully took off. "Isn't she worried about what you're doing in here?" Swinging my legs off the side of the bed, I sit, cringing when the used condom hits my leg.

"Nah. I'm planning on sleeping here tonight, so it's not too out of the ordinary for me to be here." She steps into her dress, pulling it up.

I pause in standing. "And you didn't think to tell me that *before* we got here?"

Her dimple pops. "Nah, it was fun letting you think we were breaking the law." Her dress flares out as she turns and walks to what I suspect is the en suite bathroom. She comes back out dressed and looking none the worse for wear, except maybe her hair is wilder than before, and tosses a tissue box on the bed. "Here." She gestures to my crotch. "You can't go back to the wedding like that."

I glance down at the wet stain on my dress slacks. "Shit."

She laughs. It's contagious enough to have me smiling.

That is, until she grabs her roll of fifties from the bed and slaps two of them in my hand. "A little something to help you get home, be it Uber or shuttle driver bribe."

I stare stupidly at the money. I'm trained to think on my feet in life-or-death situations, but Rose makes me feel slow, like my brain is moving through microgravity. "But you didn't even—"

"Orgasm?" She nods, frowning. "Yeah, that sucks." She reaches in her neckline and adjusts her breasts before sticking the rest of her money between them.

"Still, I—"

"But you got me good earlier, so no worries." She walks to the door, turning to finger-gun me. "Later." And then she's gone.

Shocked, whether from being treated like a male escort or from witnessing someone actually using finger guns, I stare at the open doorway.

What the hell just happened?

FOUR

STELLAR PARALLAX

Vance

"Bodie, you with me?"

"Hmm?" Blinking, I break away from the view of Munich, Germany outside the large window and glance around the room. The whole of the European Space Agency EVA team is looking at me. *Shit.*

ESA lead Sebastian DuMont frowns. "I was wondering about the connectors."

Connectors? I have no idea what he's talking about. I was too busy thinking of coral chiffon and finger guns.

Clearing my throat, I try to think of how to stall for time.

Luckily, Ian shifts forward in his seat, drawing the group's attention to him. "Personally, I think there will be plenty of slack in the cabling to route and wire-tie cleanly before mating the connectors."

"Yes, that's right." I throw Ian a grateful smile. He raises one questioning brow but doesn't say anything, which is one of the many things I like about working with Ian. He and I have worked together here and there over the years, but now that he's been promoted to EVA director, we'll be working a lot of the same projects.

Even so, as the group continues their discussion on the order of operations, I curse myself for being distracted. I'm on point for this spacewalk mission to build out Bartolomeo, the International Space Station's first outside payload hosting platform.

As a mechanical engineer and scientist, I'm excited that the spacewalk on the outer payload hosting platform is right in my wheelhouse. I've been waiting for such a moment to highlight my special skill sets.

It never once bothered me being second to Julie Starr or whoever the point man was on the spacewalks. I mean, I was going out into *space*, what did I care whether I was calling the shots or following them? But ever since they named me lead on Bartolomeo, I've been looking forward to being more than a helping hand or a 'gloried flashlight,' as Jules likes to joke.

And now I'm letting myself get distracted by a one-night stand.

True, it was an *epic* one-night stand. But still.

"ESA is on board with all the safety checks," Sinan, my European counterpart, declares, helping the meeting come to a close.

At the start of this trip to Germany, I spent my off-time going to beer gardens with Sinan. And although Sinan is one hell of a wingman, the image of the busty blonde leaning back against the barn wall with her hand under her gown just won't quit. Not even the local Fräuleins could scrub the image from my memory.

Astronauts are explorers at heart. So it makes sense that I love to figure out the who, what, when, where, and why of things. Maybe if I just find out more about Rose, I can satisfy my curiosity and stop replaying our time together.

The last slide of the presentation goes up on the screen, and I glance at it, making sure I know what's going on. When I'm sure I won't be caught off guard again, I pick up my pen and start working on the Rose problem.

All I have is a first name, she's friends with Jackie, and she was a bridesmaid.

I write *Rose, bridesmaid, Jackie's friend* and *West family guest* on my notepad. I try and think of something else, but I don't think *roll of fifties in her cleavage* or *likes to go commando* is going to help me out here. I drop my pen and pinch the bridge of my nose.

It was only supposed to be one night. As such, I made it a point that night not to ask more about who she was at the wedding. Keep the mystery and all that.

Reading over my notes, I'm seriously regretting that decision right now.

The screen goes black, and the meeting winds down. I catch Ian eyeing the paper in front of me and quickly shuffle stuff on top of it. I guess I could ask him; his girlfriend was a bridesmaid too. But it's rather embarrassing asking one co-worker if they know the full name of the girl you cut out of your other co-worker's wedding with to have sex.

People talk about what sights to see and where they're going for dinner as they gather their things. Someone brings up a group outing. Even European space agencies like to work hard and play hard, just like NASA.

"What do you say, guys?" Sebastian looks expectantly at Ian and me, trying to get a group together for pub hopping in town.

"Sorry, DuMont, I'm sightseeing." Ian gathers his notes. "My girl wants to check out Frauenkirche."

"Ah, the Cathedral of Our Lady." Sebastian nods. With his longer hair falling into his face and his thick accent, he's quintessentially European. "A great starting point in Old Town for sightseeing." He assesses Ian. "Though I didn't know you had a daughter."

Ian's phone lights up and he grabs it. "I don't," he says, distracted by his text.

I laugh at Sebastian's confusion, and step in for Ian as he did for me. "Kincaid means his girlfriend." I nudge Ian. "Though, who knows, maybe Ian likes to be called Daddy."

"I see." Sebastian laughs with me, but by the look on his face, he doesn't see at all. Some things are just lost in translation, I guess.

Ian doesn't look up as he texts back.

"And what about you?" Sebastian asks me. "*If* you think you can keep up with us Germans, that is."

Ian puts his phone down to gather his notes. His phone is still open to the text screen. Trish's name at the top.

An idea forms.

"Any other day I'd take you up on that challenge, DuMont." I lean back in my chair, hands behind my head. "But I've got plans."

———

"Is this a coincidence or what?"

The look of dismay on Ian's face is priceless as I saunter up to him and Trish exiting the south tower of Frauenkirche, one of the most visited sights in Munich.

"Why, hi-ya, Bodie." In contrast, Ian's girlfriend lights up with a smile when she sees me. "Are you here to see the Devil's footstep too?" She points to where I'm standing.

Glancing down, I grin. I hadn't realized my foot was nearly on top of the tile with the legendary fallen angel boot imprint.

"Something like that." I lean down to greet her, bending over more than I'm used to.

I've only ever seen Trish in sky-high heels, so standing next to her in sightseeing sneakers is a bit of a shock. Even with her hair pulled up in a top-knot, she barely comes up to my shoulder.

Ian quirks a brow at me, much like he did at our meeting.

"We went up the south tower first since a large group of tourists came in before us and were taking pictures of the tile." She thumbs behind her. "You want to go up? We'll wait for you."

"Thanks, but that's okay." I step back out of the way for her to snap a picture of the boot print. "Want me to take a picture of the both of you?"

"Really? That'd be great, sugar." She hands me her camera, and Ian, still looking wary, puts an arm around her.

I hold up the camera and step back, getting them and the boot print in the shot, along with the large arched wooden door in the background. It's a pretty cool picture. "You won't mind if I tag-along with you guys, will ya?" I hand her phone back, trying not to laugh as Ian frowns.

"Of course not." Trish looks at the screen. "Sheesh, babe, why the serious face?"

I have to cough to cover my amusement.

Thirty minutes later, we've seen everything there is to see at Frauenkirche, and Trish excuses herself to the restroom. No sooner does she turn the corner down the hall than Ian faces me, arms crossed.

"All right. What are you really doing here?"

I shrug. "Sightseeing."

"Like hell you are." His words sound annoyed, but he's given away by the smile on his face.

Remembering him looking at my notes, I have a feeling Ian

knows exactly why I'm here. I play dumb, leaning against the church pillar. "This is a beautiful church. A top sight to see in Munich."

"So this has nothing to do with you hearing me tell DuMont where I was going?"

I shrug.

"Uh huh. So why haven't you taken one picture while 'sightseeing'?" The man air quotes me.

"Thought you'd appreciate all the pictures I was taking of you and Trish." I look over his shoulder. "Speak of the devil."

Trish emerges from the restroom before Ian can call bullshit. When I decided not to ask Ian for help, the next easiest starting place was Trish. Not only is she here in Germany, but she was the one I saw Rose interacting with the most at the wedding. Plus, if I can get her to bring up the subject herself, maybe I can keep my interest quiet.

"Be polite somewhere else," Ian mutters right before Trish reaches us.

"So." She looks back and forth between Ian and me. "Where to now, boys?"

"Why don't we check out New Town Hall?" I gesture to the church exit. "It's only a few minutes' walk from here, and there's a cool astronomical clock in the tower."

"New Town Hall?" Trish asks.

"He means Neus Rathaus." Ian's German dialect is perfect. The guy is annoyingly cool sometimes.

"Oh goody." Trish bounces on her tiptoes in her sneakers. "I wanted to go there."

"Then by all means, shall we?" I offer her my arm. Ian scoffs.

Trish throws her boyfriend a reproving look before praising me with a smile. "Such a gentleman." When she takes my arm, Ian rolls his eyes. It's kind of hilarious to see my normally strait-laced co-worker looking more like a jealous teenager than the grown son of a senator that he is.

Having been here a few times from previous trips, I lead the way out of the cathedral and toward Old Town Center.

Ian's shoes drag on the cobblestones behind Trish and me as we walk down the pedestrian-only street.

"Oh, a hat shop." Trish points to the window front, where mainly traditional German hats are on display. "They even have fascinators." She points to a feathery bright pink tuft of fabric that I'm guessing is what she means. "I didn't know those were worn here too. I thought they were just for British weddings."

Weddings.

"Jackie's wedding was pretty great, huh?" I try for nonchalance, pretending to look at the sights while watching Trish out of the corner of my eye.

Trish closes her eyes and lets out a wistful sigh. "Wasn't it?"

"It must have been a lot of work for everyone, including you bridesmaids."

Ian snorts.

I ignore him.

Turning away from the store front, Trish laughs. "Not really. Between the wedding planner and maid of honor Jules—who'd make a great drill sergeant by the way—Rose and I didn't have much to do."

Before I can celebrate Trish bringing up my target all on her own, Ian steps between us and wraps his arm around Trish's shoulder, throwing me a knowing look. He kisses the top of her head. "Hey babe, show me that picture you took."

I scowl, and he smirks.

Dick.

When Trish is done showing him, she turns the camera for a selfie of her and Ian, kissing his cheek when she clicks.

Ian turns and deepens the kiss.

I give them a second or two before clearing my throat.

Trish pulls back. "Oh." She ducks her head, looking embarrassed. "Sorry, Bodie."

"I'm not," Ian mumbles, nudging me farther out of the way with his shoulder and taking Trish's hand, making me chuckle.

It's nice seeing two people in love. Their kind of love may be something that I've willingly cut out of my present and future, but that doesn't mean I don't appreciate it when I see it. Even if lately it's been making my chest tight.

"Oh, what's that statue for?" Trish skips over to read the placard, pulling Ian along with her.

The rest of the walk through town is easy with Trish's enthusiasm over every tourist sight and quintessential German knickknacks displayed in all the store window fronts.

But after a minute, my mind is back on the Southern blonde with killer finger guns.

"Tomorrow."

"Huh?" I look at Trish, a feeling of déjà vu from being caught not paying attention in the meeting earlier.

Trish tilts her head, her top-knot falling to the side. "I was just saying how tomorrow Ian and I are going to see the castle that inspired Snow White. Isn't that cool?"

"Uh, yeah. Very."

"Maybe it will inspire my next book." Swinging Ian's hand, she looks at me over her shoulder. "You should come with us, Bodie."

Ian nearly chokes to death on his next breath.

Trish pulls her hand free and pats Ian on the back. "You okay, baby?"

Ian controls his breathing while I try and control my laughter. "Yes," Ian says, giving me a warning look. He clears his throat. "Yes. Fine. Just, ah, thought Jackie might like something from over there." He waves toward a shop window. "I know you've been trying to find souvenirs for the girls."

"Cool." Trish fairly bounces over to the shop.

"You are *not* coming with us tomorrow." Ian's voice is low as he keeps his eyes on Trish, who's staring intently at a window display of what seems to be a jewelry-slash-figurine store.

"I don't know." I rock back on my heels. "Looking at fairy tale-inspiring sights could be my new hobby." I feel bad for messing with him, but he so obviously has something planned for tomorrow, it's too hard not to tease him.

He looks panicked. "I—"

Trish runs into Ian's side, pulling on his arm. "Sugar, you're a genius. They have Hummels. And not just *any* Hummel. They have two with a little boy looking through a telescope!" She pulls again, tugging him toward the store. "Help me pick out the best one for Jackie. It will go perfect in her new office Flynn set up for her."

Once Ian's legs start moving, she lets go and jogs into the shop, expecting Ian to follow.

Instead, he stops, turns, and puts a hand on my chest, holding me back.

I rub my sternum after he drops his hand. I may have pushed the man too far.

But instead of threats or violent curses, he takes out his phone. In a few seconds, my own phone dings.

"There." Ian pockets his as I take mine out. "That's Rose's contact information."

I catch myself smiling and shrug, trying to play it off. "I don't know why you sent me that. Who says I need her number?"

Ian scoffs. "Please."

"You coming, sugar?" Trish calls from the store's doorway.

A large smile on his face, Ian waves. "Be right there, baby."

When he turns to me, it melts off his face. "I swear to God, Bodie, if you follow me into that store, or even think of coming to Neuschwanstein Castle with us tomorrow, I will make life hell for you."

Secretly, I'm triumphant. I should leave them to their souvenir hunting and get back to the hotel. Maybe catch Sinan before he heads out to the pubs. But messing with Kincaid is fun.

Shrugging, I take a step around him toward the store. "I don't know. Castles are pretty cool. And I've never been that far south before." I stop and throw a smirk at him, as he did to me earlier. "Might want to check it out."

Ian's eyes narrow.

"Besides, you care too much about the job." I nudge his shoulder, chuckling. "You don't have it in you to mess with me at work." And he doesn't. The man crosses every T and dots every I. There's a reason he was promoted.

Ian raises one eyebrow. The look of a man with a trump card up his sleeve. "Why do you assume I meant at work?"

A sense of foreboding hits me. "Then what are you talking about?"

"I hear your mother is a real ball buster." Ian rocks back on his heels. "Thanks to one Miss Jules Starr, I happen to know what a Mamma's boy you are."

Fucking Starr. She met my mother once and has been obsessed ever since. Calling my mother her hero. Why, I don't know. They couldn't be more different. One is a career-minded astronaut with a penchant for perverted jokes, the other a retired teacher and longtime single mom who loves to cook.

But what Jules said is true: I do look after my mom. One, because that's what any good son does, and two, since losing Dad while he was serving in the Army, I've taken great pains to try and fill the void.

I give my co-worker, whom I have severely underestimated, a wary once-over. "What exactly are you threatening me with, Kincaid?"

When Ian smiles at me, I can see the political upbringing in him. There's a lot happening behind that smile. "Let's just say I happen to have access to a certain Mrs. Bodaway's phone number." He wiggles the phone in his hand. "I'm sure she'll appreciate a call. Tell her how helpful her son is being getting in between a man and his proposal plans."

"You'd call my mother?" My mind stalls and mouth drops open. "Wait. You're *proposing* tomorrow?"

"Shh!" Ian steps forward, covering my mouth with his hand, and looks over his shoulder at the shop.

I may have yelled that last part.

When Trish doesn't come running out of the store in hysterics about him proposing, Ian sighs in relief. It takes him an extra second to realize how ridiculous the two of us look, one man holding his hand over another man's mouth.

He jerks his hand back.

I move my mouth around, trying to erase the feel of Ian's palm. "First, well played with my mom, Kincaid."

He fights a smile but loses.

"And second, congrats man, that's awesome." I stick out my hand.

He shakes it, the smile on his face growing. I've never seen him so openly happy before. It must feel great to let yourself fall in love.

"Thanks, man." His lips twist to the side, like he's thinking. "I mean, we kind of already agreed to get married, but I'm not sure if that really counted."

I laugh. "Don't tell me you asked during sex?"

The look he gives me has my jaw dropping. "Are you serious?" Who would've thought Kincaid could be so spontaneous?

"Shut up." He nudges my shoulder, pushing me a step down the street. "And get the fuck out of here."

I laugh some more but nod.

Satisfied, Ian walks to the shop, throwing a hand up to wave as he goes. "I'll tell Trish you can't make it tomorrow."

"Yeah, yeah." Still smiling and shaking my head, I walk toward the bus stop. Leaning against the stand, I open my phone and thumb over to text messages, feeling quite pleased with the turn of events.

Ian's going to go down with one of the coolest proposals of all time, and I'm one more step closer to figuring out who Rose is. One more step to getting her out of my system—luscious curves, finger guns, and all.

Then I'll be able to give all my attention to the upcoming mission. No distractions.

I tap the contact bubble Ian sent, Rose's name popping up on my screen.

Rose West.

West? Why does that...

Recognition hits, and the smile melts off my face. *Fuck.*

The bus's brakes squeal, the sound intensifying the hollow feeling in my gut while my mind tries to reconcile to the truth.

Holy shit. I banged a billionaire.

FIVE

#LOTUS

Rose

ONE PERK about being a billionaire is that you can be eccentric, and people don't bat an eye.

Like coming to see your college advisor in a turquoise leotard, fishnets, rainbow leg warmers, stripper heels, and a not-so-thin veil of body glitter.

"Have you thought any more about the MBA program?" My advisor, John Mallory, taps his fingers on his desk. He is forever tapping his fingers on his desk. I think it's an anger management strategy he picked up somewhere. But I love it, and secretly I love him for sticking with me. I'm not easy to stick with, just ask my mom, my dad... oh wait, you can't, because they left.

But John has stood the test of time. The test of time being three and a half years. So kudos, John, kudos.

I recross my legs, my feet heavy from the thick acrylic heels. Glitter rains down on the chair and carpet.

More finger tapping.

"I have." Honestly, I'll probably register to get my MBA, if only because I haven't a clue what else to do with my life.

John's fingers stop tapping, and he actually smiles, launching into a well-practiced sales pitch. "Rice University has one of the most selective MBA programs in the country. The smaller size allows for faculty and students to work together more intimately and cover a more exclusive, detailed curriculum." He brings both hands together as if in prayer and tips them toward me. "The program would be an excellent choice for you, seeing as you'll be working at West Oil soon."

But will I?

Holt's working the ranch side of the West family business while starting a non-profit, and Flynn's busy growing his car restoration company and planning to be a stay-at-home dad whenever Jackie and he decide to have kids and she launches into space. Both my brothers have made it pretty clear that it isn't actually necessary for a West to work nine to five at West Oil.

Glancing over John's shoulder, I can just see the Houston skyline. If I squint, maybe I'll be able to see the West Oil building, situated uptown. Right by my penthouse condo.

"Miss West?" John frowns, then looks over his shoulder to see what I'm staring at. He turns back, confused.

I lean forward and prop one elbow on my advisor's desk. "Hmm?"

John sighs at my antics, all too used to them at this point. Poor man should've been given a raise when he was assigned as my advisor. "Rose, you already know everything I'm saying right now. We've had this talk a million times. But your decision really comes down to one thing." He looks at me expectantly.

I've got nothing, but I smile nonetheless. When in doubt, smile and flutter your lashes. "And that would be?"

He blinks but shakes it off. "What is it that you *want*?"

I sit back, thinking. A fine sheen of glitter remains on his desk where my arm was. "What do I want?" I repeat the words back to him slowly.

He nods.

My mind blanks.

Huh. Isn't that the billion-dollar question? I don't think anyone's ever asked me what I want. I don't even think *I've* ever asked myself the question. I mean, I'm a billionaire, I have everything. Right?

Lately I've been obsessing over what I *should* do. How to live up to all the expectations. How to not disappoint while hopefully making a difference with my life and all its privileges.

But what I *want*? I don't think I've thought about my future in those terms before.

John raises his brows at my silence, looking pleased with stumping me.

"I have everything I want." It sounds more like a question than a statement.

"Yes, but what is it you want to *do*?"

"I..." I've got nothing.

I'm saved from awkward silence when my boob vibrates. Reaching into my cleavage, I pull out my phone and shut off the reminder alert.

I shake off the feelings of uncertainty that have been plaguing me for months and that John just made worse. "At the moment this girl wants to go learn how to pole dance." I shove my phone back in my boobs and stand, a living disco ball.

I leave to the sound of his fingers drumming across his desk.

————

Vance

I'm TAKING my mother to a strip club.

My flight had barely touched down on the runway when she called. And it wasn't to ask how my trip to Germany went. No. It was to tell me she needed a ride. To a strip club.

It's my fault really. I left her too long without a call or visit.

So when she called, the guilt was already there to lay on, making it impossible for me to say no. And now here I am, jet-lagged, irritated, and guilted, pulling my 4Runner into the near empty parking lot of Heartbreakers.

A few cars from people too drunk to drive home last night are scattered like stars in the night sky. One in particular catches my eye. A gold Aston Martin. What idiot leaves a car like that in a strip club over night?

"There's a spot."

I say nothing, just raise my eyebrows at my mother and her outstretched arm thrusting toward one of the many parking spots available. But if she wants that one, then that one it will be. "Thanks." I nod and pull in.

Mom smiles.

I've learned not to argue with my mother. It's useless. Probably what makes me such a good fit to work with Jules in space. Between my mother and older sister, I'm used to being around commanding women. I pause after throwing the gear shift in park. Huh. Maybe *that's* why Jules likes my mom so much.

Shaking my head at the thought, I hop out.

Like every time I drive my mother, I circle the front of my car to open her door for her. The small, old-fashioned gesture reminds me of my dad. Whether it's from time passing or how young I was when he died, I only have a few memories of him. But I do remember waiting in the backseat on multiple occasions, watching him circle the car to open the passenger side door for my mother. It fascinated me.

Although, if he'd had to help my mom out while she wore platform stripper shoes, I probably would've been scarred instead.

Once my mom's steady on her teetering shoes, I hold out my arm for her to take.

"Helen?"

I glance up, my chin dropping to my chest.

Rose, *my* Rose, the woman I haven't been able to purge from my mind, or found the stones to text or call, is... is standing there. Dressed like Mom, but with higher platform heels, way less clothing, and a lot more glitter.

My mother beams. "Rosie, dear. So glad you made it today." She steps forward, frowning when I don't move.

I try clearing my throat, but it doesn't help me speak. My eyes feel ten times their size as I take in her blue spandex one-piece that clings to all her curves. At least, I think it's blue. It's hard to tell with the morning light reflecting off her like a disco ball due to the copious amounts of body glitter.

But whereas I can't seem to look away from her, Rose can't be bothered to spare me a glance. Instead she plants her hands on her belted waist and narrows her eyes at Mom. "And just *how* do you know Bodie?"

"Bodie?" My mother's eyes ping-pong between Rose and me. "You mean Vance?"

That pulls Rose up short. I'd laugh if it wasn't for the brief flash of hurt I saw cross her face. "Vance?"

"We met at Jackie's wedding," I say, finally finding my voice. "She's the groom's sister."

Rose's eyebrows shoot up. "Finally figured it out, huh?"

I shrug, not wanting to admit that I couldn't get her off my mind. Especially since it's clear she hadn't felt the same since she doesn't even know Bodie's my nickname.

I mean, it's not like I was looking for a stalker, but I thought I left enough of an impression that she would've asked someone about me like I asked about her.

I nod at her stiffly. "Yep."

Her lips purse in annoyance.

"Well, isn't that lovely." My mother steps forward, ignoring the hostility radiating off Rose, and trades my arm for hers. "Come on now. Let's not keep Angela waiting."

If anyone had told me that on my first day back from Germany I'd be following my mother and the last woman I brought to orgasm into a strip club bright and early on a Sunday, I'd have thought they were crazy.

And yet here I am. So who's the crazy one now?

———

MY POINTER FINGER on my right hand is slightly longer than the one on my left. Fascinating? No, of course not. But my hands are a safer place to look than at the stage where my mother is stretching out in different yoga positions in acrylic shoes and yoga pants.

Out of the corner of my eye, I track a pair of sparkling heels walking toward me. They stop less than a foot from my table, one toe tapping the dingy carpet.

"What are you doing here?"

I smile at her annoyed tone. "What are *you* doing here?"

She huffs. "I'm taking pole dancing lessons. Duh."

"Who even takes pole dance lessons?"

"Who fake names someone at a wedding?" She snaps back. "Besides, I wouldn't look down on pole dancers." She crosses her arms under her chest, smirking. "Your *mother* is one."

A chill races down my spine, and I shiver. "Bodie's a nickname. Vance *Boda*way."

She scoffs. "What, you gave me your nickname in case I turn into a stage-five clinger?"

I smile remembering that line from the movie *Wedding Crashers*. "Well, *are* you?"

She thinks it over. "When needs must."

I frown, expecting a vehement denial. "What does that mean?"

"It means that if I'm in the middle of the lotus position, I'm going to cling for all I'm worth, seeing as the more I do the more my clit gets stimulated."

My mouth drops open.

"Oh, poor dear. You haven't tried lotus yet?" She pats me on the shoulder, a look of faux sympathy on her face. "Don't worry, maybe one day someone will take pity on your old man ass. Now, if you don't mind, I need to go move my youthful goods around a pole to music." She shimmies, her sparkling cleavage shaking. "So you just sit here like a good boy and keep quiet, hmm?" She adjusts her breasts behind the taut spandex, and my mouth waters. "Your mama and I have to shake and twirl what God gave us."

The reminder that my mother is on a strip stage jars my thoughts away from the various mental images of Rose working her way through the *Kamasutra*. My dick is so confused.

Before I can reply, she saunters over to the stage where Mom is waiting with an older lady in a fuchsia Adidas track suit and a younger woman in a string bikini.

"Hey, Angela!" Rose calls out to the bikini lady on her way to the stage. "Why don't we work on the spread-eagle backbend Helen's been wanting to master?"

And I'm out.

Rising, I tune out the rest of their conversation and make my way to the door. I don't even risk a backward glance at Rose, decked out in Jane Fonda bedazzled workout gear. Nothing can make me watch a class that involves my mother doing anything spread eagle.

Rose's loud cackle is the last thing I hear as I march through the front doors.

SIX

FUTURE LIGHT CONE

Rose

HELEN GIVES ME THE EYE, but I avoid it.

"Wait. *Is* there a spread eagle back bend?" Myra asks, hands out as she tries to balance on sky-high platform shoes. "'Cause that sounds like something I could get into."

"No, Myra." Angela sets up a balance chair next to the pole for the eighty-something-year-old woman. "And for the love of God, please put your sneakers back on. The last thing you need is a broken ankle." She mumbles something about not wanting to be sued under her breath.

Myra's thin red lips pout. "Hmph." But she sits and begins to unstrap her shoes. "I may have been a tad ambitious with this heel height. I'll have to go back to Cindy's and get the lower pair."

The thought of Myra in Cindy's, the local sex toy and apparel shop, is going to keep me smiling for days.

Once Myra's back in sneakers, Angela claps her hands. "Let's start with some stretches."

We all touch our toes. Myra and Helen met in an advanced silver sneakers yoga class, so they breeze through the stretches.

I go through the motions, but my mind is still on Bodie. Or Vance. Whatever the hell his name is.

I hate when one-night stands show up like a bad penny. I mean, the guy said he was more co-worker than friend to Jackie, so I honestly didn't think I'd see him unless it was at some NASA sanctioned event. And considering how the last NASA event I went to ended up with me in the back of a police car, I hadn't been planning on attending many more. Which meant he *should* have been a relatively safe choice.

"How do you know my Vance, Rosie?" Helen asks, her long, dark braid swinging forward as she places her leg on the chair seat and bends forward as graceful as any ballerina. She's aged that way too, if she's old enough to be Vance's mother. They don't look much alike, Helen far more delicate and feminine than her son, but their coloring is the same.

I stand, swaying a bit as the blood rushes away from my head. I've been so caught up in my thoughts I hadn't realized we'd moved on to a new stretch.

Myra, sitting on the ground doing a butterfly stretch, leans back and gives Helen a sly smile. "Ooo, I smell a story, Rosie."

Helen and Myra are the only ones I let call me Rosie. In my opinion, if you've spent the majority of your life paying your dues and your taxes to Uncle Sam, you're entitled to say whatever the fuck you want.

I drop my three-pound heel on the chair in front of me with a thunk and bend over it.

"Apparently they met at a wedding." Helen's tone is way too nonchalant to be normal.

"Oh?" Myra draws out the sound. "Is that right?"

Every marriage-aged person would be able to hear the tone and hidden meaning in that seemingly innocuous syllable. I may only be twenty-one, but in Texas, a lot of people count that as settle-down time.

Taking a breath and letting it out, I keep my eyes focused on the glitter floating in the platform of my heels. "I already boinked him, guys. I'm not going back for more." That may be TMI for Vance's mother, but I need to nip this in the bud now before any matchmaker machinations start forming in their minds.

However, it is a testament of just how awesome my retiree friend posse is that they don't flinch. Not even Helen.

Instead, she throws a glare in the direction of the door Vance just left through that would make any grown man wary. "Don't tell me my son doesn't know how to please a woman." She pulls her leg off the chair and places her hands on her hips, looking like a petite general of war. "I already had the sex talk with him when he was fourteen, after I caught him in my kitchen with his hand up Minnie Frey's blouse."

I bite my lip at that mental picture.

"I even made him take notes."

I give up and laugh, straightening beside the chair. "If I ever have kids, I'm totally doing that. You're total mom-goals, Helen."

That gets a smile out of her. "My in-depth and detailed talk ensured he was safe, knew what he was doing, and that everyone would be happy." Helen's grin turns evil. "Of course having your mother describe what the clitoris is, where it can be found, and how to stimulate it also helped kill whatever pubescent hormones were raging inside him at the time." She folds her chair and moves it to the side of the stage. "Gave me a few more years before I had to worry about him knocking someone up."

I continue laughing, leaning on the back of my chair for

support. "This is why we are friends, Helen. You have so much to teach me about the ways of adulting. You're a genius."

"You're doing fine on your own, Rosie. You just need to have more confidence in yourself."

I scoff. "Not to question your wisdom, Helen, but no one has ever accused me of lacking in confidence." I gesture to my tight, sequined spandex attire before folding up my chair. "Case in point."

"Rosie, Rosie. I'm not talking about confidence in your body, I'm talking about confidence here." She taps where my heart would be, making my left boob jiggle.

We both bite our lips to keep from laughing.

"If you two are done feeling each other up, I've got a pole I'm ready to mount." Myra, standing stage left, circles her pole like a boxer waiting for the bell.

Nelly's "Hot in Here" blares from the speakers, and Myra jumps, holding on to the pole with both hands, spinning. She's a blur of fuchsia jumpsuit.

"Myra!" Angela jogs out from the back in her teeny bikini and eight-inch platforms like only a well-seasoned professional can. "I told you to wait for me before you mount." She throws her hands in the air, exasperation written all over her face.

"You're never gonna rein her in, but it's fun to see you try." I glance down at her chest. "Also, wardrobe malfunction."

Without taking her eyes off Myra, who's still in spin mode, Angela reaches down and slides her top back over her nipple. "Thanks. Sorry about that."

"No worries, dear." Helen, more carefully than Myra, places both hands on her pole and spins slowly, coming back to the starting position and stopping after one rotation. "We've all had a nip slip or two in our day."

———

Vance

IF A POLICE CAR comes by right now, I'll probably be arrested.

There's no obvious reason for an adult man to be sitting in his car in the parking lot of a strip club with his head tilted back and eyes closed that isn't perverted. I don't think any officer would believe me if I said I was waiting for my mother to get off her pole.

They'd probably tase me.

Maybe the pain would help my raging attraction to Rose West. In my thirty-six years, I've never had a problem forgetting about one-night stands. As much of an asshole as that makes me sound.

I made the decision years ago. If I was going to have a dangerous job, I couldn't have attachments. No wife, no kids, no one left behind in tears if I didn't make it back home.

That resolve has helped dull any attachment urges I may have had over the years. Light, easy, no strings attached. That's how I live when I'm on Earth.

Rose West is anything *but* light and easy. And definitely unforgettable.

Ding.

I grab my phone from the cup holder.

A text from my mother. *I'm ready to go.*

I frown at my phone. This is her way of telling me to come get her. *Why* I need to come to her, I don't know. If she can swing on a pole in those heels, makes sense she can walk out of the strip club in them, but I'm not about to text that.

Heaving myself out of my 4Runner, which I love even though Jackie assures me that true astronauts only drive Corvettes, I walk back into Heartbreakers, bracing myself for the visual assault of Rose in her pole dancing attire.

I blink, my eyes adjusting to the darkness. Rebecca Black's raunchy and profane song "Girlfriend" blasts from the speakers.

Even though I braced, when my eyes focus on the stage, I feel gut-punched all the same.

Nothing could have prepared me for Rose, one leg hooked high, the other splayed out, spinning upside down from the pole like a tornado of glitter.

I'm both aware that I'm standing there like a kid in a candy shop drooling over things he can't have, and also not aware of anything but her. My eyes are laser focused on her flowing hair, her gravity-defying boobs, and the thin strip of blue spandex between her legs.

But then something goes wrong. Rose squeals as her leg slides down a foot, the spinning coming to a stop. Throwing her hands out to catch herself, she slides the rest of the way down, catching herself in an awkward handstand.

I've already taken a few quick steps toward the stage before I realize it, but the younger woman in the bikini beats me there. Bracing Rose's midsection, she helps Rose fall carefully over to the side without hurting herself.

Rose, though rubbing her wrists, comes up laughing. "Whelp. I guess I haven't mastered *that* yet."

The older woman next to my mother claps. "Great job, Rosie-girl!" She looks to the bikini woman. "I want to learn that next, Angie."

"No, Myra." From the way the woman sighs, I can tell this isn't the first time Myra has asked to bite off more than she can chew.

Frowning, but with a gleam in her eyes, Myra crosses her arms. "You're no fun."

They all laugh.

"Shouldn't you practice easier moves before you break your neck doing spins like that?" I ask, my tone reprimanding.

The three women on the stage look at me, eyebrows raised.

My mother jabs me in the ribs. I hadn't even noticed she'd walked up next to me.

Luckily, she's on my right. If she'd jabbed my left side, she might have put my racing heart into cardiac arrest. Because my poor heart, the heart that's carefully monitored and trained by the best medical staff and physical trainers in the country, is racing at an abnormal level.

One thing is perfectly clear. Rose West is not good for me.

The laughter fades from Rose's face. "Do I tell you how to float in space, *Bodie*?" She scoffs. "No, I don't. So don't start telling me how to pole dance."

The woman has a point.

And with her youthful glow and billions of dollars, she's also not a safe bet for what I have to offer.

Even so.

"Go out with me tonight." Out of the corner of my eye I can see my mother's head turn to me *Exorcist*-style.

Rose laughs. "Sorry, no can do." She tosses her hair off her shoulders with both hands, showering the stage with glitter. "I have to wash my hair."

Myra chuckles, and Angie ducks her head, trying to hide her grin.

I narrow my eyes at her. "Tomorrow then?"

Mom's mouth drops open. In my thirty-six years I've never taken anyone home, never talked to her about my love life, and definitely never asked anyone out in front of her. Though at this point, it's more like begging.

"Nope." Rose saunters off, stage left.

I follow her, blocking her exit at the foot of the stairs. "Anytime this week."

She frowns at me then shifts left. I shift right. Her eyes narrow, and she shifts right. I shift left.

Crossing her arms over her sparkling chest, she begins tapping her platform on the stage. "Listen, buddy, don't think because your mama is here I'm gonna take it easy on you."

I mirror her stance. "I don't think you know *how* to take it easy on someone."

She purses her lips, like she's contemplating what I said. "Huh." She drops down a step, stopping two from the bottom. Eye-level with me. "You know, you may be right." One more step and I can make out the individual droplets of sweat mingling with her body glitter. Her breasts are rising and falling faster than normal. It's probably from pole dancing, but I'd like to think I have something to do with it.

That is until in one quick flash, she backhands my junk. She barely touches me, but what she does hit is dead center of pain town, and I hunch over, nearly going to my knees.

Two of the women gasp in shock, the third laugh/coughs. I'd like to think that wasn't my mother.

Rose, taking advantage of my protective cower, pushes me against the wall and out of her way. "I have two brothers, Vance. You should know better than to try and bully me." She sashays past.

Well-honed survival instincts keep me still until Rose shoves the double front doors open. The sunlight glints off her body like the fire trail of a shooting star. Even with my adrenaline pumping from the near emasculation, I can't help but appreciate her exit style.

When the doors close and I finally look away, I'm met with my mother's disapproving eyes.

She tosses her long dark braid over her shoulder and crosses her arms, just like she used to do when I misbehaved as a child. "You and I need to have another talk about the clitoris."

SEVEN

#IAMCAESAR

Rose

"What the actual fuck?" The neon red, white, and blue Big Texas Saloon sign, which is usually lit up like a beacon to all those in search of a good time, is dark.

I grab my boob flask from my bra and take a swig.

"When did they close?" Jackie asks, turning to Trish and Jules.

We're on our first girls' night since the wedding, and it is not off to an auspicious start.

"Don't ask me." Trish shrugs. "Must've happened while Ian and I were in Germany." She twists her new, very shiny, very *large* engagement ring on her finger.

Yeah, Trish getting engaged in Europe was a surprise. It also sounded sappy as hell, but Trish deserves all the romance Ian can muster and then some. I'm happy for them. For my best friend. I *am*.

It's just... did Big Texas have to shut down *now*? After Holt and Jules decide to raise a pet cow and Jackie and Flynn's promised till death do we part, and Ian and Trish's having a magical castle engagement?

Can I get a well-earned, drunken girls' night break from all the happily ever afters?

I twist my lips to the side, trying to look like I'm pouting. Pouting is more acceptable than the tears threatening my eyes. Even though Big Texas was shady as hell, had police stationed outside every night in case shit broke out, and the drinks were basic as fuck, this was *our* place. The place where the group first came together. The genius, the astronaut, the wanted felon, and the billionaire party girl.

And now it's closed.

Fuck you, Big Texas. Fuck you.

"Not a problem." Jules pulls her phone from the back of her leather pants. "I've got the details of another honky-tonk closer to town." Her thumbs fly over the screen. "We'll go there."

I'm too upset to even poke fun at Jules' use of honky-tonk. I simply take another large gulp from my flask and let Jackie lead me back into our UberXL.

———

TWENTY MINUTES and an empty flask later, we arrive at Whiskey River. Where there's a line out the door and along the covered front porch.

Of course there is.

Waiting in line is not my thing. Which I know makes me sound privileged as hell, but I don't care. I don't understand the concept of waiting hours in line just to give someone more of my money. I reach into my cleavage, wondering how much cash will be needed to get us through the door when the line erupts in surprised shouts and laughter.

"Whoa!" Jules points to the entrance. "Get a load of that!"

At least a dozen Vegas-style Elvis impersonators pour out of the double doors, their sequins flashing under the streetlights, followed by a rush of country club dressed customers.

"What in tarnation is going on here?" Trish asks, her eyes wide.

"Beats me, Yosemite Sam," Jules deadpans.

They bicker while Jackie and I stare, open-mouthed. Jackie is probably calculating the odds of triangulating each Elvis with the orbit of Mars, or some other such genius thing, while I'm simply astonished in the best possible way.

And happy.

Their cheap polyester capes flare out behind them as they hightail it to a nearby shuttle bus, and my hope grows with each twinkle and sparkle.

This place might not be so bad after all. I mean, a bar that has cheesy Vegas-style Elvis impersonators has gotta be fun, right?

Maybe this place will be even better than Big Texas. Maybe this girls' night will—

"Darlin'!" We all turn to see Flynn standing in the door the Elvises just ran out of, arm outstretched and waving in our direction. Holt's beside him, slipping the bouncer a bribe in the guise of a handshake.

My hope dies hard and fast.

Jackie waves back and bounces over in her Chuck Taylors. The rest of us follow.

I don't even ask. From the look on Jules' face as she lets Holt put his arm around her and walk her into the bar, it's obvious she knew the boys would be here.

This night is circling the drain faster than Elvis could eat a peanut butter, banana, and bacon sandwich. God rest his soul.

Trish's red lips curl up into a wide smile. "Ian's here too."

Et tu, Shortstack?

———

"Rosie West, we meet again."

I close my eyes against the image of Vance Bodaway, one arm stretched out across the back of the empty chair next to him, hair tumbling forward in his eyes.

For the love of God. My one-night stand is haunting me.

Vance, nonchalant as you please, is sitting next to Ian in the coveted back corner table, looking way too good in a plain blue T-shirt among a sea of button-downs and ten-gallons.

Jules grabs one of the beer bottles from the tub of ice by the table before spinning a chair around with her other hand. "Again?" She plops down, straddling the chair. "When did you meet the first time?"

Trish slides to the right of Ian. "Rosie?"

Sighing, I sink into the only vacant seat, the one next to Vance.

Vance nods at Trish and taps his beer bottle against Jules'. Ignoring my friends' pointed interest in us, he leans into me. "Thanks to you, I got another memorable lecture on the female anatomy during the drive home Sunday."

That has me rolling my lips in to keep from laughing.

Seeing my amusement, he nudges me with his elbow. "And yes, it was just as awkward and unnecessary as it was when I was fourteen, in case you're wondering."

The laugh I'm suppressing turns into a snort. "God, I love your mother."

"What happened Sunday?" Trish, whose eyes have been ping-ponging between us, probably trying to memorize our dialogue for her next book, looks riveted.

"And how do you know Vance's mother?" Jules takes another swig. "She's my hero by the way. Met her when Vance and I were given our astronaut pins."

Her admission irritates me for some reason. More so than her springing the boys on me during a girls' night. I shrug, trying to play it off. "I pole dance with Helen."

Jules' mouth drops. She turns to Vance. "Your mother *pole dances?*"

I smirk, feeling victorious.

Vance doesn't even take note of the rare sight of Jules being gobsmacked, his eyes still on mine, those damn sexy crinkles deepening. "You did a good job washing your hair. I don't see a speck of glitter."

I shrug, smiling despite myself, trying hard to ignore Trish and Jules, who share a WTF look.

Vance cocks one brow. "That mean you'll finally make time for me?"

"Ever heard the term hit it and quit it?" I try to keep the smile off my face, but I don't think I succeed.

Jules chokes on her beer, Trish's mouth drops open farther, and Jackie's brows pinch together. Ian looks amused but unsurprised. *Hmmm.*

"Isn't that the colloquium for a one-night stand?" Jackie pushes up her glasses.

"As usual," Jules says, tilting her beer bottle at Jackie, "you are correct." Pointing the mouth of her bottle to me, she asks, "When was the hitting and quitting? Because though Vance Bodaway is a friend, I'm not sure he's good enough for you."

Vance's eyes cut to Jules. "Are you serious?"

Probably paying him back from earlier, this time Jules ignores him. "You hold a mean flashlight in space so others, like *me*, can get the real spacewalk work done"—she smirks when Vance rolls his eyes—"but what else do you bring to the table? I mean, this is Rose West. Billionaire and best friend of Julie Starr. She deserves more than a flashlight hand job."

I know she's saying all of that to get a rise out of Vance, but it pleases me nonetheless, nullifying any annoyance I was harboring from her, including the boys on our girls' night.

"He was mentored by John Herrington," Jackie pipes up, not realizing Jules was joking.

"Who's John Herrington?" Trish and I ask at the same time. When Vance raises his eyebrows at me, I regret my obvious interest.

"He was the first Native American in space." Jackie tilts her head in that way she has when she's trying to recall facts. "Now in retirement, he does a lot of recruiting on government preserved reservations, doesn't he?" She looks at Vance.

"Yeah, he does." Vance nods, the crinkles around his eyes disappearing. "But I didn't meet him until after I was selected as an astronaut candidate." He takes a sip of his beer. "But he was a big inspiration of mine. Even though he's Chickasaw and I'm Zuni, it was life-changing watching the first Native American fly into space."

Not liking how serious Vance has gotten, I nudge him in the ribs with my elbow. "I'm surprised they had televisions back then."

"Back then?" He looks mildly affronted. "I'm only thirty-six."

I try not to let the surprise show. "And I'm only twenty-one."

His surprise does show.

Honestly, his Native American heritage is working for him. I really hadn't thought him that old. I just liked giving him shit.

I grab my glass and salute Vance with it. "That's what they call a generation gap, old timer."

Holt and Flynn come back with a handful of rum and Cokes.

"What'd I miss?" Holt asks, eyeing the mixture of surprise, amusement, and confusion we're all expressing.

"Rose wham, bammed, and thank you, ma'am-ed Flashlight here." Jules pipes up. "Though he doesn't seem to know that the 'thank you' implied that she was done with his ass."

"Or how young she was when the whamming and bamming happened." Trish sips her drink through the miniature cocktail straw.

Without a word, Holt turns and walks back toward the bar. Jules gets up and follows him, laughing so hard she stumbles.

Flynn stands frozen, eyes narrowed on Vance.

"Yo, big bro." I kick out with my boot and connect with Flynn's shin, making him wince. "Just remember all the times I have to hear about *your* sex life from Jackie." I shiver and take a big gulp of my drink. "So just be thankful this was a one and done."

My brother's frown turns upward in what I think is supposed to be a smile but doesn't quite make the mark. "What?" Flynn's grimace is frightening. "It's cool. I'm cool." He shrugs awkwardly. "Besides, we all make mistakes." He throws Vance some serious side-eye. "No offense."

Jackie tilts her head up, her eyes confused behind her glasses. "How is that not offensive?"

Her naïve question busts the table up laughing. Flynn pulls her to her feet. "I'll explain it while we dance." He takes her hand and leads her to the dance floor.

Ian puts his beer down. "Dancing sounds like a good idea."

"You go ahead." Trish waves him away without looking at him, her eyes still moving between Vance and me. She tends to take people watching to a whole new and creepy level.

Sighing, Ian tugs an unwilling Trish up and away from the table. "Good luck," Ian mumbles to Vance as they move past.

Vance does that personal space invasion that some men do, where they turn their whole body toward you and lean forward, blocking you in so they can't be ignored. It's usually annoying as hell and a good reason for a well-placed knee into their junk.

But this time, a thrill runs through me.

I'm a disappointment to feminists everywhere.

"You look good." His eyes travel low and high, taking in my high-waisted skinny jeans and one shoulder cropped T-shirt with my hot pink bra strap on display.

I fluff the wild blond mess that is my hair over my shoulders. "I do, don't I?"

He smiles. It's a good smile. A smile that does things to a woman's lady parts. Made worse by the fact that I know all too well just how happy my lady parts could be if I gave in to it.

I shift in my seat and regroup. "So what was with the Elvis impersonators earlier?"

He huffs out a laugh. "To be honest, I'm not all that sure." He runs a hand through his hair. "The boys and I just arrived when they were dancing. Then someone yelled 'rat,' and we were nearly trampled by the horde of sequins and pleather."

"There was a rat?" I push my drink across the table.

"No." He laughs and slides it back to me. "Turns out someone snuck in a cat."

"A cat."

"Yep."

I pick up the drink and take a large swallow. "Huh." I look around, soaking in rustic night club glamor—antler lights over our table, a cowboy hat-wearing DJ, and a mixture of crystal chandeliers and disco balls over the crowded dance floor. This place definitely has a cooler vibe than Big Texas. "You come here often?"

"Never been here until tonight." The crinkles are back around his eyes. "Came here just for you."

"Hmmm." I was afraid of that. At the wedding it was easy to compartmentalize him as "man I'm done with." But now, knowing he's Helen's son, finding out tidbits of his upbringing and career motivation, seeing first-hand how well he holds his own with my somewhat intrusive, wisecracking girl posse—I'm *interested*. He doesn't fit in the box anymore.

A waitress comes by and asks if we need anything.

He shakes his head, the silky black hair moving as he does.

I want to touch it. I tighten my grip on my glass. Because even if I acknowledge my expanding interest in him (interested enough to want to hit it a few more times), I also know that our six degrees of Kevin Bacon is a lot closer than I'd previously thought. Which means complications are inevitable.

I pole dance with his mother.

I'm best friends with his co-workers.

He was in high school when I was born.

He turns his attention back to me, his deep brown eyes holding mine. His eye crinkles deepen.

Ah, fuck it.

Like flipping a switch, I get my flirt on, fluttering my lashes at him. "Blow Job?"

He chokes on his own saliva. "Excuse me?"

———

Vance

MY LIP CURLS INVOLUNTARILY when the bartender slides the Blow Job shots across the bar.

"What, your masculine pride can't take it?" Rose smirks, grabbing one of the shots.

"No, my teeth." I eye the heavy dose of whipped cream on top. I'm not a health fanatic per se, but it's a professional hazard to keep in shape. "How much sugar you think is in there?"

"Sure, the sugar." Rose rolls her eyes. "Just admit you don't wanna do a Blow Job."

Leaning against the bar, I give my best condescending look. "Listen, Rosie-girl, as you love to point out, I'm older than you. I'm not one of the immature boy-men you're used to. I'm secure enough in my masculinity to shoot a whipped cream topped drink, no matter what it's called." To prove it, I push off the bar and turn to line up my shot. "You want to shoot Blow Jobs? Let's shoot Blow Jobs."

Rose looks impressed by my words, proving there's a first time for everything. She follows suit and centers her shot glass as well. "Fine, old man. Let's do this." But when she reaches for her glass, I slap her hand away. "Hey, wh—"

I tsk. "If I remember Jules and Jackie explaining this to me, and I should, because their aside during an EVA briefing about sexually named alcoholic drinks was *fascinating*"—I roll my eyes remembering that particularly long training session—"the correct way to drink a Blow Job is hands-free." I arch a brow at her, daring her with a look. "Am I right?"

"Are you mansplaining a Blow Job to me?"

"Are you not doing it right?" I fire back, clenching my abs at the look she throws me, expecting a gut punch. I turn my hips in toward the bar in case she decides to aim lower like she did at the strip club. It's a dangerous business riling Rose West up.

She glares at me a second longer before squaring up to the bar, shot glass lined up to her center. "Fine." A few tendrils of hair fall forward when she begins to lean over.

"Wait."

She huffs, straightening up. "Now what?"

I bite my lip to keep from laughing at her exasperating expression and brush her hair back, fisting it in a ponytail. "It's the gentlemanly thing to do."

If her eyes narrowed any more, they'd be closed.

With her hair out of her face, she bows forward, her rear end snuggled nicely against my crotch. I grunt at the contact, and she wiggles her ass, probably paying me back for irritating her.

But she really doesn't need to, because as comical as I imagined the whole process of doing Blow Job shots would be, the reality of watching her lips wrap around the rim of the glass as she sucks just hard enough to form a seal so she can lift the glass off the table hands-free is torture enough.

She straightens, tilting her back toward me and swallowing the whipped cream and Baileys in one go before leaning forward and dropping the glass back down.

Shrugging my hands off her hair, she turns to me. "Your turn."

By the look on her face, I can tell she knows that the last time she said that to me, she rode me like a champion rodeo queen in her family home.

The vivid memory has my eyes locking on her lips.

She licks them. Slowly.

I want nothing more than to kiss her. And if I had brought my 4Runner out tonight, maybe I would. But with no place to take this kiss any further, I pull my gaze away and square up to my own Blow Job shot.

One, because I told her I would and I'm not going to back down. It's like I have to prove to her, and myself, that just because I may be more years older than her than I'd originally thought, I can still hold my own.

And two, because I'm still reeling from Jackie's reminder on why I became an astronaut. And the sacrifices I knew I'd have to make when I became one.

I was seventeen when Herrington flew up and determined not to follow in my dad's military footsteps. I was going to be an engineer. I was going to build things, not bomb things or be bombed. I wasn't going to leave the people I loved behind.

And then Herrington changed it all. Photographs and videos of him carrying the Chickasaw flag in zero gravity lit up the news stations. I watched him, on NASA TV, help build the spine of the International Space Station over various space-walks. He was a builder, just like me, but he was building in *space*. And that called to a part of me I must've inherited from my fallen in action father.

"Chicken?" Rose taunts, pulling me away from my sobering thoughts.

The crowd that gathered around a hot girl doing Blow Job shots "the right way" laughs as Rose begins to bawk, bent arms flapping.

And just like that, Rose has me smiling and living in the moment.

I bend over and suck the shot up and back, managing not to choke on the large lump of whipped cream sliding down my throat. When the shot glass pops away from my mouth, the crowd's applause is louder than their previous heckling.

"Fucker," Rose says with a smile. I laugh, pulling her into me for a side hug, getting a high off the energy she emanates. She's like the sun, radiating energy on all the people in her orbit. I can't help being drawn to her.

The blaring music changes to a slow song. Across the bar, Jules is shuffling her motorcycle boots in time with Holt's cowboy ones, Trish's eyes are closed as she rests her head on Ian's chest while he rocks her to the music, and Jackie's mouth is in constant motion. Probably applying a multi-nuanced algo-rithm to the two-step's rhythmic oscillation. The thing they all have in common is the grin they've put on their dates' faces. A grin I'm pretty sure is just like the one I'm sporting.

A glance in my peripheral shows Rose also looking at her friends, a frown where her smile should be.

I'm not too sure what to make of that. And I'm too caught up in Rose's orbit to find out.

"Another round?" I ask, bringing her eyes up to mine.

Sighing but now smiling, she turns back to the bar and slaps the surface. "Line 'em up, old man."

EIGHT

VERTICAL LAUNCH

Rose

Two Blow Job shots in and I'm pandering to the newly formed crowd. The retelling of the fight during Jackie's bachelorette party at the strip club is going over fairly well. Both men and women are hanging on my every word.

Well, the women are. The men are probably stuck on the strip club part, their minds in the gutter.

"You're saying that girl over *there* launched herself off a strip stage and took down a three-hundred-pound thug?" A woman points at Trish on the dance floor.

"Yep." I nod like the proud mama I feel like when I remember Trish's sexy airborne scissor kick takedown.

The crowd stares at my petite brunette friend two-stepping in a demure, knee-length pleated skirt, silk tank top, and black platform pumps. She looks more like a kindergarten teacher with a heel fetish than a vigilante stripper. "But don't mention it to her. She'll get all embarrassed, which will make her fiancé mad." I heave a long-suffering sigh. "Things do tend to escalate when the menfolk get snippy."

Vance chokes on a sip of beer while the women in the crowd nod knowingly.

"Now, y'all scoot." I wave away the crowd. "I have a feeling this particular member of the menfolk"—I thumb over my shoulder to Vance—"has ulterior motives for showing up tonight, and I am *just* intoxicated enough to hear him out." I give Vance the once-over, as if daring him to say otherwise.

He just smiles.

The women laugh while the men murmur words of encouragement to him as they disperse.

He returns my once-over. "You think I have ulterior motives, hmm?"

"Yep." I grab my fresh rum and Coke from the bar, the empty shot glasses still resting next to it.

"I can't just be here having a good time?"

"Nope." I sip pinky out, like the lady we both know I'm not.

"And just how did you come to that conclusion?"

I heave another sigh, slightly worried I'll hyperventilate. "Because, Vance, you have never, not once, shown up at any of our gatherings. It is too coincidental that you're here tonight after I rocked your world in my family's guest bedroom, then shot you down at Heartbreakers in front of your mom."

The bartender walking past stops, looks at us, shakes her head, then keeps walking.

I tip my drink toward him. "And let's not forget that earlier you admitted to showing up tonight just for me."

He laughs. "Oh yeah. I did."

I hitch an elbow up on the bar and lean on it. "So what is it you want?" I wave my drink-free hand down my body and try and keep the hopeful note out of my voice. "Seconds?"

"Seconds would be good." His eyes roam over my face, and I can feel the heat of his gaze touch on my eyes, my mouth, the length of my neck and pause an extra second on my exposed shoulder and the visible hot pink bra strap. "Thirds and fourths even better."

My internal temperature gauge just spiked. "Listen." I put my drink down and straighten from the bar, clasping my hands together, trying to look solemn. "I appreciate the prior use of your penis, and even applaud the confidence it took to down Blow Jobs in a crowded cowboy bar, but I need to make this clear. I am *not* looking for a boyfriend."

Vance winks. "That's great, 'cause I'm not looking for a girlfriend."

"Good." I drop my hands, ignoring the sting of his acceptance. "We're on the same page then."

He looks into the neck of his beer bottle. "Just out of curiosity, though, what *are* you looking for?" His question sounds too casual to be believable.

Annoyingly, that sparks a flash of unwelcome hope. But if he wants to play games, so can I. Laying on the dramatic flare I'm known for, I heave yet another sigh. "I don't know. But if you want to be a big strong man and tell me what I *should* want, I'll listen."

The music changes, and we both watch Ian, Flynn, and Holt take their fiancée, wife, and girlfriend into their respective arms and sway, shuffling their feet to another slow two-step.

Something that isn't quite lust but leaves me wanting all the same crashes over me. It's the same feeling I had at Jackie's wedding. It feels like—

Vance's bottle hitting the bar top makes me jump.

He takes a step closer, and his scent covers me, bringing lust back to the forefront.

"Well." He leans down, his breath tickling my ear. "For

starters, how about you want more of that fun we've had together?"

Fun. For a brief second, I feel hurt, but one look at his sly smile and I shake it off.

"What?" I step back, taking a deep breath and trying to gain control. "Breaking and entering in search of orgasms wasn't enough fun for you?"

He chuckles, and my eyes clock the way his shoulder muscles bunch as he does. "Oh no, that one goes down in the record books for sure. Even if you were just messing with me."

I pick up my drink, wrapping my mouth around the small straw. His eyes narrow on to my lips, making me feel triumphant.

"But I'm sure we have a few more record-breaking moments in our future." He closes the distance between us again. "Weren't you saying something about the lotus position?"

Trying not to let him see how he's getting to me, I don't retreat. Instead, I joke. "Oh, Vance, Vance, Vance." I pat him on the shoulder in a consoling fashion. "I'm not sure an old man like you could handle lotus." Shaking my head, I tsk. "In fact, I'm not sure you could handle me more than once—*period*."

Instead of him taking the bait and retreating back to what I'm comfortable with—sarcasm and banter, he leans in even closer, our chests touching. "Well, you know what they say, don't you?" He nibbles my ear.

I swallow hard. Hopefully he doesn't notice. "Probably, but why don't you tell me anyway?"

He grazes my jaw line with the tip of his finger. "There's only one way to find out."

I'm pretty sure I've just been outplayed. Huh. I don't think that's ever happened before. And even more surprisingly, I'm not annoyed about it. I'm pleased.

My eyes flick to the dance floor again, finding my friends and their men still there, still all loved up.

Probably too in love to notice if I disappear early, right?

I slide my arm between us, my hand reaching into my bra. Vance and a few men in the vicinity do a double take when I pull out the wad of cash I keep there. "I'll get the bill, you get the Uber."

The sexy eye crinkles deepen. "You got it, Rosie-girl."

———

Vance

WE'RE a tangle of limbs and hot breath as we enter my bedroom.

I was worried how this would go when Rose and I climbed into the Uber. Would there be awkward silence? Would she cry wolf and leave? Would I?

It seems I worried for nothing, because Rose wasted no time filling the twenty-minute drive to my apartment with stories of her party days, recaps of how her friends all fell in love (and the vital role she played in each happily ever after), and how much she loves messing with her college counselor.

Granted, she wasn't talking to *me*, but rather the Uber driver. A man closer to Rose's age than mine, who kept giving me nods and smirks that I assume were to signal how impressed he was by my catch of a young, hot co-ed, all the while using his rearview mirror to look down Rose's shirt.

Still, her talk managed to kill time before we arrived at my place, situated a minute from NASA on the north side of Clear Lake. And when I stiffed the driver on the tip and gave him a one-star review noting 'misuse of review mirror,' I felt vindicated, if extremely petty.

Rose skipped up to my apartment on the third-floor whistling, acting like her coming home with me was a common occurrence.

But as soon as my key turned in the lock, it was like a bell went off in her head, and it was game on.

I was nearly tackled from behind as she pushed me through the nearest door.

When I flicked on the lights, she paused in her attack. She glanced around, finding herself in the bathroom. "Whoops."

When I backed her across the hall into my bedroom, she regrouped, attacking me once more.

And now here we are, her hands busy pulling at my shirt, undoing my belt, fisting my hair.

She's a tornado. It's all I can do to stay on track, guiding her to the side of the bed and knocking her back onto it. Déjà vu.

I take a deep, lust-scented breath, needing to slow down, plan my next move.

But as always with Rose, she gives me no quarter. With me now out of reach, she crosses her arms, whipping her shirt off and throwing it somewhere over my shoulder. Her hot pink bra that's been teasing me all night is lace and sheer and holding the weight of a thousand fantasies.

That comes off too.

"Are you just going to stand there, or are you going to take off your pants?"

I push aside the belt buckle that she already undid but pause when I reach for my top button. "Actually"—I drink in the sight of her topless on my bed—"I think I'll take yours off instead."

She raises her hips in invitation. "By all means."

It takes me a second to get a good enough hold on her waistband and the right leverage to peel her skinny jeans off her. They turn inside out as I pull, and with each new inch of skin revealed, my dick presses more urgently against my zipper.

Once her legs are free, I drop her pants and reach out for her panties.

"Ah, ah." She wags a finger at me. "Tit for tat." She shimmies, her breasts swaying. "And as this is a lot of tit, you owe me a lot of tat." She laughs, her head dropping back. "God, I crack myself up."

I find myself laughing with her as I reach back and tug my T-shirt over my head.

"Keep going, old man. Let's see if your carpet matches your drapes or if you're Just for Men-ing your Johnson."

"Jesus, I'm only thirty-six, I'm not going gray yet." I shake my head, exasperated, but still smiling.

She shrugs, her tits bouncing. "Yeah, I know. But you're fun to rile up." Her tongue rubs her bottom lip, her eyes bright with lust on my chest. "Now hurry up and show me the goods."

I reach down and tug off my boots first, then shove my pants and boxer briefs to the floor in one move.

"Holy anaconda." She sighs a happy sigh and slides off the side of the bed to her knees. She murmurs something that sounds like, "I knew it would be life-changing," but I'm too turned on by the sight of Rose on her knees, her breasts rising and falling with each breath, her eyes locked on my dick like it's the key to happiness, to process her words.

I haven't been this on edge since my high school days. The fleeting thought that Rose was only just born when I was just learning how to control myself in the bedroom nearly has my dick flagging.

That is, until she deep throats it in one go.

She comes back up gagging. "Whelp." She cough-laughs. "That didn't go as planned."

I've never had so much fun with someone in bed before. I push her hair back, my thumb at the corner of her upturned lips. "Easy there. You don't have to—"

"Are you about to mansplain a blow job to me again?" She plants her hands on her hips. "'Cause I'm just saying, if you do, I'm out." Her mutinous expression would be cute if I didn't think she'd follow through on her threat.

"Nope." I shake my head and zip my lips with my hand, knowing I look ridiculous. "Not mansplaining a thing."

"Hmmph." Frowning, she shifts her thighs farther apart, dropping her butt down lower between her heels. "Better not."

And then I'm in her warm mouth again, her slick tongue running up and down my cock, flicking the underside of the tip.

"Jesus."

She hums a sound that I'm sure is supposed to be words, but my brain isn't functioning. She's deep throating in earnest now, her slightly lower positioning allowing my cock to glide down her throat.

Through hooded eyes, I watch her nostrils flare as she breathes in through her nose, her hands coming up to grip my ass and pull me toward her.

All I can do is hold her hair back and mumble incoherently until my balls start to tighten.

Before I embarrass myself and come, I pull out, the shock of air to my wet dick dialing back my desire enough to reach down and lift Rose up, tossing her on the bed once more.

"I wasn't finished." Her pout, still glistening from her expert blow job, is sexy as hell. I'm certain if I let her, this woman would run me ragged for the rest of my life, and I'd love every minute of it.

I shake off the thought and spread her thighs with my hands. "But I haven't even started yet." I drop down, licking at her clit.

"Hmm, yeah." She pulls her thighs up and widens them even more, giving me room to work. "I'll let you win this round."

I smile as I go down on her, building her up to a maddening pitch, pushing her hard and fast into orgasm. Lapping at her while she screams.

It isn't until she's twitching from light aftershocks that I pull open my nightstand drawer and grab a condom.

She's only just opened her eyes when I enter her, the fast thrust of my cock arching her back, ripping a moan from her lips. "Ah, fuck yes. Do that. More of that."

I do. Still smiling, I pull back and pound, a slow, hard rhythm that has her twisting beneath me. Her smart mouth opens in a silent scream as another orgasm rips through her.

And when her inner walls clamp down around me, I see the stars I've only ever seen in space.

But somehow, they're brighter.

NINE

OUTER SPACE TREATY

Rose

I'm not hung over. So that's something.

Vance snores, looking sexy as hell sprawled out on his back, one arm over his head.

That's something too.

I would've thought, in the cold light of day, I'd regret my decision to come home with him last night. Or at least my laziness to not vamoose after he wrung the fifth orgasm from my body in the wee hours of the morning.

But I don't. Instead I shiver as a long-lost orgasmic aftershock runs through my body. I close my eyes and enjoy the superpower of orgasm muscle memory that only surfaces after a stellar bout of sexy times.

Well done, Vance. Well done.

Rolling toward the nightstand, I look for a clock. Nothing but a lamp. But seeing as the sunlight's soft outside, it's probably early. I can sneak out and Uber my way to Flynn and Jackie's, where I left my car before "girls' night." Catch some more sleep in their guest room or just head to the city.

Hashtag walk of shame time.

I hang over the side of the bed and swat at the floor, hoping my phone's somewhere down there, all while wondering if I can even get an Uber this early in the suburbs.

The snoring comes to an abrupt stop, and Vance rolls toward me, throwing his arm over my waist and pulling me into his morning erection. "You up?"

"Well, it's clear that *you* are."

He laughs, the shake of his body doing great things for the long and hard appendage rubbing against my ass.

Wanting to stay, but not wanting to cross any lines about what this is, I shift to the edge of the bed. "I better get going."

He lets me slip out of his grasp but sits up when I stand. "Why?"

I glance around the bedroom, looking for my clothes. "It's easier this way. I'll just go to Jackie and Flynn's before they wake up and tell them I was there all night and they just didn't notice." I find my panties and pull them up.

"But why?"

I ignore the sexy morning rasp in his voice and snatch my jeans off the floor. "Are you only thinking with your small brain this morning?"

He looks down at the erection popping a tent in the sheets, then back at me, perplexed.

"Ugh." I huff and pull the legs of my pants right side out and step into them. "If my friends know I stayed here, there'll be questions. Questions I don't feel like answering. Questions you should be wary of because they will be coming from your co-workers." At least, those are *some* of my reasons. I leave out the one where, as much as I loved last night, I don't want to get used to it. Because in my experience, all good things end.

True, my friends have helped me witness the power of true love (insert cheesy Hallmark trailer here), but that's *them,* and this is *me.*

And let me just remind myself how much older Vance is than me. Which doesn't matter in the sack, 'cause all those life experience skills have *really* paid off. But his age does mean he's established in life. He already had his quarter life crisis. He not only figured out what he wanted to do, he became the best at it and then flew into space for it. He's a high-profile person due to all his career accomplishments. Not like me—a benefactor of someone else's success.

He's also surrounded by people, *women,* just like him. People like Jules and Jackie.

Which is fine. Great, even. I love Jules and Jackie. But I'm not them.

I'm well aware of what I am. I'm the good time. The laughs. The remember-when girl.

I'm cool with that. It got me this far. But now I should be more. *Do* more.

I jump up and down to shift my weight into the tight denim. Fuck, skinny jeans are the worst.

Vance apparently doesn't think so because his eyes are on my bouncing boobs, all but drooling.

I roll my eyes at him and find my shirt on the bureau.

Vance's big brain must finally kick into gear because he gets out of bed and walks to my side as I tug on my shirt.

"Listen, Rosie." He drops his big hands on my shoulders, stilling my movements. "I like you."

It's *my* big brain's time to stutter. That rising panic in my chest is back. It's probably because he's standing stark naked in front of me. And if I thought he was impressive last night, in the pale light of morning, Vance is hypnotizing. Unlike the boys I dated or banged in the past, he's full-grown. Dick and all.

His muscles are filled out in a way that speaks of experience and maturity. I want to reach out and see my pale hand sweep along his darker skin. Caress each ridge and tweak each peak.

But I don't.

Instead, I snort, trying to act unaffected as I shake off his hands to unhook my bra strap from the corner of the mirror. "What are you, twelve?" I slide the hot pink lace into my back pocket.

He lets out a long-suffering sigh, running a hand down his face. "Can you stop being a smart ass for five seconds?"

Tilting my head, I pretend to contemplate the question. "I don't know. I've never tried."

He steps closer, his hard-on still raging and now less than an inch from my waist. "As I was saying, I *like* you. And since you were willing to go a second round with me, I'd say you don't dislike me." He waits, keeping eye contact.

I purse my lips. "True, but considering that last night I gave you the third and fourth helpings you wanted, I thought this"—I wave my hand between us, the back of my hand making contact with his chest—"was over."

"Do you want it to be over?" He cups my shoulders once more.

My mouth stays shut. Because even though the throbbing between my thighs and the handsome, imploring man before me makes me want to say no, I'm smart enough to know the answer should be yes.

His thumbs graze my collarbone. "We have fun together."

I grunt noncommittally as the unintentional barb hits home. *Fun.*

Then Vance kisses me.

I have no idea how long we stand there kissing, but when he finally slows the kiss, leaning back to meet my eyes, the light coming in from the windows is much brighter than when we started.

His lush lashes fall heavy over his dark eyes, still hazy with lust. "Be with me until I leave on my next mission."

He says nothing more. Just waits me out.

Mentally I shake my fist at him for knowing silence is my enemy.

Finally, I speak—slow and wary. "Are you thinking of like... a friends with bennies situation?"

"Yeah." His ab muscles tighten, and I'm pretty sure he is trying not to laugh. "Friends with bennies."

My lips twitch in spite of myself. Fucker.

But as adorably vexing as he is right now laughing at my particular vernacular, he is also a tall, dark drink of orgasms.

I glance down, confirming the impressiveness of his cock. Yep, ready and waiting.

"So..." I say to his dick. "This is temporary?"

"Yep. I'll be going up to the ISS in a few months, so why don't we just..." He waggles his eyebrows when I look up at him.

"Oh my God." I laugh. "You look like a lecherous old man when you do that."

"But a hot lecherous old man, right?" He waggles them some more.

Laughing harder, the fight drains out of me. He's fun. And apparently thinks I am too. So why shouldn't I enjoy this? It's not like I have anything else to do. My friends are all in the honeymoon phase of their relationships. I have time to figure out what I need to do next. What I *want*.

And while I figure that out, I'll have sex until my clit falls off from overuse.

Sounds like a good time to me.

And a good time *is* what I'm known for, after all.

Decision made, I whip off my shirt, nearly blinding him with the fabric.

It's like waving a red flag at a charging bull.

Vance backs me up against the bureau, hands sliding into the back waistband of my jeans, grabbing my ass, going from zero to hero in a second flat.

Not to be left behind, I grab his dick and pump, enjoying his hard grunt.

Yeah, friends with bennies is a great idea.

Vance drops to his knees and with one hard tug takes my pants with him. He stays down to pull my ankles out, kissing the tops of my thighs as he does.

"All right, old man, you win this argument." I funnel my fingers through his hair and bring his mouth closer to where I need it. "Now make it worth my while."

And he does.

———

Vance

"You're very good at that."

"What?" Rose's eyes never leave her phone, her thumbs flying. She's been on her phone for the past fifteen minutes, while I lay in postcoital bliss.

"Ignoring me."

She snorts, still not looking at me. "Aw, is the poor little astronaut feeling neglected?"

Even her baby talk is a turn-on.

I roll over, trailing my fingers up her thigh. "Maybe."

It's a sad state of affairs when after a round of early morning sex to celebrate our new friends-with-bennies relationship at my apartment, and another fun sexcapade after I drove her home to her penthouse, that I'm pouting over her obvious disregard for my presence. I should be happy she's so unattached. In fact, I should be driving home right now congratulating myself on this epic turn of events.

Instead, I'm looking around the room with a frown. This doesn't seem like a room Rose would live in. I mean, it's huge and luxurious, as any penthouse apartment would be. But even with all the fancy furniture and décor, it feels kind of empty.

The only thing that seems like Rose is an impressive floor-to-ceiling bookcase stocked with romance novels and pictures of her and her friends. Dead center is a gold framed photo of Jules, Trish and Rose in their bridesmaid dresses on either side of Jackie in her wedding dress.

Everything else in the room and what I saw of the apartment looks straight out of a rich and famous interior design book.

I tap her with my foot under the covers. "Did you read all those?"

Rose's thumbs stop so her index finger can scroll. "No, I just have them for show."

Her sarcasm is not lost on me.

I nudge her again.

Sighing, she drops her phone and turns to me, her shoulder against the stack of pillows propping her up. "Yes?"

"What are you working on, anyway?"

"My thesis." No smile to tell me she's joking.

"Thesis?"

"Yeah, remember?" She quirks an eyebrow. "You're banging a co-ed." She turns back to her phone.

I try and cover my shock with a joke. "Must be going senile in my old age." I hadn't really thought of Rose as the studious type. Which makes me a dick.

She smiles as if reading my thoughts and turns her attention back to her phone.

Inching up, I look over her shoulder and read as she toggles over to her student email account. One inbox heading reads: *Business Fellow Program.*

Once, during a social compatibility session during astronaut training (required as NASA is effectively launching a bunch of high-achieving individuals into space to live in tight quarters with each other for months on end), I read a research paper on different personality strengths. One of them was humor. The paper delved into the intellection levels of famous comedians. Almost all of them have an above average IQ.

It makes sense when you think about how fast funny people's minds have to work. How, in order to hit just the right note of hilarity, they need to have a firm understanding of their contextual landscape while taking into account the variables of the audience.

I reach for my own phone on the floor next to the bed, still in my back jean pocket, and google Baylor Business Fellows. A minute later I have a newfound respect for the woman next to me.

The Business Fellows program is a separate division of the standard business degree that you have to apply for even *after* being accepted into Baylor University, a prestigious school in its own right. A student needs to be ranked in the top three percent of their class and have National Merit status.

In other words, Rose West, billionaire and National Merit scholar, is going places. She'll have no problem letting me go when it's time for me to fly. I'll be a small blip on her way to world domination.

No wonder she's so good at ignoring me.

She lets go of her phone long enough to slap my shoulder.

"All right, old man. You need to head out. I gotta go see your mamma about a pole."

"Ugh." I sink back on my pillow, arm over my eyes. "I forgot it's Sunday."

Rose laughs, getting out of bed. I watch as she walks over to the en suite bathroom door.

"Are you gonna drive your mom again?" she calls out once she closes the door.

"No, thank God." I raise my voice but stay in bed, too comfortable to contemplate moving quite yet. The sheets smell like sugar, spice, and glitter. "I only drove her last time because her car was having its tires rotated."

"Hmmm." Water starts running, and a minute later she emerges, walking toward the closet. "Are we doing this on the down-low or are we lying to people?" As she's still naked, it takes me longer to answer.

"What do you mean?"

She pulls open the double doors and steps inside. From my vantage point on the bed, her closet looks bigger than my entire apartment.

"I mean, the questions. Everyone always has questions." She moves farther in so I can't see her, but I hear drawers opening. "Like your mother. I may have told her we banged."

I cringe.

"Sorry not sorry," Rose adds. "*Plus* you asked me out in front of her."

"Yeah, I forgot about that," I mumble.

Another drawer closes. "Besides giving you a sex education refresh, I'm sure she's gonna have lots of questions."

"Thanks again for that, by the way." I shiver, remembering my mother's 'talk.'

"You're welcome," she sing-songs.

Brat.

"And then there are the girls. You came on pretty strong last night. There is no way they're just going to let that go."

"Why don't we just tell them the truth?" Seems simple enough.

"Yeah, that'll work." Rose clears her throat. "Hey, Helen, don't mind me, I'm just banging your son like a tasty side-piece."

"Tasty side-piece?"

"You prefer old man?"

"Tasty side-piece works."

I hear her chuckle and more drawers opening and closing. What the hell is she doing in there?

After a minute of thought, I come up with a solution. "How about we tell people we're dating?"

"Dating?" she calls out, and her voice has an odd edge to it.

"Not for real," I assure her, not wanting her to think I'm asking for more than she wants. "But people date all the time, you know. Doesn't mean they get married. So when it's time for me to fly up, we'll just say it didn't work out."

A drawer slams hard. "Huh."

"And by the time I get back"—I lean back, hands behind my head, feeling pretty smart—"you and I will be old news."

The only sound I hear is of fabric rustling.

"Rose?" I slide my hands out from behind me, worried, wondering if I'm not as clever as I thought I was.

"I'm still here." She emerges from the closet.

My jaw drops.

Rose is decked out in a leopard print leotard, gold belt, black fishnet stockings over sheer neon pink tights, and black patent leather platforms. Her hair is in a messy top-knot, complete with a braided neon pink sweatband.

She's every *Weird Science* fantasy come to life. And I've had quite a few in my time. Hello, eighties teenager.

She runs her hands down the slick sides of her leotard. "You better leave before I set off the glitter bomb."

"Glitter bomb?" I blink, breaking the stare.

"Yep. Glitter bomb." She spins on her heels and walks out.

I grab my pants off the floor and shrug into them, nearly falling over when I see how high the leotard is cut in the back.

"So, uh, what did you think of my idea?" I run my hands through my hair as I follow her down the hall. The glare off the white marble floor makes it look like she's walking on a cloud of pink.

"The fake dating one?" she asks, still walking ahead of me, still not sounding one hundred percent like Rose.

"Yeah." Now that we aren't ripping each other's clothes off, I get a better look around the place. White walls, neutral furniture.

"Sounds good." She pauses in front of a closed door.

The only things on her shelves in the main living room are gaming stations. Every gaming station ever made. And rows of games.

Besides those things, the room is devoid of life. No personal pictures or touches. "How long have you lived here?"

"About four years."

I'm about to question the flat tone to her voice when she opens the door.

I'm blinded.

Glitter walls, glitter ceiling, glitter floor. It looks like it might once have been an office, with wall-to-ceiling built-ins along the back wall—which are also covered in glitter. I can't tell if it's paint or dust.

Holding my hand up as if to ward off the light, I back up a step. "What *is* that room?"

"My glitter room." She looks at me like I'm slow.

"Ah, I see." I don't see. Probably because my retinas are

scalded by the light reflecting off the billions of mica particles. It's like I went on a space walk without my sun shield. On one hand, who has a glitter bomb room? On the other, it's the only room I've seen that seems remotely Rose-like.

She steps inside and wiggles her fingers at me. "Booty call me later." And with that, she closes the door.

I'm left pants-undone and dismissed.

This is starting to become a habit of hers.

TEN
#TBD

Vance

How do you booty-call a billionaire?

I've been staring at my phone for longer than I care to admit asking myself that question. My cubical on the astronaut floor of building five is quiet, the silence broken by my intermittent typing and the sound of book pages turning. My phone rings, and I nearly throw it across the room in surprise.

A few cubicles down, Jackie, with various books and manuals stacked in front of her, is deep into the informational part of astronaut training, one of her black high-top Converse shoes bouncing like a jackhammer as she reads. At the ring, her foot stills, and she looks up, her head titled.

I hit the side button, silencing the phone. "Sorry."

But Jackie's already looking down at her books again.

My shoulders brace when I see the name on the screen. I slide my thumb across my phone and hunch forward. "Hello, Brittany."

"Don't you 'hello Brittany' me." My older sister's condescending tone, which she has perfected over my lifetime, comes across loud and impatient as ever. "Why haven't you called me back?"

The better question is why did I answer her call now? I pinch the bridge of my nose. "Sorry, I've been busy." Busy trying to smooth talk a billionaire.

"You're always busy." Brit's tone is swimming deeper into annoyed territory. "Every holiday, every birthday, every soccer season and family get-together—you're *busy*."

I rub the hand at my nose down my face. "Well, I am."

"Bullshit." I hear someone over a loudspeaker talk about turkey prices.

"Where are you?"

"Grocery shopping for Thanksgiving."

Ah, fuck. That's this week.

"You remember Thanksgiving, don't you?" Her voice gets sweet, letting me know I'm in for Brit's classic sarcasm. "Your favorite holiday. The one where you show up just as dinner's ready and leave before pie is served."

"I'm watching my diet."

"You're such a girl."

"How chauvinistic of you."

She groans, causing me to pull the phone away from my ear. "Listen, bro."

I very much doubt that other forty-year-old women with two children use the term 'bro.'

"I want to see my brother. Your nephews want to see their uncle. So tell me you are coming to Mom's this Thursday and *not* just for an hour."

"I'll be there."

"Uh huh, sure." Brit tests her heavy sarcasm skills. "I've heard that before."

As my sister grumbles about past holidays and other get-togethers where I was a no-show, I glance back at Jackie, wondering if she can hear my sister from her desk. She's still studying with a furrowed brow of concentration, so I doubt it. I notice a black-and-white picture of Neil Armstrong in a pilot jumpsuit, wearing the same shoes she's wearing, pinned to her corkboard. Next to it, a picture of Flynn and her at the wedding, standing in front of the West mansion where Rose rocked my world.

"Are you listening?"

I spin in my seat. "Of course I am."

Behind me is Jules' desk—a mess of papers both stacked and spread out everywhere like a tornado went through. Her corkboard is decorated with pictures of a cow wearing a rhinestone collar, standing next to a small pink barn. Pictures she likes to show me every time we happen to be in the office at the same time. Also in one of the cow pictures is Rose, alongside Jackie and Trish.

I lean closer.

How did I never notice that before?

Everything is Rose. And it's only been two days since I've seen her.

"So you'll be there on time, right?" My sister's voice cuts through my thoughts.

"Where?"

"I'm going to kill you."

Sighing, I spin back to face my computer. "I'm just messing with you, Brit. Yes, I'll be at Mom's for Thanksgiving. On time."

She finally lets me go, and we hang up.

Tossing my phone on my desk, I lean back and squint against the sun blazing in through the windows along the perimeter of the mostly empty floor.

Not only is it the week of Thanksgiving, but the astronauts that are still onsite are either training, traveling, training, studying, training, public speaking, or training. Some of my colleagues are in the gym, running through their detailed weight training regimes, or in a class somewhere being briefed on a new science experiment they'll be doing in zero gravity sometime in the future, or in the Neutral Buoyancy Lab running through the order of operations for an upcoming spacewalk.

My high-priority tasks have dwindled now that the Bartolomeo's mission has been set eight months out. NASA isn't usually one for last-minute procedures, so with everything in place, there's just a lot of email double-checks and yes, more training. But today is not a training day. I may have told my sister I'm busy, but today I've got nothing but time to think about Rose. And the fact that I want to spend all that time thinking about her is concerning.

I refresh my emails, checking for anything new. There isn't.

I think about distracting myself with the gym, but I've already been. My most arduous self-appointed task today has been avoiding Jules, who's dogging my every step, trying to get me to break first about why I was so friendly with Rose at the bar.

"Houston, we have a problem." Tom Hanks' voice rings loudly around the empty floor.

"Oops." Jackie reaches for her phone. "Sorry."

Whatever she reads on the screen makes her smile, then pack up all her stuff.

"Hot date?"

"Hmm?" She glances up. "Oh, no." She pushes up her glasses looking more like a college student than an astronaut. "I'm meeting the girls for lunch."

"Girls?"

"Uh-huh. Trish just got approval for her spousal support badge."

NASA finally got hip to using less sexist vernacular and

renamed the Wife Security Badge that all partners are allowed to apply for to the Spousal Support Badge. I've seen Jackie eat lunch with Flynn a few times, so he must have one, too.

"That's cool." I watch Jackie putting away her notes and books. Everything in its proper place.

"Ian even got Rose a day pass so we can all eat together first."

I stand. "Rose is here?"

Jackie frowns, tilting her head again. "You know, *I'm* the one who isn't supposed to pick up on social cues, and yet even I hear the note of excitement in your voice whenever Rose's name is mentioned."

I can't argue, so I just shrug at being called out.

Jackie slings her bag over her shoulder, calling out over her shoulder, "You can come if you want."

Oh, I want.

———

AFTER A FEW SECURITY clearance swipes and a short walk through the quad, Jackie and I arrive at the cafeteria parking lot. Rose and Trish are part of the small crowd waiting in line at one of the food trucks set up on the side.

Yep, NASA has food trucks. They are on a rotating schedule, a different two each day of the week. It's a clever way for Uncle Sam to cut down on the cafeteria budget. Today it's chicken and waffles and Asian fusion.

Rose is in line for chicken, wearing Birkenstocks, denim shorts, and one of those threadbare T-shirts that like to drive men crazy. It's a dark olive-green color, but due to the thin fabric, I can easily see her black bra underneath.

What really catches my eye, though, are her pigtails. Her wild blond hair is caught up in two low ponytails draped over her shoulders, the ends hanging right above the shadow of her bra cups. She looks both seductive and adorable.

"There you are, Flashlight." Jules comes up behind me, clapping me on my shoulder. "And here I was thinking you were avoiding me."

"Me?" I put my hand on my chest in a dramatic fashion. "Never."

She snorts. "Uh huh." She glances over to where I'm looking, a sly smile growing on her face.

Before she can ask, I close the distance between Rose and me. Jules and Jackie follow.

When I reach her, Rose is holding one of those red-and-white checkered cardboard containers, filled with a large chicken and waffle sandwich and an unhealthy helping of french fries, a can of Coke shoved in her back pocket.

She stops short when she sees me. "What are you doing here?"

"Seeing as I work here, I think I should ask you that question."

Rose rolls her eyes.

"I was going to call you right before Jackie told me you were here."

Her eyes cut to Jackie, who, oblivious, is now waiting in line at the Asian fusion truck. "Was and did are two different things."

Her tone has me smiling. "Do I detect disappointment in your voice?"

"No." She sticks out her hip, leveling me with a look of annoyance. "You detect an admonishment for not having the balls to pick up the phone."

Jules' eyes are bouncing between us as Trish walks over with a plate from the waffle truck.

"No balls, eh?" I raise a brow. "That's not what you were saying Saturday night."

Rose straightens, her eyes widening before she shoots a quick glance toward her friends, whose mouths are hanging open.

"When we were taking those Blow Job shots."

Her shoulders relax, and she snorts again. "Yeah, it did take balls to give good head in a bar."

"Trish!" We turn to see Ian jogging up. He takes Trish's plate of food from her with one hand, wraps his other arm around her shoulders, and kisses the top of her head. "Hi, babe."

Trish sinks into him. "Hi, sugar."

It isn't until my nostrils flare that I realize I'm annoyed. Not because Ian is here, but because he can so easily show affection to Trish. I've never wanted to have that level of relationship with someone before. But now that I do, I'm annoyed I can't.

Or can I?

Mimicking Ian, I sidle up to Rose, grab her food, and drape an arm around her.

Jules smirks. "And just what—"

"Rose and I are going to eat in the quad." I tip her basket food in the direction of the green space nearby.

Rose, looking quite unimpressed by my show of chivalry and affection, raises an eyebrow at me. "We are, huh?"

"Yep." I kiss the top of her head, and she stiffens.

Jackie bounds up with a container of egg rolls. "What'd I miss?"

"Rose is ditching us for Flashlight." Jules, hands on hips, frowns at me.

Jackie just nods. "Yes, that makes sense."

"It does?" Trish asks.

"Yes, that is what newly-formed couples do. They excuse

themselves from the group to continue growing their level of intimacy."

Trish sputters. "New couple?"

Even Rose blinks before asking, "Intimacy?"

It's Jackie's turn to frown. "Yes. I read various books on relationships after Flynn and I got together."

"Of course you did," Jules deadpans.

Jackie nods at Rose and me. "Those two show all the signs of a newly-formed couple."

"Is that true?" Ian finally speaks up, his tone amused.

Rose opens her mouth, but I beat her to it. "You can't argue with a genius." I tighten my arm on her when she starts to pull away. "Now if you'll excuse us, my *girlfriend* and I have a lunch date."

I tug Rose toward the benches in the quad, leaving one verified genius, two shocked women, and an apathetic engineer behind.

When we reach a bench situated in front of a small pond filled with ducks and turtles, we sit, Rose removing her Coke from her pocket first.

There's a beat of silence before Rose's head turns to me, her eyes narrowed. "I was only going to tell them that if it came up. I wasn't planning on announcing it. I don't like lying."

I lean back on the bench, feeling oddly satisfied with the way things turned out. "This way I get you all to myself, and they won't think it's weird."

She huffs. "No, they're just compiling their questions for the inquisition later." She takes her food back from me, allowing me to stretch out my arm behind her.

I chuckle. "When do you think that will be?"

She takes a large bite of her sandwich, pushing it to the side to answer. "Who knows?" She chews some more. "The NASA peeps are taking Trish and me on a tour after lunch. They'll probably throw some questions at me then. Thankfully, as it's Thanksgiving this Thursday, I'll get a bit of a reprieve before they can launch a full attack."

The conversation with my sister is still fresh in my mind. I switch gears. "What does Thanksgiving look like at the West Ranch?"

Rose cracks open her can of Coke and takes a sip. "Thanksgiving is usually spent in sweats, with a heaping pile of turkey, stuffing, and mashed potatoes in a Styrofoam container balanced on my knees while watching football with my brothers."

"That sounds great." It would be a lot easier for me if my family's Thanksgivings were like that.

Rose smiles, as if thinking of the time fondly. "Yeah, it was."

"Was?"

She pops a fry in her mouth. "This year Trish decided to ring in her first Thanksgiving being engaged to Ian by turning into Suzy Homemaker and hosting a large feast at their house." Picking up her sandwich again, she eyes it, like she's trying to strategize where her next bite should be. "Knowing how whipped my brothers are, I'm sure Jackie and Jules will rope them into going."

I frown. "You weren't invited?"

She looks at me like I'm stupid. "Of course I was." She takes another bite, and I watch her cheeks puff out like a chipmunk. A drop of maple syrup slides down her chin. "But I'm not going."

"Why not?" I wipe it off with my thumb, sucking the syrup off.

We both stare at each other, the moment charged.

Finally, Rose looks away, chewing fast. "Trish is a deplorable cook, so it's probably better to fly solo this year." She gets very engrossed in the turtles bobbing up and down in the ponds.

Rose says she loves being single and independent, but like the mechanical engineer I am, I can't help noticing the pieces that don't fit.

1. Sad at her brother and best friend's wedding.

2. Wistful glances, followed by looks of annoyance whenever she spies her friends and their significant others together.

3. Her agitation when the men crashed their girls' night.

4. How she is always staying over at someone else's house when she has a penthouse to herself.

5. Not wanting to be the seventh wheel.

All those elements add up to someone *not* okay with being alone on Thanksgiving. I may not like going to my own family's holidays and get-togethers often, but I have my reasons. Rose, on the other hand, looks anything but satisfied with being alone.

"Why don't you come to my mom's house for Thanksgiving?" The words are out of my mouth before I can think them through. But once I do, I realize it's a great plan. I keep my promise to Brittany about staying longer, and Rose, acting as my buffer, doesn't have to spend the holiday alone. "That's got to be better than celebrating solo."

Her chicken sandwich pauses halfway to her mouth. "I didn't think we were doing those sorts of things."

I shrug, trying to play off my sudden nervousness. "We're *friends* with benefits, aren't we? We can call it a Friendsgiving." As my heart rate ticks higher, I remind myself of what Rose said. She isn't looking for a boyfriend. I'm not looking for anything serious. So as long as we both remember that this is casual between us, there's probably no harm in spending Thanksgiving together.

Rose takes a bite, frowning, like she's mulling it over. Probably trying to come up with more excuses.

"Plus, if I tell my mother I invited you, but you said no, Sunday Strip Day will get real awkward."

I wouldn't, but that doesn't stop Rose from pausing mid-chew and speaking without even trying to shift her food aside in her mouth. "Oo oudn't!" Her garbled exclamation is hilarious.

Smirking, I lean back, closing my eyes and soaking up the sun. "You up for taking that chance, Rosie-girl?"

I peek from behind my lashes as she grabs her Coke to help wash down her large mouthful.

She purses her lips, considering me. "Are you serious right now?"

I can't tell if she's annoyed or pleased. Maybe both. "As serious as a stripper without glitter."

That gets a small smile out of her. "That *is* serious."

I watch the ducks and turtles moving around and over the small pond in the middle of NASA's campus courtyard as I wait her out, knowing she hates any lengthy silence. I'm proven right when, after a moment of my continued reticence she heaves a large, annoyed sigh, her breasts threatening the thin fabric of her T-shirt.

"Fine." Rose pulls away from me and stands, tossing the rest of her lunch in the nearby trash can. "I'll go." Hands on hips, she faces me. "But after, you better fuck me like a stranger."

I choke on my saliva.

Two employees walking behind her do a double-take.

When I can breathe again, I ask, "And how in the world does one fuck someone like a stranger?"

Rose crosses her arms, the move pressing her breasts up, making the outline of her bra more pronounced. "You hit it hard and beat feet. And by it, I mean me." She thumbs to herself. "No feelings, no afterglow."

Chuckling, I stand, guiding her back to where the others are camped out with their lunches on a picnic bench, all nervousness gone. This is why Rose and I work so well together. And why Thanksgiving won't be laden with expectations.

Right before we reach the girls and Ian's table, I celebrate with a kiss to her cheek. "Deal. After Thanksgiving, Operation Stranger Danger will be in effect."

But as I drop her back off, Jules giving me more side-eye and Trish looking dreamily between Rose and me, the jitters return.

'Cause nothing about Rose so far has me wanting to beat feet.

Rose

TRISH WASTES no time after Vance heads back inside and Ian begins the NASA tour. "You two make *such* a cute couple." She's leaning in close so only I can hear as Ian and Jackie point out the different buildings and what people do inside them.

"Couple of people having sex is all," I mutter, ignoring Vance's plan to lie and say we're dating.

I've learned the hard way that if you say something often enough, you start to believe it. Like when I was little and I told myself if I was good enough, if I was perfect enough, if I just tried hard enough, that Mom would stay. And if Mom would stay, so would Dad. Lying to yourself takes an emotional toll, and I can't afford to start lying about Vance and me.

It's better not to try.

I'm smart enough to know that every time Vance throws an arm around my shoulder, teases me, or does sweet things like invite me to Thanksgiving dinner, that it's not gonna end well for me once he boards that space shuttle.

"This is where the Virtual Reality Lab is," Jackie says, her steps more like hops in her excitement. "I'll begin observing training sessions next week." She points to a nondescript brown building that looks like a high school built in the seventies.

In fact, most of the buildings here are boring and boxy. I find it ironic that on the inside, they house some of the most state of the art equipment ever invented.

"Just sex, huh?"

Trish and I jump, not having seen Jules sneak up from behind.

Jules squeezes between us, draping an around each of our shoulders. "Is that what Bodie thinks too?"

I pretend to be interested in what Ian is saying about the Cold War era causing the lack of windows due to security issues. "His idea, actually."

"And that's okay with you?" By Trish's tone, it's apparently *not* okay with her.

I must not have come across as flippant as I thought. I shrug off Jules' arm. "No biggie."

"Huh." I can feel Jules' side-eye. "So did you actually come to NASA today for lunch and a tour or are you really here to see your boy toy?"

I laugh, nearly choking. "I'm not sure boy toy is the right terminology." I think of our fifteen-year age gap. "Maybe geriatric gismo?"

Jules' hands land on my shoulder, stopping us. "Dude, he's my age." She looks mortally wounded. "Uncool."

"Yeah, but much to your dismay, you and I aren't dating."

"I always forget how much younger you are than the rest of us," Trish says.

"Thanks?" I make a note to buy more eye cream on the way home.

"It's a total compliment," Trish says. "It speaks to your maturity."

"Yes." Jules scoffs, rolling her eyes. "Because nothing says maturity more than a Blow Job shot taking college student who takes pole dance classes."

"Says the woman who owns multiple rhinestone collars for her pet cow," I deadpan.

"Cookie isn't a pet." Jules looks affronted. "She's family."

I take an interest in my surroundings. "Uh huh."

"Speaking of *family*," Trish butts in. "What is this I hear about you not coming to my Thanksgiving dinner?"

"Yeah, and be the odd man out again?" I roll my eyes. "I don't think so."

"Just bring Vance," Ian says, startling the rest of us by joining the conversation. Jackie is gazing at an ugly brown building with pebbled cement siding like it's Santa's workshop.

"He's having Thanksgiving with his family." I omit the part about me joining him. Lying by omission is okay. I do that all the time. That's how I stay one step ahead.

"Did you miss the part where Rose said she and Vance are just friends with benefits?" Jules asks.

Ian shrugs. "That doesn't sound like the guy who stalked Trish and me in Germany until I gave him your number."

Trish straightens to her full five feet five inches in her four-inch platforms. "What now?"

Ian raises an eyebrow in his fiancée's direction. "You didn't think it weird that Vance just happened to show up at the church in Munich right when we were there and followed us around?"

Trish frowns. "But he said—"

"And then declared he wanted to come with us on a day trip to Neuschwanstein Castle before suddenly leaving while we shopped for souvenirs?"

Trish frowns harder.

Ian looks at me. "It's because I gave him your contact information. That's what he really wanted." He tilts his head, looking very much like a lawyer giving his closing argument to the jury. "That doesn't sound like a guy who just wants friends with benefits, does it?"

"I agree with Ian," Jackie adds, turning away from the building and sliding into the conversation as if she was always listening. Which she probably was. "If you think about it logically—"

"As one does," Jules murmurs.

"From Bodie's contrary actions, he is either unable to say what he really wants or is oblivious to it," Jackie continues. "'Man is a confused creature; he knows not whence he comes or whither he goes, he knows little of the world, and above all, he knows little of himself.'"

Jules nods. "That sounds like one badass feminist quote right there."

"Who said that, sugar?" Trish smiles at our genius friend.

"Johann Wolfgang von Goethe." Jackie pushes up her glasses. "A German poet, politician, and scientist."

"Do tell." Trish loves when Jackie gets lost in her genius. We all do, really.

But my heart is beating too fast to listen as Jackie ventures on about an eighteenth century man's accomplishments while we walk down a tree-lined sidewalk.

As I try not to lie to myself, I can't help but admit that I *like* what I just heard. Which my street-smart sixth sense is telling me will only bring trouble my way.

We are just friends. Friends who slap uglies on the regular.

So Ian and Goethe can suck it.

ELEVEN
#FEMINISTSGIVEGOODTHANKS

Rose

THIS ISN'T SO BAD.

"Dude, how are you so good at this?" Jacob, Vance's eleven-year-old nephew, tosses his Xbox controller on the orange shag rug.

Turns out Helen's house is just a few blocks over from Flynn's in the coveted Clear Lake Forest neighborhood near NASA.

Vance was relegated to plumber, being sent upstairs where Helen ordered him to stop her master bathroom sink from dripping. Shortly after, Helen shooed me out of the kitchen after I cut myself slicing cheese for the charcuterie board I brought. I've been in the seventies-style living room since.

Thankfully, Brittany, Vance's sister, showed up a few minutes later with her boys in tow, dropping them off in front of the TV before scurrying out back with her husband Matt, each rolling a large cooler behind them. I'm not even sure she saw me sitting on the couch in her hurry.

"*Dude*. What can I say? Fortnite is my jam." I lean over and nudge him with my shoulder, nearly falling into him. Helen's couch is tweed and plaid and all things cozy. Which means deep divots in the couch cushions where people have sat over the years. Unlike my penthouse, Vance's childhood home looks lived in. It looks *real*, rather than magazine worthy.

I love it.

Jase, Jacob's older brother, snickers from the brown leather recliner off to the side of the living room. "Man, you let a girl beat you?" He laughs harder. "And five times, too!"

"Oh Jase, Jase, Jase..." I shake my head at him, all dramatic disappointment. "There's so much wrong with that misogynistic attitude of yours."

Both Jacob and Jase, their dark hair, brown eyes, and high cheekbones making them look similar enough to be twins, tilt their heads to the right. Seeing as their dad Matt is blond and blue-eyed, the Bodaway genes are strong with these two.

"What's miss-ah-ga—" Jacob shakes his head. "What did you say?"

"Misogynistic." Placing my controller next to me on the couch, I crook my Batman Band-Aided finger at them. "Gather 'round, boys, and let Auntie Rose tell you all the ways in which women rule the world and men need to just sit back and love it."

———

Twenty minutes later, I leave Jase and Jacob openmouthed and blinking in the living room to go see where else I can be helpful. Along the way, I take in family photos hung on the wall. Most are of Jacob and Jase at varying ages, but there are some older ones too.

There's a family portrait from Vance's childhood. I recognize Helen, not looking much different than she does now, and Brittany, looking like a pre-teen. And a scrawny kid. Vance.

He's probably about six or seven. His silky hair is styled in a hilarious bowl cut. He's wearing an orange, blue, and white striped shirt—à la Bert and Ernie from Sesame Street.

So cute.

But there's also a handsome man with his arm around Helen. He's standing tall, his face more serious than happy, but the corners of his lips are tilted up just enough to let you know he's proud to be standing with his family.

"Did the boys scare you away already?"

I jump at Vance's voice, coming from right behind me.

"Those two rugrats?" I thumb over my shoulder toward the living room. "Please. Ask them later who scared who."

He shakes his head, laughing. "Why doesn't that surprise me in the least?"

"Because you know I'm a winner?"

"You're something, all right."

We smile at each other a beat longer.

"So..." I glance around, a sudden heat overtaking me. "Is that your dad?" I point to the old family portrait.

I regret my question when the smile falls off his face. "Yeah. That's my dad."

"Um... what happened to him?" I'm aware I shouldn't have asked. But things just got awkward, and when things get awkward, I tend to make them awkwarder. Not a word. I know. But whatever. It's what I do.

"He died in action when I was little." He stares at the photo. "A few weeks after that photo was taken, actually."

Yep, I was right. I shouldn't have asked. "Sorry."

"It's all right." Vance shrugs, still staring at the photo.

"What was his name?"

"Lonan Bodaway." His voice seems devoid of all emotion.

"Lonan?"

"Means cloud or blackbird in Zuni." He gives me a wry smile. "I'm guessing his soul leaned more to blackbird."

"Why do you say that?"

"Blackbird's more ominous, isn't it? And he did die young."

I look back at the picture, unsure how to respond. "He was very handsome." I lean closer, noticing the crinkles around Lonan Bodaway's eyes. "You look like him."

Vance hums in acknowledgement but doesn't say anything else.

"Why don't Helen or your sister have Zuni names?"

"They do. My mother's real first name is Elu, meaning full of grace."

"I can see that." I nudge him in the ribs, trying to lighten the moment. "She sure is graceful on the pole."

He rolls his eyes. "Har. Har."

Having succeeded in making him laugh, I breathe a sigh of relief. "Why does she go by Helen?"

"Always did when she wasn't on the reservation." He shrugs. "At least, that's what she told me. And then, when we moved here, it was easier to introduce herself as Helen. That's her middle name."

Huh. I look at the girl with heavy dark bangs in the picture next to Helen. "And Brittany?"

"Mom flipped it when Brittany was born, gave her a Zuni middle name, Tacia. It was my great-grandmother's name." He snorts. "Means quiet."

"Why is that funny?"

"You'll see."

I smile at the frustrated affection he has for his sister. "And you? What's your Zuni middle name?"

His smile disappears again. "Lonan, like my dad." He nods

back at the portrait. "Let's hope it means more cloud than black-bird this time."

My heart drops at that inauspicious comment.

"You know"—Vance tilts his head, studying the family portrait—"I never understood why Mom hung this."

He sounds like he's talking to himself, so I say nothing.

"I still remember coming home from the funeral." A V forms between his brows. "Mom started going through all the mail that had been piling up since we got the call that he died."

I reach out and hold his hand. Second-guessing myself, I try and pull it back, but his grip tightens on mine.

"The picture was buried beneath some overdue bills, and when she saw it, my mom just lost it." He shakes his head, as if trying to dislodge the memory, still not letting go of my hand. "Cried so hard she passed out. My sister had to help her to bed." He swallows. "Stayed there for months."

"Helen?" It's hard to imagine such a strong woman having a huge breakdown.

"Yeah."

We're quiet for a moment before I get the nerve to ask another question. "What branch in the military?"

"Army."

A few feet away, the back screen door slams, Brittany coming in wearing what looks like overly large work gloves with her black leggings, fitted T-shirt, oversized cardigan, and Nikes. I'm glad Vance wasn't lying when he said to dress casually. I was nervous when I traded the silk dress I was going to wear for jeans, sandals, and a cotton wrap blouse.

"We have a problem." Brittany blows a strand of near-black hair out of her eyes.

Vance is alert in a second, no trace of the lost little boy look he wore a moment ago. "What's wrong?"

Brittany sees me and does a double-take. Then her eyes flick to our clasped hands.

She smirks.

Together Vance and I let go, me clenching my hand tight, feeling somewhat odd without his to hold on to.

Vance clears his throat. "Well?" he prompts his sister.

Adopting another dramatic expression, Brittany throws her hands in the air, one glove flying off. "The turkey is still frozen."

I catch the glove.

Brittany slumps against the wall. "Mom's going to *kill* me."

I like Brittany. She's got good dramatic flair.

And I also see why Vance finds her Zuni name amusing.

"Everything all right out there?" Vance and I turn to see Helen peering out from the kitchen. "Nothing's wrong with that turkey, is there?" Helen's normally jovial expression narrows on her daughter. "I let you talk me into this deep-fried turkey fad, you better not make me regret it."

"No, no." Brittany straightens, trying to smile but looking more like a hyena with bared teeth. "All good. I just came in to see if Rose would like to come out and have a beer." She punches me playfully in the arm, hitting a sweet spot that has me wincing. "Save her from my video-gaming sons."

Seeing someone in need of a lifeline, and not wanting to get dead-armed again, I jump in to throw it. "Yes, I'd love to, thanks." Still holding the glove, I usher both Vance and Brittany out the door and away from their mother. In the short time I've known Helen, I've come to see how very astute she is. Retreat is the best option at this point.

The screen door slams behind us, and from our position on the back porch, I can see Matt standing in the middle of the yard where it looks like a fire pit would normally be, surrounded by lawn chairs. But instead of a fire, there's a large silver pot with a temperature gauge set up over a burner. Next to it are the two coolers from earlier, one with a naked turkey sitting on top.

Matt takes one look at us and chuckles.

"It's not funny, Matty!" Brittany wipes her forehead with her gloved hand. Matt bites his lip.

The closer we get, the more heat I feel from the flames under the pot. But sure enough, when we touch the bird, it's ice cold.

"Mom's going to kill me." Brittany plops down on a lawn chair.

"I told you to stay off that Pinterest, Brit." Matt still looks amused. He turns to Vance and me. "She's always on that thing, discovering do-it-yourself projects and weird-ass food to cook." He twists his back, stretching. "Just last month, I pulled my back when she had me adding shiplap to the dining room."

Brittany sits up and narrows her eyes at her husband. "You didn't say that when I turned the attic over the garage into your man cave. I found *that* idea on Pinterest."

Matt shrugs.

"And besides," Brittany continues, "fried turkey is not 'weird-ass food.'"

Matt just takes a swig of beer. "Well, who told you that soaking a frozen turkey in water for just three hours would defrost it?"

His wife holds her glare, but her nostrils flare when she mumbles, "Pinterest."

Vance chuckles. Which sets Matt to chuckling.

I pull out my phone.

Brittany slumps back again. "Fine, laugh it up. I'll just be known as the person who ruined Thanksgiving."

Vance, his laughter dying, runs a hand through his hair. "I mean, maybe Mom'll laugh about it?"

Brittany and Matt both look at him with eyebrows raised.

Vance grimaces. "Or, you know, maybe not."

Brittany looks at me, and I glance up from my phone as Google Maps loads my location. "For as casual as we are at holidays, Mom is rather stringent on certain things."

"Like having a turkey," Matt adds, making Brittany glare at him again.

The address loads. If I'm right... I check the distance to the West Ranch's nearest customer. The blue line between Vance's mother's house and them is short and doable.

"What are you looking at?" Vance asks, peering over my shoulder.

I click the screen off. "No one freak out. I have a plan." Pointing at Brittany, I walk backward toward the side yard. "Can you stall your mom for a bit?"

She must hear the confidence in my voice because she suddenly looks hopeful. "Yes I can."

"Awesome-sauce." I turn and sprint toward the driveway.

"Wait, what?" Vance calls after me. His footsteps follow, catching up with me at the gate.

"Where are you going?"

"Shhh." I put my finger to my lips then point to the window above us, where his mother is probably still in the kitchen, cutting radishes into roses. "I'll be back," I whisper, finger gunning him.

Vance snorts. "Oh, no you don't. You're not leaving me this time, Rosie-girl. Not again." He covers my hands with his, pulling me to him. "Besides, what are you? The Terminator?"

I feel my smile dim, his words making me pause. *Me* leave *him*?

In a flash, all our previous interactions wash over me. Me leaving him in the guest room at the wedding, turning him down for dates at the strip club, declaring I wasn't looking for a boyfriend at the bar, trying to sneak out in the morning after sex rounds three and four, kicking him out of my apartment after declaring friends with bennies.

I've been pushing him away, making him leave. But he keeps coming back. Does... does that mean he cares? Like Ian said?

"Rosie?" He tilts his head, frowning, oblivious to the emotional shock I've just had.

Shaking it off, I pull my hands from his and unlatch the gate. Reaching back to him, I deepen my voice in my best Arnold Schwarzenegger imitation. "Come with me if you want your turkey."

———

Vance

"Where are we going?" I hold on to the oh-shit handle above the door as Rose takes a turn at high speed. "Also, side note, turkey is not worth dying over."

She rolls her eyes at me. "You strap yourself on top of a tank full of rocket fuel. You can't tell me you're scared of little old me behind the wheel, can you?"

She weaves in and out of holiday traffic like a drunk sailor on leave. It would be frightening if she didn't do it so flawlessly.

"Of course not," I lie. "Just wanted to make sure you're aware of the limit on how far we'll go for a bird."

She revs the engine.

"*Death.*" I glare at her. "Death is the limit in case you didn't get that."

Exiting the neighborhood by taking a right on Lake View Boulevard, Rose simultaneously thumbs the buttons on her steering wheel. The car speakers start ringing.

"Hello?"

"Mr. Robert Vincent?" Rose guns it to the traffic light. "This is Rose West of West Ranch."

A beat of silence. "Uh, hello." He clears his throat. "Yes, Ms. West, what can I do you for?"

Thankfully she stops at an intersection at NASA Road 1. "Well, Bob, I need a turkey."

"A turkey." Pause. "On Thanksgiving." He sounds dumbfounded.

"Yep. And I know you're just the guy who can help me." The light turns green, and the back of my head hits the car seat when she stomps on the accelerator.

"Well, Ms. West, the shop is closed and I—"

"I'm two minutes away."

"You're what?"

"I'm two minutes away from your butcher shop, Bob, and I'm telling you now that if you meet me there with a turkey, I will make it worth your while." She makes the left onto NASA and immediately changes lanes and shifts gears, shooting ahead. "Not just for today's turkey, but for your next order of beef from the ranch."

"I... I mean, I would, but you see—"

We pass by Jules' apartment building on the right.

"How does fifteen percent off wholesale sound?"

Silence.

Rose downshifts, slowing as she hits a red light. "Did I lose you, Bob?"

"Um no. I was just wondering, could you repeat what you—"

"Fifteen percent. Plus whatever you deem a last-minute turkey worth." The light turns green before she stops, and Rose revs the engine once more, passing a stopped minivan and an old pickup truck on the left.

"I'll see you at the shop in five minutes, Ms. West." He hangs up.

Rose coasts on a flashing yellow across westbound NASA Road 1 and onto Kirby Drive. A few seconds later the engine ticks as it cools in the parking lot of Bay Area Meat Market. I manage to pry my fingers off the panic bar.

She turns to me, all smiles, and pulls a wad of cash out of her bra. "And now we wait for the goods to be delivered." She starts counting out her money in a calm, unaffected manner.

Meanwhile, my mind is reeling as fast as her car's acceleration. "You don't seem at all fazed by this turn of events."

Rose shrugs. "Just another Thursday for me." She pauses in counting her fifties. "Too crazy for you?"

Huffing out a breath, I laugh. "Not in the least." Then I hide my shaking hands under my thighs.

TWENTY MINUTES after we sped off in her Aston Martin, we arrive back at Mom's victorious, wheeling a fifteen-pound turkey, already brined, trussed, and ready to fry, in a fold-out wagon.

"Oh my God!" My sister runs over to Rose, throwing her arms around her. "How did you manage this?"

Rose shrugs. "Just knew a guy."

I scoff. "Knew a guy, my ass."

Rose glares at me, annoyed that I hadn't agreed to keep quiet on how she essentially hijacked a turkey on Thanksgiving Day.

"It wasn't a big deal." Rose hardens her voice, evil eye still in effect.

"You call arranging a discount price on the next order of

beef the butcher buys from your family's ranch just so he'd be willing to open shop and get us a turkey no big deal?"

Rose takes a menacing step toward me, turkey in tow.

I raise my hands in surrender. "Okay, okay."

She holds the glare a second longer before tugging the wagon toward Matt, who's already pulling the lid off the pot.

"And they just had a turkey lying around?" Brit asks me out of the corner of her mouth. "On Thanksgiving?"

"Nope." I shake my head in amusement, the scene replaying in my head. "They'd sold out. But seeing as the owner hadn't cooked his own turkey yet, he handed over the bird his family was going to eat in exchange for a number Rose typed into her phone and flashed him." I whistle, remembering the way the man had nearly thrown the turkey at Rose, even giving her the wagon in which to haul it. "That bird probably costs more than a car."

In shocked silence, which is a rare occurrence for my sister, she watches Matt help Rose do the honors of lowering the bird into the oil.

"How am I supposed to pay her back?" Brit says, exhaling long and loud.

"If you even offer to, she'll tit punch you."

My sister chokes on air, turning to me wide-eyed. "What?"

"Her words, not mine." I nod at Rose, who puts the lid on the pot, then takes a beer Matt is offering from a second cooler by the fire pit.

She smiles, eyes on Rose. "I like her for you."

"It's not really like that, Brit. It's not serious." I frown, wondering why when I say that in my head it sounds fine, but when I say it to my sister it doesn't ring as true.

"I don't care how serious it *was*, I care about how serious you're going to make it."

I open my mouth, but Brit talks over me.

"She got my baby brother to finally show up to a family gathering for more than just a plate of food and a good-bye." Brit throws me some serious side-eye. "I'm smart enough to know that if Rose wasn't here, you wouldn't be either." She punches me in the bicep before I can object. "Don't fuck this up."

Rubbing my arm, I wonder why I surround myself with such strong, violent women. "Sorry to burst your bubble, sis, but Rose and I are just friends." I side-step in case she tries swinging for me again.

Instead, she laughs in my face. "Sure, sure. *Friends.*" She shakes her head, looking at me like she did when I was little and in trouble. "Well then, you better step it up, little brother, because between Rose taking pole dance lessons with Mom, playing video games with the boys, and her willingness to buy a butcher's turkey for me, I'd say the Bodaways are more likely to kick you out of the family and adopt her if you're too stupid to lock her down."

I throw her a sardonic look. "First, thanks for that. Second" —I glance up at Rose, who has her head thrown back in laughter, looking youthful and stunning—"it would be a crime to lock her down. She's only twenty-one."

"Hey, if she's okay with you robbing her cradle, so am I." Brit turns to watch Rose stop laughing long enough to taunt Matt into a beer-chugging contest.

Huh. I thought for sure Brit would give me shit about her age. Thought she'd agree with how illogical it would be to get serious with someone so much younger than me. "Well then," I say, my tone much more defensive than I mean it, "Not only is she young, but she's a billionaire who is about to graduate college with a prestigious degree." Instead of reassuring me, my logical reasons for not being anything more than friends with Rose pinch at my chest.

I'd call it heartburn, but I haven't eaten anything yet.

Brit simply throws her hands on her hips, looking condescending as hell. "So what you're telling me is that she's a great catch and you're too chicken-shit to step up." She claps me on the back so hard I stumble. "Good to know."

"I—"

But she's gone, walking over to Rose and Matt, leaving me on the sideline with my lame excuses, dead arm, and bruised shoulder blade.

Rolling my shoulder and shaking out my arm, I ease the pain from my sister's attack.

But it doesn't do anything for the pain in my chest.

TWELVE

SYMBIOSIS

Rose

"There." Brit sets the platter, holding the perfectly golden turkey, to the left of her mother. "What do you think of that?" For someone who was near tears a little more than an hour ago, Vance's sister looks pretty smug.

Though it could also be due to the four beers we drank out back while we waited for the turkey to fry.

"Wow, Mom." Jacob, sitting one seat over to my right, smacks his lips while holding a knife in one hand and a fork in the other. "That looks *good*."

Everyone's situated around the mahogany dining table. The matching chairs are ornate with upholstered seats and wooden backs. There's a china cabinet to match, filled with long-ago collected knick-knacks and the extra place settings of good china we aren't using. As is usual with older houses, the formal dining area is its own room, separated from the rest of the living spaces. And although it has that untouched, slightly museum-like quality of a room used mainly for holidays and big family gath-

erings, with our casual attire and everyone's relaxed attitude, it's
like I'm part of a long-standing tradition. It's homey.

It's awesome.

"You know, Brittany"—Helen, looking very matriarchal in
khaki slacks and a sweater set, surveys the bird as Vance carves
it—"I was wary of this whole fried turkey fad, but it does look
delicious." It's hard to believe that this is the same woman I hug
a pole with every Sunday morning.

"Yes," Matt says, catching his wife's eye. "Just like Pinterest
said it would."

He jumps in his seat across from me at the table, Brittany
having no doubt just kicked him in the shin, though his smile
never wavers.

"Well, to give credit where credit is due, it wouldn't have
turned out half as well if it weren't for Rose's help." She nods
graciously at me.

I smile, my cheeks tight. The whole point of challenging
both Brit and Matt to a chugging contest was to beat them into
submission so they wouldn't be able to mention anything about
my turkey procurement. The last thing I want is to make this
day about anything I did. Or about how much money I spent. It
should be about Thanksgiving. About family.

Helen pats my hand, and my face heats. "Yes, such a good
girl, my Rosie."

I can't remember the last time I blushed.

"But isn't your family missing you today?" Helen asks me,
her concern only making my cheeks hotter.

I finger the napkin on my lap with my free hand, trying to
muster up some levity. "Oh no, my brothers are with their
womenfolk today."

"But what about your parents?" Jacob asks. "I tried
asking Mom if I could go to Billy's house today." He leans in
conspiratorially. "He got a new hoverboard rider for his

birthday," he whispers, as if that explains why he should've been allowed to miss a family holiday. He straightens. "But she said kids were required to be with their parents on Thanksgiving." He finishes with a masterful pre-teen roll of his eyes that encompasses both his exasperation at not being allowed to go and his appreciation at being wanted by his mother.

"My parents are dead."

Jase's eyes bug out, and Jacob looks down at his plate. "Sorry."

Well, shit. I hadn't meant to say that. "Ah, don't be." I smile widely as if proving just how okay I am with my parents' passing. "It was a long time ago."

"Here you go, Mom." Vance serves her a few slices of breast meat. His eyes are soft on me before he winks and asks the table, "Who wants a leg?"

The sad tangent forgotten, Jacob and Jase raise their hands and call out, "Me! Me!"

Brittany pouts. "Between the two of you, I'll never get to have a turkey leg on Thanksgiving again."

I catch the boys' eyes. They blink and sit up.

"You can have my leg, Mom." Jase elbows Jacob, who nods fervently.

"Yeah," Jacob adds. "You can have mine too."

Brittany and Matt stare at their boys like they've each grown another head.

"Isn't that nice?" Helen beams. "Such gentlemen you two are turning out to be."

"True gentlemen are feminists," Jacob says with a solemn look on his face. "And should always make sure a woman has the first choice when he can."

Jase nods. "Especially as most of their choices were taken when patriarchal societies were first established to suppress female rights and power." He looks at me. "Isn't that right, Rose?"

"That's right." I roll my lips in to keep from laughing and raise my water glass to them. "Always knew you boys would make great feminists."

Jacob and Jase beam at me and raise their water glasses in return. "Cheers!"

Brittany turns to me as I sip, her mouth open. "I'm just saying"—she leans across the table, resting her hand on one of Helen's, which is still on one of mine—"that if my brother's an idiot and doesn't put a ring on it, *I'm* going to marry you."

My face heats again. I search for something smart-ass to say to deflect, but my mind blanks. I can't meet Vance's eye.

"I'm that replaceable, huh?" Matt nudges his wife, saving me from having to respond. "Thanks for that, babe."

Unrepentant, Brittany sits back, smirking at her husband. "Any time, honey."

"Here you go, Brit." Vance hacks the legs off the bird and tosses them both on his sister's plate. He throws his sister an indecipherable look.

"Ah..." Brittany frowns at the massacred legs. "Thanks?"

Before I can shake off whatever awkwardness is taking control of my brain and further assess Vance's expression, Matt lifts his plate for turkey. "White meat for me. You know I'm a breast man." He chuckles while Brittany rolls her eyes, looking very much like her sons.

"Jeez, Dad." Jase shakes his head at his father. "Don't be such a mis-o-gin-iss."

"Yeah, Dad." Jacob rolls his eyes with dramatic disgust. "Really."

The whole table laughs.

"Seriously, Rose." Brittany toasts me with her wine glass. "We can elope right now."

———

"VICTORY IS MINE!" I stand as tall as my flat sandals allow me in the inch-deep shag carpet and raise my game controller in the air.

"She's like a Jedi Master of Fortnite," Jase whispers to his dad.

"Undefeated I am." I try to nod sagely, but it's no doubt ruined by my shit-eating grin.

What can I say? I love winning.

"Har, har," Jacob deadpans.

Vance's lips twitch, but he's still pouting from when I took him out in the first round. He may be able to put shit together in space, but he sucks at video games.

My stomach churns from my sudden movement, so I sit back on the well-worn sofa. If I'd known there were going to be three kinds of pie for dessert, I wouldn't have had seconds on everything at dinner. But not wanting to be rude (and unable to help myself), I still managed to eat a slice of each flavor before settling in to whoop on some Bodaway butt in a knock-out round of Fornite.

"Just you wait, Aunt Rosie." Jase, sitting on the floor next to his brother, waves his fist in the air with mock anger. "I'm gonna practice so hard that when Christmas comes, I'll take you down!"

Aunt Rosie. Christmas. His words hit me like a gut punch from his little fist.

I blink back a sudden wave of emotion. Seriously, between the blushing and the wet eyes, it's like I've become a different person.

"Practice never hurts." I grasp for my normal smart-ass self. "But you'll need more than a few weeks of it to beat someone on *my* level." I point to Vance, sitting in the recliner. "Just ask your uncle how to overcome such overwhelming defeat. He's gotten loads of practice since meeting me."

"Har, har," Vance mimics his nephews' earlier sarcasm. Then, lightning-fast, he pounces on Jase and Jacob, wrapping a long arm around each and pulling them to the floor. Then the tickling starts.

Matt gets pulled into the pile by his older son, letting Jase hold him down so Jacob can jump on top. Brit and Helen watch from their spots next to me, sipping on their wine, wide smiles on their faces, giving me the impression that what I'm witnessing right now is a rare sight.

I'd jump into the wrestling/tickling pile myself, but as I've already reached under the hem of my shirt and popped the button on my waistband, I'll sit this one out. Besides, I'm gonna pass out in a food coma if I don't leave soon.

"Ahhh, no.... Uncle Vance—ahh!" Jase's peals of laughter ring out over the video game's soundtrack.

"Get 'em, Vance, get 'em!" Brit eggs him on. She catches my eye and mouths *Thank you*.

I don't know if she's thanking me for the turkey again or for something else, so I just smile.

Then I ponder how serious she was earlier at dinner and whether I should book us a flight to Vegas.

Because I can't remember the last time I had this much fun at Thanksgiving, and I very much would like to find out what a Bodaway Christmas is like.

———

Vance

Rose falls asleep during the car ride back to my place.

It's odd sitting next to a sleeping Rose. She's usually so vibrant, reverberating spontaneity, fun, and enthusiasm for life.

Rose snore/snorts, turning her head toward me. "Victory..." she mumbles.

Smiling, I make the turn toward my apartment.

The quiet is nice too. It's peaceful occupying the same space as her. It reminds me of this cool astronomy project NASA is doing at the Marshall Space Flight Center in Alabama. They've been studying the star R Aquarii, which, originally thought to be just one star, is actually two—a dense, white dwarf star and a cool red giant star.

R Aquarii is a volatile stellar relationship, or symbiotic stars. Stars so close that they interact with one another in a similar way.

The white dwarf is about ten thousand times brighter than the red giant, and has stronger gravitational fields, though it's smaller. A red giant star is a dying star in the last stages of stellar evolution. As the star exhausts the helium within its core, the shell containing the gases burns carbon, getting hotter and hotter, heading toward supernova.

But because of the white dwarf's gravitational force, it sloughs away the carbon layers of the red giant, pulling them onto its surface to burn away. Essentially extending the red dwarf's life.

I've always thought I was doing just fine, great, even. I'm doing the work I love and living a healthy, satisfactory life. But today, going on a high-speed chase for a turkey, sitting beside Rose at dinner, hearing her regale the group with stories of my mother's pole dancing successes to everyone's horror, and then beating all our asses at a video game, I realized how much I hold myself back. I was a red giant until Rose's strong gravitational pull burned away my blinders.

But, just as with the stars, I'm not sure how long both of us will last if this continues.

The wind through my 4Runner's cracked window plays with her blond hair, which she put up in a messy bun during the tournament. I have a feeling if I tried to explain symbiotic stars to Rose, all she'd hear is me comparing her to a "white dwarf" and she'd straight-up junk punch me. She's funny like that.

Her humor has made me laugh more in the past few weeks than I have all of last year, probably.

Tonight, I realized that I'd made myself a loner long before I met Rose. By not wanting a lasting romantic relationship, I'd inadvertently walled myself off from most any relationship with people. Even my family.

My SUV bounces over the speed bump in my apartment complex's parking lot. Rose's open mouth lets loose another snort/snore. There isn't much lady-like about Rose, but she is definitely all woman. She's one of a kind. And as much as I don't want to dim her burning light with my dying one, I wonder if maybe we can't prolong what we have going on.

I told myself that inviting her to Thanksgiving dinner with my family was to keep her from being lonely, but I have a feeling it was more to keep me from being alone.

Maybe it doesn't have to end with my next flight. Maybe we could just let this run its course, until Rose is ready to move on, until she's found what it is she wants.

But then the memory of my mother, crumpled on the floor and crying, telephone in her hand, rears its head, and I shake off my doubts. It's better to end things when we said we would. It would be nothing but selfish for me to hold on.

I park and cut the engine, contemplating my next move. Since we didn't drive to her penthouse, Rose told me she'd be the one to beat feet with an Uber after we played stranger danger at my place. But after today, I really hate the idea of Rose leaving.

She snort/snores again in her sleep, jarring me away from my thoughts and making me smile as only Rose can. I slide out, closing my door carefully, and round the hood to open her passenger side door. Rose stays asleep through me unbuckling her and swinging her legs out, but when I turn and squat down, trying to hook her arms around my shoulders in a piggyback, she stirs.

"What's happening?" Her breath tickles my hair.

I shift her weight forward and grab under her thighs. "I'm taking you to bed."

"Stranger danger time?" On her own, she turns her upper body toward me and wraps her arms securely over my shoulders and around my neck.

Standing, I hike her higher and more securely on my back and kick the door closed. "Sure, stranger danger time."

"Awesome," she mumbles into my neck, then promptly falls asleep again.

It takes quite a few minutes and some precarious balancing to get up the steps to my apartment and drop Rose gently on the bed.

"Imma rock your world," Rose mumbles into the pillow.

She snores through me taking off her sandals and jeans.

I leave her to go to the bathroom, and by the time I'm back she's shucked off her remaining shirt and bra and has lain diagonally across my king-size bed in just her panties.

Though Rose is near-naked and on my bed, it isn't exactly how I planned this night to go. However, I'm not annoyed. If anything, I'm kind of relieved. As much as I like fulfilling orgasm guarantees with her, I also like just being with her. It makes me feel more alive. Even if she's passed out in a food coma.

It takes some maneuvering on my part and some inventive sleep-cursing by Rose before I finally wrestle the covers out from under her and have us situated—Rose on one side of the bed, me on the other.

Sighing, stress about today's dinner drains away. I'm tired in a different way than I usually am when I hang around my family. Instead of anxiety, I feel... content? It's an odd change of pace.

Though, as content as I might be, I'm still awake ten minutes later.

Something's not right.

I run through my usual nighttime routine, wondering if I missed a step along the way. Did I forget to lock the front door? Was there something I was supposed to set my alarm for tomorrow?

Before I can figure out exactly what's missing, Rose rolls over and lands half on top of me.

"Vance?"

"Yeah?" I curl my arm around her.

"Thanks for Thanksgiving."

I smile up at the ceiling. "You're welcome." I kiss the top of her head. "Thanks for the turkey."

She answers with a snore.

I fall asleep a moment later.

———

HUAHH. *Huahh.*

It sounds like a large animal is in the throes of sex.

Huahh.

Or maybe someone vomiting? It's hard to tell.

Rose must have moved, seeing as I can move my left arm, so

I roll that way, searching for her. The sheets are warm, but she's not there.

"Rose?"

Huahh.

Either the sound is getting louder or I'm waking up. Prying my eyes open, I see the barest beginning of sunlight making an appearance through the window.

The sound of the toilet flushing starts my brain firing, and I jump out of bed and stumble into the bathroom.

Rose is kneeling in front of the toilet, head lying on her arms, which are crossed and braced over the rim. Her eyes are closed, her brow sweaty.

"Rose?"

"Uh, no." She doesn't open her eyes, but she turns her head in the opposite direction. "Go away."

I drop to my knees beside her. "You sick?"

"No, I'm vomiting out my internal organs for funsies."

I'm glad her eyes are closed because I don't think she'd appreciate my smile. "Yeah, sorry. Stupid question."

She suddenly rises and hunches over the toilet again. I smooth loose strands of hair back from her face while she gags.

"How long have you been in here?"

"Maybe an hour?" She spits but doesn't throw anything up again. "I don't know."

"Maybe you got it all up."

She lays her head back down, and I stand, grabbing a washcloth from the closet. "Want to try coming back to bed?" I soak the cloth with cold water and wring it out. "I can bring a trash can and set it next to your side. You'll probably be more comfortable there." I rub her forehead with the cloth, and she sighs.

"I should go home. I don't want to get you sick."

"No way you're going home like this." I drag the cold cloth

over the back of her neck. "What do you think it is, food poisoning?"

"If it is, and you tell your mother I got sick from her Thanksgiving dinner, I'll kill you." She raises her head off her arm and glares at me. "Like legit run you over or something."

Clad in only neon green lace underwear, hunched over a toilet, shaking and sweating from being sick, Rose still manages to make a mean death threat.

Things are never boring with her around.

"Come on, Rosie-girl. Up we go." I lift her up by her armpits and brace her weight on me as she gets her feet under her.

"Damn it." Rose shakes her foot out in front of her. "Pins and needles." She tries walking, but it's more a limp-hobble.

We make it to the bed, where I lay her down and tuck her in. "Just lie close to the edge. I'll be right back with the trash can in case you need it."

She mumbles something about embarrassment and curses three kinds of pie.

By the time I change the bag on the tall trash can from the kitchen and bring it to her, she's out like a light. Not snoring like before but breathing deeply. She looks even younger when she isn't cracking jokes and being a smart-ass.

Her wide brown eyes are closed, her thick lashes resting on her cheeks. Her brows, usually moving with expression, are still and delicately arched. A handful of freckles are scattered across her nose and high cheekbones. And full lips, the color of her namesake, are parted, giving her an innocent look. It almost seems impossible that such a force of nature lives inside this peaceful beauty.

Sometimes with Rose, I get lost in all the showmanship, the glitter, the jokes, the hair, but now, still and peaceful with nothing to distract me, I can see just how stunning she really is.

She glows. Like a star.

THIRTEEN
#EMOTIONALPANIC

Rose

THERE WAS no stranger danger sex last night.

That's my first thought upon consciousness taking ahold of me.

Hell, there wasn't even regular sex. I squeeze my eyes shut as the events of last night unfold in my mind. Fuck.

Maybe it was all a dream. Carefully, I open my eyes. Instead of the bare, light gray bedroom wall of my condo, where I was supposed to sleep last night, it's the bare, white wall of Vance's apartment. Fuck. Fuck.

Nope. Apparently, I really did pass out in a food coma, only to later blow chunks into my friend-with-bennies' toilet in the wee hours of the morning. *Awesome.*

I burrow deeper under the covers.

My skin feels too tight, and my chest is all fluttery. Is this... embarrassment? It's a new feeling for me. I mean, I do ridiculous things *all* the time. I'm the queen of the outlandish and in-your-face-ness. And never, not once, have I been so embarrassed that I felt like dying.

Until this moment.

I huff out a large sigh under the covers and regret it immediately. My breath is hot and foul like a metal garbage can left out in the Texas sun. Just another fantastic morning revelation. I pull the covers off for a breath of fresh air and catch sight of the windows above the bed.

Okay, maybe I don't want to *die*, but I do find myself contemplating how to jump out of a three-story-high window without legit bodily harm. A sprained ankle would be a fair price to pay for bypassing a walk of shame.

Especially as my side of the bed has a towel draped over the edge and a trashcan pulled up close. There's even a tall glass of water on a coaster on the nightstand.

So not only did he not get stranger danger, but Vance took care of me? That's weird, right?

I slide my foot across the sheets in search of another body but find no one. Okay, good. Silver lining. I can sneak off to the bathroom before he—

"Rose?"

Slamming my eyes shut, I lie still and feign sleep.

I can't hear his footsteps on the carpet, but from my awkward position, on my side with my back leg extended, I can feel him getting closer.

Breathe in, breathe out. Relax your eyelids. Do not react to his unfair, delicious morning scent.

He taps my nose. "No use pretending, Rosie-girl. You are *not* that graceful a breather."

I try to fake snore, but the air gets caught funny, and I start coughing.

Hashtag fail.

Vance chuckles, soft and deep. Not only is it an awesome

sound, but it's a fantastic visual when I open my eyes, even though I'm embarrassed as fuck.

"You're a nut, you know that?" His eye crinkles are deep and sexy.

I grunt, not sure what to say. Because on top of being disgusted with the aftermath of being sick, embarrassed that he took care of me, and ashamed that I didn't make good on my stranger danger plans, I'm now turned on.

He laughs again. "The great and mighty Rose West isn't feeling embarrassed, is she?" His right eye crinkles more as his smile turns into a smirk.

"Maybe," I say into the pillow, regretting it instantly when my breath blows back at me.

Instead of more laughter, which is what I'm expecting, Vance runs his hands through my hair. Or tries to—it's kind of a knotty mess. "No need to be embarrassed."

I grunt again.

"Come on." He lightly shakes my shoulder. "After being sick, nothing feels better than a warm shower."

I don't move.

"*And* I've got a new toothbrush with your name on it."

That perks me up. Lifting my head, I chance a good look at him. He doesn't seem annoyed. His smile is gentle, almost... loving? I don't blink, trying to memorize this moment. The embarrassment fades, and I feel—

He slaps my ass over the covers. "Come on. You stink."

Well, then. Moment over.

Twenty minutes later, I feel great. Nay, fabulous.

Conditioner and a toothbrush. Is there really anything else a girl needs?

Well, maybe orgasms. Yes, definitely orgasms. But one thing at a time.

I'm sitting at Vance's counter in one of his T-shirts and a pair of his boxers—washed, cleaned, conditioned, and eating oatmeal.

Not a trace of nausea to be felt.

Hashtag win.

"Are you sure you should be eating that?" Vance eyes my oversized bowl. "I mean, oatmeal by itself wouldn't be so bad when you're not feeling well, but did you even measure how much brown sugar and maple syrup you put on that?"

"I feel great," I say with my cheeks full of sugared oats. "I don't think I was actually sick. I think my stomach just revolted because I ate so much last night." I manage to swallow, the hot cereal making my eyes water a bit. "Otherwise there is no way I'd feel better so quickly."

"That would explain why no one else got sick."

I pause, a large spoonful halfway to my mouth. "How do you know?" I glare at him. "You didn't tell Helen I was sick, did you?"

"Calm down, champ." He holds out both hands toward me. "I only texted Brit and told her *I* wasn't feeling well."

"Oh." I jam the spoon in my mouth. "Thanks," I mumble around the oatmeal.

Vance is making me uncomfortable. And this time it has nothing to do with waking up with vomit breath. Rehashing all my past relationships, it isn't like I dated losers. Okay, I never really *dated* dated, but then neither are Vance and I. And it isn't like any of the guys I've been with were jerks. No one talked shit to me or was overly aggressive. But they also didn't invite me to family Thanksgivings or hold my hair back while I threw up (which, during my younger, pre-legal party days, they had plenty of chances) or took the blame for something to save me embarrassment. And they sure as shit didn't ask me to stay around for breakfast in the morning when they caught me trying to Uber my way home.

I eye the phone in question, its glitter case turned over and placed out of my reach. "So how long are you going to confiscate my phone for?"

He pours milk over his Mueslix. "When you promise not to high-tail it out of here until you feel better."

"Like I said, I feel fine." I scoop another spoonful into my mouth. It's mostly maple syrup. So good.

He gives me an eye roll worthy of myself. "Uh huh, sure."

"Okay, *Dad*."

He shivers. "Please don't ever say that again."

"Yeah." I nod, feeling cringey. "It was weird for me too."

We smile at each other. Another moment I'm unsure about.

Music blasts, and we both jump.

"'Whip It'?" Vance's lips quirk as he grabs my phone when I lean over to get it. "I didn't know you were a Devo fan. Isn't that a little before your time?"

"It's my ringtone for Flynn." I reach out, making the gimmie motion with my hand. "You know, 'cause he's so whipped."

Chuckling, he ignores me, answering the call before I can stop him. "Hey, Flynn."

Even I can hear the foreboding silence emanating from the phone.

"Flynn?" Vance repeats.

A deep rumble, but one I can't decipher, comes through the other side.

Vance's smile gets bigger. "She's fine, she's with me."

More rumbling. I'm impressed by how unperturbed Vance is over my brother's posturing. Flynn's newfound brotherly protectiveness can be intimidating.

Vance laughs. "Rosie will be with me all day, so don't worry about it."

I will? Sitting up on my stool, I frown at him in question.

Vance winks at me.

What the hell does *that* mean?

I have an odd sense of the shoe being on the other foot. *I'm* usually the one keeping people on their toes, calling the shots. How did I get myself into this, this... *situation* with Vance?

My eyes travel down to his crotch, where his big-ass dick rests behind a fine netting of sports shorts material and silky, athletic boxer briefs. I shift on my stool, uncomfortable now for another reason.

"Talk later. Tell Jackie I said hi." Vance hangs up.

I try to mask my arousal with an amused tone. "You know, he might have let you live until you mentioned his wife."

"Jackie?" Vance mulls it over. "Nah, him saying good-bye after I mentioned her was the only time he didn't sound like he was going to castrate me."

I quirk a brow at what he thinks is an exaggeration. "He knows how, by the way."

"How what?" He pauses with his spoon halfway to his mouth.

"To castrate you." I take a sip of water. "Part of growing up on the ranch."

Vance cringes and lowers his spoon back to the bowl. "Thanks for that."

I chuckle. "Relax, I'm just messing. Flynn's all talk really. He just acts that way out of guilt."

Vance frowns, taking a bite of his Mueslix. My lips curl as it crunches. He might as well eat twigs and dirt, in my opinion.

He swallows. "What guilt?"

My next bite of oatmeal is mostly brown sugar, so I try and stir it. It's hard to do as I like my oatmeal near paste-like without much milk. "He just feels bad that he wasn't around when I got back from boarding school. He doesn't mean it when he gets like that. You're safe." I finally get the spoon going, but Vance's silence stops me.

He's looking at me like I'm crazy. Which is not an unusual look for me to receive, but one that I don't think I deserve at this particular moment in time.

I put my spoon down. "What?"

"I think you underestimate your brothers." He pats his cereal into the bowl with the back side of his spoon, probably trying to get his cardboard breakfast to soften in the milk. "They both really care."

"Yeah, sure." I shrug, my skin feeling tight again. "I know."

His penetrating gaze intensifies for a sec, but thankfully switches to his gross, healthy cereal again. We sit in silence for the rest of breakfast, me wondering how much side-eye I'll get if I add more maple syrup to my bowl, him staring down at the counter as if lost in thought. We finish our breakfasts at the same time, and before I can hop off the stool, Vance takes our bowls and rinses them in the sink. He needs a sponge to clean the sticky syrup and sugar off mine before he can put it in the dishwasher.

It's very domesticated. And new to me. I've never just shared space with someone in silence like this. It's a simple thing, compared to me having previously deep-throated him, but somehow more... intimate?

"Want to watch TV? *Price is Right* should be on soon."

I perk up, my musings forgotten. "I love *The Price is Right!*" I jump off the stool and move over into his small living room area, flopping onto his overstuffed leather couch. "I'm so good at this game. You're gonna go down, old man."

He grabs a blanket off the back of an armchair and drapes it over me. "I didn't realize it was a competition."

"Duh." I roll my eyes for effect. "Life is a competition."

"Is that so?" Lifting my legs, he sits, dropping them back down on his lap, making sure they're covered by the blanket. "Then I guess I'm already winning."

I pretend he's talking about being an astronaut. "Okay, astro-boy."

But as he holds my eyes for a moment longer than I think necessary, I have a sneaking suspicion he's not.

FOURTEEN
SPLASH DOWN

Rose

"The price is WRONG, Bob!"

I point to Vance and celebrate my "win" with an awesome victory dance. He overbid on the showcase showdown, and I got within three hundred dollars. I wiggle my body as I jump from foot to foot, slapping the air in front of me like I'm riding someone doggy style.

I never said I was a gracious winner.

"Bob Barker isn't even the host anymore." Vance rolls his eyes. Something he's probably doing more now than he ever did before he met me.

I tend to bring out the best in people.

"And I can't believe you just quoted *Happy Gilmore*." Vance shakes his head. "I'm pretty sure you weren't even *alive* when that movie came out."

If he pouted any harder, he'd look like a blowfish.

Turns out, between this and the Fortnite battle last night, Vance isn't a gracious loser.

I find that hilarious.

I stop air slapping and shrug, my cheeks hurting from smiling so hard. "Adam Sandler movies are timeless, old man."

"I'm pretty sure there are a lot of movie critics that would argue that statement." Pout forgotten, he shakes his head and grins.

I shimmy closer to him and bend forward until I'm nose to nose with him. "Stop looking at me, *swan*." My imitation of Adam Sandler in *Billy Maddison* is eerily accurate if I do say so myself.

"All right, all right, enough." He holds out his hands, laughing when I change up my victory dance to the running man. "I guess it's safe to say you're feeling better?"

I take a break from dancing, a little out of breath. "I told you I did." Flopping down next to him on the couch, I rub my tummy. "I just ate too much last night is all."

"That's good, then." Putting his arm around me, he pulls me in. I let myself be embraced, enjoying the cuddle time.

Until I realize that I'm enjoying the cuddle time.

I stiffen, about to get up, grab my clothes out of the dryer, and beat feet when his arm tightens around me.

"You're leaving?" There's a resigned note in his voice that makes me pause.

I think about what he said at Thanksgiving, about how I'm always running out on him. I don't want to hurt his feelings, but I'm not sure if my emotionally stunted heart can handle cuddle time.

"I won't leave." I struggle to sit up. "But I do have a suggestion."

He narrows his eyes like he doesn't quite trust me. "Okay."

Nervousness sets in, and I bite my lip. "Wanna go people watch?"

"People watch?" Vance frowns.

"Yeah, it's Black Friday." I push back, putting more space between us. "I've heard that's when all the crazies come out." I hug a pillow to my chest. "I just thought it might be fun to do... together."

When he doesn't say anything, my heart rate quickens.

"Never mind. It's cool." I jump up from the couch. This is why Thanksgiving was a bad idea. Why hanging out without sex is all kinds of confusing. It gives me ideas. Dangerous ideas. "You can just booty call me la—"

"No." Vance lifts off the couch, grabbling my hand before I can jet. "Let's do it."

———

I'M LOSING MY MIND.

Honest. It's the only explanation for one, not going home after my *Price is Right* victory and two, jumping Vance's bones the minute I saw him put on that old man cardigan.

Like, seriously. How is an oatmeal colored, rolled collar cardigan with large wooden buttons so fucking sexy? It's something I imagine wrinkly old men wearing when they play chess in the park.

And yet, I told him to keep it on while I banged him on the kitchen counter before we left.

Hashtag sorry not sorry.

"I thought we just came here to people watch?"

I ignore Vance's bemused tone and throw the laser tag kit in my cart.

I came Black Friday shopping with good intentions. Our trip was to show Vance that I don't always run, while also spending time with him in a public place where he can't get all cuddly with me. We were going to get a latte, wander around the anarchy of sales, and maybe I'd even surprise a few people by paying for their carts like I normally do when I venture out to big box stores. Easy. Fun.

Then one by one, all my carefully thought-out plans were ruined as the dark magic of Black Friday washed over me.

There are people running, not walking, but *running* in all directions. Mother-daughter groups tag-teaming in a divide-and-conquer approach, men pushing two carts, one in each hand, while holding a list between their teeth as they jog around the store. There are no kids. Not even in the toy aisle. Just adults looking exhausted and freakishly intent.

It's an adult-only Thunderdome of retail madness.

Love. It.

Latte forgotten, I now have a cart stuffed with laser tag, a high-tech back massager, an at-home beer brewing kit, and an industrial-sized KitchenAid mixer.

A llama piñata pillow catches my eye. "Ooo!" I grab it fast, even though there are five others, and it isn't even on sale. Without stopping, I toss it in my cart, already looking to see what's next.

"Do you like llamas?" Vance strolls beside me, still looking sexy as hell in his cardigan and relaxed as always. I don't see how he can't feel the energy in the air. The panic. The rush. He's totally failing at Black Friday.

Not looking at him, I push my cart into the electronics section. "It's from Fortnite." This area is much more crowded than the rest of the store. My pulse quickens.

"Why are llamas in Fortnite?"

"They're loot boxes," I answer absentmindedly, checking out the gaming consoles. "Probably why you haven't seen one yet."

Vance snorts.

"They're how you earn gear and money in—" I freeze. Two

pairs of Sennheiser GSP 600 gaming headsets are sitting on a near empty shelf. Half off.

They are the same ones I use. And honestly, when I bought mine, I didn't even look at the price. (Hashtag billionaire.) But something about seeing half-off spelled out in big, red block letters kicks my adrenaline up another notch.

Abandoning my cart, I rush over to the shelf and grab one of the headsets. It's even the updated model with its signature noise-cancelling microphone and sonically accurate high-fidelity audio, compatible with all gaming consoles.

"Sweet." I reach for the other set, only to be hip checked by something very large and in charge. I stumble to the side, catching myself before hitting the floor on a stacked display of big screen TVs in boxes. "What the f—"

"*Shit.*" Vance jogs over, helping me up. "You okay?"

My knee throbs where it hit the corner of one of the TV boxes.

"What the hell just happened?" I rub the spot where I'm sure it's already bruised. This is going to put a real damper on how my legs look in fishnets for pole dance classes.

Vance glares over my shoulder where the headsets are. I follow his gaze to where a woman is tossing *my* headset into *her* cart.

Oh hell no.

"Excuse me." I shake off Vance's hands. "That's mine."

The woman, an inch taller and twice as large, gives me a once-over, looking like what she sees does not impress her. "Doesn't look like it." With an expression of superiority that would make the Queen of England feel like a peasant, she starts to push her cart away.

Oh fuck no.

I sidestep her, grabbing the side of her cart. "You stole that headset out of my hands. I want it back." I hold my free hand palm up.

She swats it away, leaning into my space. "Last I checked, your hand wasn't on it, missy."

My anger boils, narrowing onto this woman like a Death Star laser beam. I can't believe she just called me missy. That as a woman she would use such sexist language to patronize another woman.

In the back of my mind, I know the headset isn't worth an altercation. I can just order it later no problem.

But the front of my mind is busy feeling insulted on all kinds of levels. Even my fashion level, seeing as she's wearing white athletic ankle socks with royal blue Crocs.

Who does that?

"The only reason my hand wasn't on it was because you hip-checked me." Out of the corner of my eye, I see Vance frowning, leaning slightly forward then leaning back, as if unsure of what to do. I tighten my grip on the woman's cart.

She shrugs, her shoulders almost touching her ears due to lack of a neck. "Little girl, if you can't hack Black Friday, then stay home."

I might look like a high school student in Vance's T-shirt, which I knotted at the waist with my jeans and flat sandals, but I straighten to my full five-foot-six height and try to look impressive. "Black Friday refers to sale prices, not WWF style of shopping, *ma'am*."

The woman jerks her cart out of my grasp. "Just fuck off, bimbo."

"Hey now, there's no need for that." Vance finally decides to step up, trying to come to my rescue.

Bless him.

But I'm Rose fucking West. I don't need rescuing.

Tit for tat, I hip-check the woman's cart into her stomach,

making her stumble back into a phone case display. While she steadies herself, I take the headset out of her cart.

"Why you..." Her eyes narrow onto the headset, now in my hands.

"Your hand wasn't on it." I cringe internally at my snide remark. Black Friday is *not* a good look on me.

I register movement at both ends of our aisle and realize a crowd has gathered. Apparently, two women about to brawl is enough to stop even the most formidable bargain shoppers in their tracks.

Vance's eyes are ping-ponging between Croc Woman and me. It's amusing enough to break the Black Friday spell I'm under. Sighing, I resign myself to buying the damn headphones online and reach out to toss the headset back in her cart. But before I can, Croc Woman surges forward, fist at the ready.

Bam.

"Ooo, damn!" Someone in the crowd cries out.

Pain surges through my chest as I stagger back, dropping the headset. Slightly hunched over, I grab my right boob with both hands. I tilt my head up, my brain not catching up to what just happened. "Did you just... tit punch me?"

Croc Woman looks completely non-repentant. Vance, whose mouth is hanging open, snaps to, stepping between us, arms out.

"That's enough." Tilting his head back he bellows, "Security!"

But my adrenaline is back in full force, pulsing through my system. This isn't about Black Friday, feminism, questionable fashion choices, or even principles anymore.

I just absolutely refuse to go down like this.

One hand still on my boob, I reach out with the other and grab the first thing I find, hurling it past Vance's head and hitting the woman square in the face.

With my llama pillow.

Whelp. That's embarrassing.

A few people in the crowd snicker.

The woman doesn't even flinch. She lurches forward on attack, but this time Vance counters her, standing in the way. Vance may be taller, but honestly, I'm concerned for his safety. Everyone in Texas knows you don't send out your QB against a linebacker.

"Um, Vance. You might want to—"

The woman kicks out her socked and Croc-ed foot and nails him in his tender bits.

Vance goes down, sounding like a wounded water buffalo.

Sympathetic moans erupt from the crowd.

"Serves you right," Croc Woman says to him as he curls into a fetal position, then she picks up the headset beside him.

Righteous anger dissolves, and I drop down to Vance's side. "Vance?"

He moans.

"Sweetie." I push his hair back off his forehead. "You okay?"

He opens his mouth, whether to moan again or answer me I don't know, because his voice is drowned out by the Croc Woman. "You dirty spic."

I black out. Or something. Because while the crowd gasps at her racial slur, my vision darkens, and a rage that I've never felt before surges through my body.

"He's Native American, you racist asshole!" someone shouts, then lets loose a war cry worthy of Geronimo himself. That someone is me.

The next thing I know, I'm airborne.

The next several seconds are a battle of leverage and suffocation as the woman holds me to her chest, forcing me to motorboat her hefty bosom until I feel myself about to pass out from lack of oxygen.

I do the only thing I can—bite.

Howling, Croc Woman rears back. I jump up in an attempt to mount her like my stripper pole so I can subdue her with a scissor pike.

My ab muscles protest, and my scissor pike morphs into some kind of bear hug. When she regains her momentum, I'm riding her like a bride-to-be on a mechanical bull during her bachelorette party.

Hashtag fail. Hashtag *major* fail.

"Ladies, ladies!"

In a blur of color as Croc Woman moves left and right, trying to dislodge me, I make out two people in blue running toward us.

Sanity returns.

I loosen my grip, but I can't jump off while she's moving back and forth. "Stop spinning!"

Not surprisingly, Croc Woman doesn't listen. Instead, she reaches back, grabbing me by my top-knot, pulling me forward like she's trying to flip me over her shoulder.

And that's when it hits me.

Nausea. Serious, gut-wrenching nausea.

The next time she pulls my hair, I hurl. I hurl *hard*. All down the front of Croc Woman's shirt.

The crowd gasps.

Croc Woman screams, arms out and leaning back as if trying to dodge my puke. But there is no dodging this puke. It is *all* over her.

With her arms out and her weight unbalanced, I'm unseated, landing hard on my feet. A shot of pain shoots up my ankle. My only thought: Oatmeal, maple syrup, and brown sugar don't taste nearly as good the second time around.

Croc woman twirls around to face me, puke flying off her

shirt in an arc, splattering the phone cases. The crowd dives to avoid the unfriendly vomit fire.

Vance is still curled up, hands between his legs.

"Did you..." The woman looks down at herself, taking in the river of vomit dripping down her T-shirt. Her nostrils flare. Then she gags. Once. Twice. On the third, she hurls.

Apparently, Croc Woman is a sympathy puker.

Other sympathetic people in the crowd gag and stumble away. Others stare, horrified. The security guards try to slow their run but end up sliding in the upchuck.

I wipe my mouth with the back of my hand and vow then and there never to shop on Black Friday again.

———

Vance

"WHAT THE *HELL* WERE YOU THINKING?" I pace the small security office. Or rather, I try to pace as best I can with the bag of frozen peas held to my junk.

Rose is on a fold-out chair with her head between her legs. "I was—"

"You could've been arrested. Or hurt." The shock has worn off, replaced by worry. I change directions, causing a twinge in my balls. "Fuck."

Rose lifts her eyes from the ground. "I know, but—"

"And what is your brother going to say?"

"My brother?" She sits up, her eyes narrowing. "What the hell does he have to do with it? I'm not a child you need to tell on." She rubs her boob. "And in case you forgot, I was assaulted. I was tit punched, for God's sake!" She rubs harder. "It's still sore."

I gesture to my pea bag-covered dick.

She snorts. "Okay, well, you might win the most grievously injured contest."

"Miss West? Mr. Bodaway?" Mr. Rodriguez, the store manager who we met earlier, enters the room followed by a security officer. One who didn't slip in vomit.

I stop pacing, and Rose smiles at the manager. "Yes?"

Mr. Rodriguez's soft eyes match his tone as he talks to Rose. "You're free to go, Miss West."

My shoulders drop in shock. "Just like that?"

He spares me a glance. "Just like that." He looks back to Rose. "How are you feeling?" He smiles at her like she *didn't* just cause a major incident in his store on one of the busiest days of the year.

"I'm fine." Rose reaches out and takes his hand in both of hers. "I really appreciate all your help with this situation, Mr. Rodriguez."

He smiles, adding his other hand to hers. "Jorge, please."

Rose smiles brighter. "Only if you call me Rose, Jorge."

They share a moment. If Mr. Rodriguez wasn't in his late fifties and somewhat portly, with a large gold wedding band on his left ring finger, I'd be jealous.

Hell, I think I am, anyway.

"You must be very proud, Mr. Bodaway," the manager says to me, *still* holding Rose's hand.

"Why's that?"

"We have several witnesses who came forward explaining how Rose only retaliated when the offender spat a racial slur at you." He shakes his head in disgust. "In Texas, that's considered a hate crime, and we take that very seriously."

"Oh, ah, yes." I have no idea what he's talking about.

He must see my confusion. "After you were assaulted, the woman currently in custody called you a 'spic.'"

My mouth drops open. Unfortunately having people comment on my darker skin isn't new to me, but I'm surprised I didn't hear it. My balls throb. Then again, maybe I'm not surprised.

"Your girlfriend here was nice enough to correct the woman on your Native American heritage and come to your defense in a very, uh"—he struggles to find the word—"*unusual* way."

Rose grimaces, and the store manager laughs.

He drops her hand to hold it out to me. "You may not be a fellow Hispanic like me, but I won't tolerate any racial slurs against my customers."

I shake his hand. "Thank you."

"Speaking of customers." Rose reaches into her bra, pulling out a black credit card. "I'd like to pay for the current purchases of everyone in the store."

He stares at her, his mouth open for a minute before clearing his throat. "That is very thoughtful of you, Rose, but it may cause a bit of a riot with everyone trying to get to the cashiers."

"Oh." Rose looks downcast for a moment before brightening again. "Then how about free coffee all day?" She thinks for a moment. "No riot, just happy, energized customers."

Mr. Rodriguez beams. "Wonderful idea." He turns to me, his eyes dimming as if he's not all that impressed with what he's seen of me thus far. "You have a very caring and smart woman here."

I toss the bag of peas in the trash. "Yeah." I feel weighed, measured, and severely lacking.

"Oh, we're just friends," Rose says.

Mr. Rodriguez's eyes light up. "*Really?* Well in that case, I have a handsome son about your age."

———

"No." Rose points to the shopping bag I just grabbed from my 4Runner. "Leave those."

After Rose politely thwarted Mr. Rodriguez's matchmaking attempts, and I apologized to her for yelling, I drove Rose to Flynn's house.

I glance down at the shopping bag with the headsets and back massager in my hand. "Why?"

"Because I have to take those home and wrap them. They're for your family."

"What?"

"I guess I got a bit excited when your nephews mentioned Christmas." She laughs, but it doesn't sound natural. "Silly, right?"

"I..."

"When I saw all the Christmas decorations in the store and people running around throwing things in their carts that were probably gifts for people, I got a little ahead of myself." A look of panic flashes across her face, and she holds out the hand not grasping the llama pillow. "I mean, I know we're not like that, but still, your family was really welcoming to me yesterday, and on the off chance that I do see them again..." She drops her hand and shrugs. "Well, I at least wanted to get them some Christmas presents."

I stare at the bag I'm holding again, then over my shoulder at the large KitchenAid mixer box still in the back of my SUV.

"Your mom was complaining about her back last pole dance class, so I thought she'd like the massager. And when Matt went outside to clean up the turkey pot, your sister mentioned to your mom that she needs a mixer but doesn't know whether to ask for that or the diamond studs she really wants this Christmas."

Rose walks over to the and pats the box. "Brit had me download the Pinterest app."

I snort.

"And I found this tutorial on it that shows you how to glitter-coat stuff. I was thinking I could go a step further and rig up my glitter room to refinish the mixer. Thought Brittany would appreciate the DIY of it." She takes the bag out of my hands and places it next to the mixer box. "And these headphones are the same ones I use when gaming. They're really good. I thought your nephews and I could exchange usernames and game together."

"And the beer brewing kit?"

"For Matt. Thought he could go head to head with Brittany in the DIY department." She holds up the bag in her hand and shakes it. "The laser tag and llama are for me, but I want to show Jackie."

I know I should say something, but once again, Rose has me speechless. How could all that have gone through her mind on our short-lived race around the store?

"Ah, this Christmas—"

"It's okay, really." She side-steps me, eyes on the ground. "I get that spending Christmas together isn't happening."

"I—"

"It's just that as great as my brothers are, we're a house full of billionaires—so the thought of presents has never been that exciting." She looks up smiling. "Shopping for your family was fun." She freezes at whatever expression I'm making, then swallows. "That's all."

"What do you usually do for Christmas?" is all I can think to ask.

She looks relieved at my question, like she was worried I'd yell at her again.

I have never felt more like an asshole in my life.

"*Die Hard* marathon." Her normal devil-may-care smirk is back in place. "While overeating Holt's holiday cakes and cookies."

That pulls me up short. "Your brother bakes?"

"Yeah." She nods, taking a step closer to Flynn's front walkway. "His chocolate chips are the best."

Two long strides of my own have me next to her again. "They're that good, huh?"

"Oh yeah." She laughs, her amusement sounding genuine this time. "Just ask Jules. I think my brother's cookies have turned into some sort of weird mating call for them." She snorts. "They're so gross."

She might say they're weird and gross, but her expression looks wistful.

"Think he'll give up the recipe?"

"Doesn't have to, I already know it. It was my grandmother's." She's back to frowning at me. "Why? You looking to make cookies?"

"Maybe you and I could." It's my turn to shrug, a sense of self-consciousness falling over me that I haven't felt since adolescence. "You know, before we head over to my sister's for Christmas dinner."

Her mouth drops open. I take a moment to bask in the pleasure of having shocked Rose West into silence.

"That's a month away." She takes a step back. "Are you sure we should make plans that far out?"

I take a step forward. "It's almost eight months until my flight. Why *not* make plans for next month?" I tilt my head to the side. "You're not backing out of our deal already, are you?"

"No?" I've never seen her looking so unsure.

She's adorable.

"Good." I shift so we can walk up the path side by side. "'Cause one of those friends-with-bennies benefits is gorging on my mom's Christmas tamales."

"Tamales?"

"Yeah, she picked it up from her grandmother, who lived in

a border town in south Texas before moving to the reservation in New Mexico when Mom was a baby."

We reach the front step. "Sounds awesome." Her grin erases all traces of my earlier panic.

"So you'll come?"

I can tell she's thinking about it. Though her smile dims, I can tell she wants to say yes.

I wait for the silence to break down her resistance.

She lasts about thirty seconds before sighing. "Okay, fine. I'll come." She says it like she's doing me a favor.

I'm pretty sure she is.

I try not to look too triumphant, but from the look she throws me, I probably fail.

The front door swings open. "Hi guys!" Jackie smiles, planting herself in front of her very annoyed-looking husband.

Rose kisses Jackie's cheek and throws some sort of gang-looking hand sign at Flynn. "Yo, bro."

Flynn crosses his arms over his chest. "Where have you been?" He's talking to Rose but glaring at me.

Rose just rolls her eyes. "Don't be lame." She pushes past Jackie and her brother. "I was just with Vance, getting into a public bitch fight and nearly getting arrested."

Flynn drops his arms, his eyes snapping to his sister. Jackie's eyebrows shoot over the top of her glasses.

"But don't worry," Rose calls over her shoulder as she walks into the house. "I came out victorious once again. No charges filed."

I brace for impact when Flynn turns my way again. But I'm surprised by his sympathetic expression.

"You poor bastard." He waves me inside. "Let's get you a drink."

FIFTEEN

HIGH SPEED DATA TRANSFER

Vance

IF YOU'D TOLD me yesterday that Flynn and I would be laughing over a beer and prime steaks, I'd have thought you were crazy.

But here we are.

That's happened often since Rose has come into my life.

And while Flynn and I stand at the outdoor kitchen set under a pergola, Jackie and Rose sunbathe. Well, Rose is. Jackie's skin has a near grayish cast to it from the amount of sunscreen she's applied, and she's settled herself under a very large umbrella.

Rose, wearing a bright pink string bikini, is basking in the sunlight.

It's not cold, but it sure isn't warm. Which is made apparent by Rose's nipples trying to poke their way through her top.

I remind myself not to stare. I don't want to shatter the newfound friendship I seem to have forged with Flynn by perving on his little sister in front of him.

"So, Vance."

I jerk my gaze away from Rose, having just done what I told myself not to. "Uh, yeah?"

"Now that you've been officially initiated into the club, how you feeling?"

"Club?"

"The 'I survived Rose West's drama' club." He turns the meat on the grill, perfectly crisscrossing the grill lines. "I love my sister, but she gets herself into some crazy situations. I've seen..."

As Flynn tells story after story, my fingers tighten around my beer bottle. I know he's saying what I was thinking just an hour ago in the security office, but hearing Rose's brother, someone who's always supposed to have her back say it, well, it really pisses me off.

I cut off his Rose antics monologue. "Sounds to me like Rose is a great friend."

Flynn's tongs pause mid steak rotation. "What do you mean?" Rather than annoyed at me for cutting him off, his tone sounds amused.

"Every story I've heard, whether it's a bar fight, getting arrested or bribery, has all been done for her friends and family." I take a breath, trying to calm down. Nothing good will come of fighting with Rose's brother, I'm sure. "Rose doesn't get in trouble just to get in trouble. There's *always* a reason, and those reasons are the people she loves."

Flynn grins like I just told him he won the lottery. "Is that so?"

"*Yes.*" My anger only increases by his sudden flippant attitude.

He gives the grill his attention again. "So what you're saying is that today's Black Friday drama had a reason."

"Of course. You should know Rose always leaves out the

stuff that puts her in a good light." I laugh at the absurdity of it. "I bet she didn't tell you that she went on a high-speed chase just to bribe a butcher for a turkey for my family's Thanksgiving dinner."

He nods. "You're right."

I freeze, my previous anger shocked out of my system. "What?"

"Rose does always go overboard for the people she loves." He points his tongs at me. "Today's drama is another example, I'm sure."

"The headphones were for my nephews." My voice lacks conviction, and Flynn knows it.

"Yes." He rotates the foiled potatoes. "*Your* nephews."

I want to say that we are just friends with benefits. That we have a time limit.

But I don't. Because how do you tell someone that their little sister explicitly said she didn't want a boyfriend? That she's into stranger danger and keeping things casual? You don't tell them. Because that is awkward and mean.

And because I don't want to get junk punched twice in one day.

"Now"—Flynn transfers thick asparagus spears onto the grill, a mean feat with tongs—"the question is, what are you going to do now that you've made it into my sister's inner circle?" He flashes me a penetrating look. "Which, I may add, is a very hard thing to do. My sister doesn't trust easily."

I swallow. "Why's that?" Glancing at the girls, I see Rose has turned over on her lounge chair. The words *KISS IT* are on the cheeks of her swimsuit.

Flynn turns his head away from the grill and stares at his sister for a beat. "Rose likes to tell Holt and me that the two of us did the best we could after our parents, then our grandparents, died." He shakes his head as if in disgust. "But that's a lie she tells us to make us feel better. We could've and should've done more."

"What do you mean?"

Jackie says something, and without looking, Rose flips her the bird. Jackie laughs.

"Every year or so, Mom would pick up and leave. Sometimes for weeks, sometimes for months. Sometimes Dad would follow. Rose was right at the stage where she really needed her mom when they both died in that car accident. She had no one to guide her through the tough, embarrassing adolescent stage except two self-indulgent older brothers too focused on their own pain and interests." Carefully, he spins the asparagus, ensuring it doesn't fall through the grate. "So we shipped her off to an all-girl boarding school, figuring the other girl students and female teachers would fill in the voids for her."

Flynn closes the grill, his hand resting on the handle for a moment.

"She was lonely. Even surrounded by all her friends and continuous socialite parties, Rose was lonely. And I hate myself that it took me so long to realize it. And when I did, all I did was yell at her when things got too crazy because I didn't know what else to do."

Rose's cackle echoes in the courtyard. Jackie's blush can be seen from where Flynn and I are standing.

"She seems okay now." I sound more hopeful then convincing.

Flynn smiles, looking at his sister and his wife. "Thankfully." He leaves me there by the grill and walks over to where the girls are sitting. He picks up his wife, sits in her chair, and places her on his lap. Rose flips another bird.

The gesture reminds me of all the times Rose was left behind at a table, all her friends dancing with their dates. Rose, the odd one out.

Flynn might have twenty-twenty vision when it comes to the past, but he fails to see how him marrying Jackie, Holt getting with Jules, and now even Trish being engaged to Ian has put Rose back in the same situation as before. She's feeling left behind again.

Memories of Thanksgiving and this morning replay in my head, now colored by this new information. I invited Rose to my family's Thanksgiving because of exactly what Flynn just said. Rose seems lonely. But hearing her brother confirm it breaks my heart a little.

And it makes me determined to fix it. But Flynn's suggestion about how Rose may feel about me puts a wrench in that idea.

I run a hand through my hair, thinking. Flynn *has* to be wrong. Rose told me she wasn't after a forever guy.

We're just keeping each other company.

Shaking off the heavy thoughts, I join the group, pulling a lounge chair closer to Rose's.

Rose turns on her butt when I sit. "You boys have fun measuring dicks?"

Flynn rubs his tong-free hand down his face. "Jesus, Rose."

She laughs, rubbing her hands up and down her arms.

"You cold?" I take off my sweater. "Here." I hold it out to her, trying very *very* hard not to stare at her pointed nipples.

I almost succeed.

"Aw, your old man cardigan?" She takes it, putting her arms through the sleeves. "Aren't you sweet."

"Old man is right," Flynn grumbles, like he's forgotten our intimate little chat just minutes ago. "How old are you, anyway?"

"Your age. That's how old." Rose wraps the open front around her.

Flynn grumbles.

"And even if he wasn't, you get no say if I want to cruise the senior center for dates."

"What the?" I lean back, affronted. "I'm not even close to being a senior."

"Well, actually." Jackie wiggles in Flynn's lap, trying to sit up straighter. "Seeing as you're thirty-six, you have less years to reach senior status at sixty-five than you have lived." She pushes up her glasses. "So it depends on your definition of close."

Fuck. She's right.

And by the look on Flynn's face, the truth hit him hard as well.

"Now, now." Rose scoots over until she's on my lounge chair, lifting my arm and putting it around her shoulders. "Don't make Vance feel bad about his age." She winks at me. "That's my job."

"Har, har." I am not amused. But like a moth to a flame, I can't help but hold her close. And pretend not to notice how well she fits.

Whether in heels, glitter, or my T-shirt, Rose fits.

"Come on." Rose snags her phone out from under the lounge chair and settles back against me. "I'll show you that Pinterest video I was telling you about. The one with the glitter refinishing for the KitchenAid mixer."

I ignore Flynn's pointed look. "Sounds awesome."

SIXTEEN

#PINTERESTWORTHY

Rose

"Did you actually get worse at this?" I hike up my midi-length skirt and curl my legs under me.

Vance's fingers fumble over my buttons.

"Give me a break. I don't do this every day like you do." He shifts up higher on his ass, bracing himself on the front of my sofa.

"Please." I shimmy over, closing the gap between us on the living room floor. The hand-knotted silk rug feels soft and silky across my bare legs. "You do too do this every day." I lift my shoulders and dip down. If he wanted, all he'd have to do was look over to get a glimpse down my shirt. "I've watched you."

He looks over, his hands still on the remote control. "You've watched me?" The Fortnite battle he's been playing and losing for the past twenty minutes rages on.

"Yep." I trail my finger up his thigh.

He tries his best not to be affected.

It's cute how he tries.

"First, that's creepy." Vance jerks his thigh away, clearing his throat. "And second, what are you talking about?"

Sighing, I lean back against the front of the couch, knowing even without my distracting efforts his game will be over soon. "You really are a newb."

Vance frowns at the screen, his fingers not hitting the buttons in the correct combination he needs to win this current battle.

"Newb. Newbie," I clarify. "New to it."

He turns away from the TV to narrow his eyes at me.

He dies.

I purse my lips in amusement and point to the game.

"Damn it." His tosses the controller between us.

Laughing, I pick it up and maneuver around to the different screens. "Look. I can see who's playing if I just go into Options and then scan the social list."

The V between his brows gets deeper. "But how did you find out my username?"

"Please." I shove him playfully in the shoulder. "I play with your nephews, remember? And although you made them promise not to tell me that you've been practicing, you didn't say that they couldn't confirm the name @NASA_starlord on their friends list was you." I scoff. "But really, it's not like I didn't know it was you." I shake my head at him. "NASA starlord? Really?"

He chuckles at himself. "Better than NASA's Flashlight."

"I don't know." I drop the controller to the side and lift up on my knees, pulling my skirt out of the way so I can straddle him. "I've started to think Flashlight is a great nickname for you." I kiss him but pull back quickly. "Don't tell Jules I said that."

He snorts, his eyes on my waist where his hands are circling. "Easily done. She doesn't need any more ammunition." He pauses, tilting his head to the side. "But why do you think Flash-light is such a good nickname?"

Poor guy looks a little hurt.

I grind on his lap. He grunts as his dick hardens beneath me. "Because of that."

His hips shift under me, moving with me.

"It's my very own Maglite." I lean forward and whisper in his ear. "Thick, heavy, and hard."

"Jesus." Vance groans, his head falling back on the couch cushion. His hands dig into my hips as I move over him.

This has become a common occurrence this past week.

Not the sex so much as the company.

When I told Vance I had finals to study for this past week, he said he understood. Honestly, I hadn't believed him. So when he took it upon himself to come over almost every night after he got off work to bring me dinner, I thought that was code for something else.

But whenever I thought he was making a move, he'd just kiss my forehead in greeting. Most of the time after dinner he'd sprawl out on my sofa to read a book while I studied at the kitchen table.

Hashtag men who read are hot.

The two times *I* tried to make a move on *him*, he left, saying he didn't want to distract me.

Hashtag what the fuck?

But today is Saturday. My self-appointed day of rest.

And by rest, I mean sex. Lots of sex.

I lean back, bracing myself on his thighs. "Take your shirt off."

"Yes, ma'am." He reaches over his shoulder and grabs a fistful of T-shirt with one hand and pulls it over his head. It's both oddly sexy and infuriating. Because really, that's a prime way to stretch out a shirt. And yet he looks so hot doing it.

"Mmmm." I lick my lips at the six-pack he revealed. "Is it just me or do you look more ripped than usual?"

His eyes shift to the side, and his shoulders jump in a small shrug. "I had to do *something* while you studied this week."

I swear there'd be a flush on his cheeks if his complexion wasn't so dark.

"Is that so?" Honestly, I could argue that. I could point out that he was here most of the time this week and that the only time he'd have to work out was either early in the morning before work or late at night when he left my place. Which he must have done, because *damn*, his six-pack is extra cut right now. Especially as he tenses, bracing for my smart mouth to embarrass him.

But why would I embarrass him when I can ride him?

Crossing my arms over my stomach, I grab the hem of my shirt and lift, exposing my new bra. One of the ones that has weird straps crisscrossed over the top of your breasts while leaving the nipples exposed. It does fuck-all for support.

But I didn't wear it for support; I wore it for effect.

"Dear God..." Vance's eyes glaze over in some sort of sex trance.

Mission accomplished.

Reaching my hands under the soft billows of my skirt, I undo his jeans. When his cock springs free, I moan at the soft skin pulled tight over his erection as I pump him up and down.

"Fuck. Wait. My back pocket." He grabs my forearms like he's going to stop me but doesn't do anything else, enjoying my handiwork.

I shake one hand off to reach under the couch and pull out a condom.

He chuckles when he sees it, which turns into a groan when I twist my wrist at the top of the next pump.

"Did you plan this?" His breath comes in pants.

"Of course." I don't need a mirror to know my smile is evil and satisfied.

Back under the pleated tent of my skirt, I roll the condom on and slide my panties to the side.

"Wait." Vance's hands reach for me, getting tangled in the material.

I slap them away. "No more waiting." I lift on my knees, centering him under me. "This is happening *now*." I sink down, impaling myself, shuddering with pleasure at the delicious sting and stretch. "Fuck that's good."

"So fucking good," Vance agrees, his eyes and hands on my breasts. He pinches his fingers, tweaking my nipples.

I whimper.

He scoots forward with me on top of him, his dick hitting my cervix and setting off a mini orgasm.

"Holy shit."

"Wrap your legs around me, baby."

I do it without thinking, still focusing on the radiating waves of pleasure coming from under my skirt.

Vance's abs tighten as he crunches closer to me, wrapping his arms up and under mine, his chin near resting on top of my boobs.

"Lotus." He smiles at me, those eye crinkles of his setting off more fireworks in my downtown. Then what he says registers, and I smile back, remembering my joke about this particular sex position on the day we met at the strip club.

I'd been kidding, having never actually done this before. It's too slow. Too close. Too intimate a position.

It scares me.

But right now, with Vance, it feels right.

Something changed between us after the night of no stranger danger sex. I can't put my finger on it, and if I think about it too much, I might have a panic attack.

So I don't think. I feel.

Digging my fingers into his back, I rock myself on him, his dick hitting my G-spot, his pelvis rubbing my clit.

Hashtag amazing.

He dips his chin down farther, sucking my nipple between his lips.

"Fuck." I rock faster. But as fast as I rock, it's a slow build.

I bite my lips, whimpering in frustration. I unhook my leg, looking to get more leverage with my heels on the ground, but Vance stops me.

"No. Like this." He sucks my other nipple.

"But... I can't..." I try to bounce but can't.

"Shhh." He blows cool air over my hardened nipple. "I got you." He takes over, rocking me against him, giving me no choice but to cling to him. To let *him* pleasure *me*.

The sounds coming out of my mouth are new to me. I plead.

He rocks.

I beg.

He rocks.

I implore him with my nails running down his back.

He rocks.

I can't see what's happening under my skirt. I can't see where we are joined, where my skin rubs and rocks against his. But I can *feel* it.

The friction. The glorious fucking friction.

He rocks.

Panic builds in my chest. Tears sting my eyes. Something is happening. I don't... I don't think I like it.

"Vance."

He must hear something in my voice because when his eyes lock on mine they soften, and the haze of desire doesn't lift but shifts, something deeper and sexier moving through them. "I got you." He rocks.

"I..."

He rocks.

"I'm going to..."

He rocks.

I fall apart, staring into his eyes, crying and begging. For what I don't know because the climax is here, and it's glorious. It ravages my body, my muscles tightening and spasming, and I have no choice but to let it take me, let it do with me what it will as Vance continues his slow, methodical rocking.

My inner walls clamp down, and Vance's body jerks then stills, his arms tightening around me like a vise, bringing us as close as possible. Merging our pleasure.

And when our bodies relax, and the pleasure ebbs, Vance and I are left staring at each other in the aftermath. I see wonder in his eyes. Wonder and confusion mixed with a little bit of fear.

All the things I feel myself.

———

"YOU'D MAKE AN EXCELLENT ENGINEER." Vance leans against the door frame, arms crossed over his still bare chest, staring at the deconstructed KitchenAid mixer hanging from the ceiling. "I can't believe you managed to rig up a suspension line." He pushes off the wall and walks over the glitter-dusted floor to study my homemade apparatus.

I pause in sandpapering so he can spin the appliance, which is secured to the ceiling by a hook-screw and three bent and twisted wire hangers. He looks at me appreciatively.

And since I put my shirt back on because sandpaper and bare tits don't mix, I know he's appreciating my ingenuity and not my body.

Oddly, it's just as satisfying.

"I'd make an excellent anything," I joke, glad to be back on more solid ground after our mind-melting lotus sex.

"I don't doubt it." His sincerity almost makes me blush.

Vance watches me work in silence for a while. It's happened so often this past week that I find it comforting. His presence is almost a habit at this point.

One that I tell myself will be hard to quit. One I don't want to quit.

"So is that the issue?"

"Huh?" I shake off my thoughts to see Vance looking down at me with concern.

"Your being good at so much. Is that the concern you have over what to do now that you're graduating?"

I grimace. "When you say it like that, I sound kind of arrogant."

He shrugs. "You can't help it if it's true."

Laughing, I toss the rag to the side. "I'd be surprised at your lack of derision, but I guess when you're surrounded by people like Julie Starr on a daily basis you've become immune to boastful people."

"Nah, it isn't boasting if you can back it up. And seeing how Starr made youngest commander ever at NASA, and you're a Baylor Business Fellow who's graduating early with honors, you're both able to make those kinds of statements without sounding conceited."

"How did you know I was a Business Fellow?" I mean, I wasn't hiding it from him, but I also never brought it up.

He looks smug at my surprise. "You're not the only one with connections."

I tilt my head to the side and shift my features into disbelief.

"Okay, okay." He holds up his hands. "I *may* have looked over your shoulder a few times while you were on your phone ignoring me."

"Should've known." I pick up the finer grit sandpaper and go over the appliance once more. "You become so needy when I'm working."

Vance chokes. "Me?" Clearing his throat, he straightens, looking affronted. "Needy?"

"You can't help it if it's true." I smirk, throwing his words back at him.

He smirks back. "Brat."

We both chuckle.

"Seriously though." He reaches around me to steady the mixer so I can sand it more easily. "Why are you so concerned with not knowing what you want to do next? Lots of students are in the same boat."

"But not all those students have the advantages that I do." I glance around the room. "Just look where we are."

"Your glitter room?"

"No, you idiot." I snort. "My *penthouse*. Which I own free and clear." I circle in Vance's outstretched arms to reach the backside of the KitchenAid. "The ability to have something as superfluous as a glitter room is just the icing on the cake that is my ridiculously lucky life." A tightness forms in my chest as I say this out loud. My hand moves faster over the metal. "I mean, I not only have no student debt hanging over my head, but I'd be able to get into any corporation just based on my last name even if I wasn't top of my class." I stop, slightly out of breath, and lower my hands. "I don't even have to work. I could just be useless the rest of my life. My mom did a good job of that." I chance a glance at him, expecting derision or confusion over my guilt for being born so privileged. I find sympathy instead.

I back up, toss the sandpaper to the side, and pick up the damp rag again. "I just..." I sigh, hating being unable to put into words what I've been feeling this past year. "I just feel like I need to do something worthwhile." I try and laugh off the rush of emotions I'm feeling. "Hashtag first world problems, am I right?" I reach up to wipe down the fine layer of dust I just created. But before I can finish, Vance draws me in for a hug.

"No matter what you do, I'm sure it'll be worthwhile."

I give myself a moment. No, just a fleeting second to enjoy his embrace. Because even though it feels great, after our lotus sex, I need to get us back on track. Back to friends with bennies, stranger danger no strings attached sex.

No more emotional eye banging during climax.

I reach down and palm him over his jeans. "Wanna do something else worthwhile?"

And as expected, he does.

———

"You almost done?"

"Yep." On my stomach, I swipe Mod Podge over the KitchenAid base.

"You know what I don't get?" Vance is still shirtless, his skin sparkling like a teenage heartthrob vampire.

There is glitter in *all* the places glitter shouldn't be.

Hashtag totally worth it.

I point my glue-coated brush at him. "The fun of do-it-your-selfing?"

He snorts. "Yeah, I totally don't get that, but that wasn't what I was talking about."

"What then?" I focus on painting a thin, even coat over the sanded metal.

"Why you don't have a Christmas tree."

My brush slips, the question unexpected. "Ah, well, I guess it just seemed sad."

"It seemed sad *not* to have a Christmas tree at Christmas?" He glances around. "I mean, you have a glitter room. I figured your penthouse would be decked out like a stripper themed North Pole."

I gaze at him in awe. "Sometimes you amaze me with how well you understand my aesthetic." I chuckle. "Stripper themed North Pole. Classic."

"So?" he asks, not letting the absence of a Christmas tree go.

Sighing, I finish Mod Podging the last section. "If you must know I just really didn't feel like buying and decorating a tree all by myself." Dropping my brush, I screw the glue cap back on and raise my hand. "Now help me up."

He takes it, pulling me to my feet.

Whether it was what I said or how I said it, thankfully he lets the Christmas tree conversation die and studies the hazy coat of glue I just spent a lot of time doing. "You probably could've paid for someone to do all this, you know?"

"But then it wouldn't be from me." I brush off my bare ass, my skirt and panties tossed and forgotten in the corner. "And besides, I—" I burp, fighting a sudden wave of nausea.

"You okay?"

"Yeah, fine." I take a deep breath, and the sick feeling recedes. "I was just lying on my stomach too long."

He gives me a concerned once-over. "Are you sure you shouldn't get that checked out? Weren't you feeling off the other night too when I brought over Jimmy John sandwiches?"

"Anyone would feel sick with the amount of food you are trying to force feed me," I say, exasperated. "I mean, do you have a fat fetish or something? Because I swear my clothes are getting too tight."

"Yeah, but in all the right places." He smiles at my glitter boobs, only to frown a second later. "What are you doing?"

"Hmm?" I glance down, not having realized that I was rubbing the right one. "Oh, I guess my boob hasn't recovered yet from the woman's fist of fury. It's sore."

His lips twitch. "Fist of fury?"

"Hey." I plant my hands on my hips, knowing the waist slimming, boob swaying affect it will have. "You weren't so amused when that woman's sock-Croc nailed you in the nads."

He busts out laughing. "Nads?"

"Gonads."

"Yeah," he says between laughter. "I know what nads refer to. I just haven't heard it in a long time."

I lift a single brow in his direction. "Seeing how many years you've already lived I find that hard to believe, old man." I rub my left one now.

"Har, har." He eyes my chest. "I thought you were punched in the other boob?"

"I was, but this one's hurting too." I shrug. "Probably getting my period." I snort. "Or I'm pregnant."

I laugh, but Vance doesn't.

His body stills, and the smile slides off his face.

I can't help but find his reactions amusing. "Relax, old man." I wave my hand over my glitter speckled hoo-ha. "IUD." Then point to his crotch. "Condom." I walk over to the built-ins where the glitter bomb controls are. "Def not pregnant."

He swallows. "Right."

Men are such touchy creatures. "Come on." I wave him over. "The engineer in you will love how this works."

His walk is slow, almost a shuffle, but he comes over. I spend the rest of my day teaching him how to glitter bomb and play Fortnite.

But the silence isn't as comfortable as before.

SEVENTEEN

FREE FALLING

Vance

"Never take both hands off the Space Station on a spacewalk."

Maneuvering my hands along the rails of the International Space Station's truss, I angle forward out of the airlock to go under the S-o truss, while the Virtual Reality Lab instructor narrates for the new astronaut class who is observing as part of their training.

Once under the nadir side of the truss, I work my way down the nodes on my way to the Columbus module. That's where I'll be installing the bridge support for Bartolomeo in a few months.

I need to be focused, even if this is just a simulation of my upcoming spacewalk. But even though I'm surrounded by a virtual, three-dimensional replication of the International Space Station, I'm seeing something completely different in my mind.

Rose, hunched over her laptop. Rose, staring into my eyes lost in pleasure. Rose, covered in glitter and joking about being pregnant.

"See how he's gripping each brace as he goes?" the Virtual Reality Lab instructor asks. "The gloves have tactile response, so they simulate the pressure of each hand grip."

"Manus gloves, correct?" Jackie asks. She's been front and center since she entered the room, analyzing everything.

There's a pause before the instructor answers, and I suppress a laugh. Jackie is going to give *all* the instructors here at NASA a run for their money. She probably knows more than they do.

"Ah, yes. They are Manus."

"I've heard they have one of the best motion tracking bracelets and finger sensors on the market." I can't see her, but I can imagine her either pushing her glasses up her nose or tilting her head in thought.

Not to be outdone, the other astronauts start talking virtual reality jargon.

I successfully climb under the truss, my gloves tightening with each grasp of the handholds on the Unity module, all the while wondering if Rose has been too busy to notice my recent MIA attitude.

This past Saturday she asked for some space until finals were over. I went from going over every day, if only to watch her study and bring her food, to nothing—no calls, texts, or visits—for five days. Her presentation is Monday. After that, there is no plausible excuse for my physical and technical absence. Even now, I'm pretty sure Rose knows the difference between giving her space to get things done and going completely dark on communication. She's too smart not to.

"Vance, pause here so that we can get an idea of your visuals," the instructor says.

I still my movements, hands outstretched mid-climb. There are two screens in the VR room that those not wearing goggles can see. One has a bird's eye view of my training session which shows my avatar pausing in its path and the other a view of what I'm seeing on the spacewalk.

"Now turn your head around, Vance. Give 'em the show." There's pride in the instructor's voice, and I get it. If you haven't been to space yet, what the new astronauts are seeing on the screen is pretty awe-inspiring. NASA got into the virtual reality game early, and their equipment has always been top of the line. Best Uncle Sam can buy.

"Look at that," the instructor says, probably pointing to the screen showing my viewpoint. I'm looking back at the moon, partially shrouded in darkness, offset by the bright blue glow of the Earth's atmosphere.

"Whoa," someone says.

With sights like this, usually I feel nothing but grateful and focused on the path I've chosen for myself. But with Rose on my mind, for the first time, those feelings waver.

Pregnant.

It's the word that's been bouncing inside my skull whether I'm geared up in virtual reality gear, pushing myself at the gym, or fielding text messages from my nephews asking to play Fortnite.

Meanwhile, Rose just laughed it off, thinking pregnancy an impossibility due to double contraception. But I still can't shake the fear that word spikes in my chest.

"Earth to Vance?"

My head snaps up, and I realize all I see are stars spinning by me like I'm flying in the Millennium Falcon at light speed.

"*Shit.*" Lost in thought, I must've lowered my hands from the imaginary handholds. And that's *after* I failed to make the all-important tether swap to the new anchor point. Basic spacewalk 101 stuff.

Now I'm playing out NASA's worst nightmare—an astronaut unattached to the station, spinning out into space in a simulated fall from the ISS.

"Ah, Vance is probably just showing you our emergency training protocol." The instructor laughs awkwardly.

I drop my hands to the chest plate I'm wearing which mimics the SAFER jet pack astronauts wear in space. "No, I'm just an idiot."

Jules jokes about me being a glorified flashlight during spacewalks. I can laugh at the joke because I know what everyone else knows—that I'm one of the most reliable astronauts in rotation. I don't make mistakes like this.

I flick the SAFER on and wait the few seconds it takes to power up. A few seconds more of spiraling away from the ISS.

Once it does, I cancel out my rotation. As soon as I'm not spinning, I swivel my head and body around until I find the station. Thanks to Newton's first law, I'm only yards and not miles away. Even so—

"The SAFER only has so much fuel," the instructor says as I switch to translation mode, using the jet pack's yawl and pitch to get closer to the station.

"I believe the estimated window of time for an astronaut using the SAFER is five to ten minutes," Jackie says. "Anything over fifteen, the chance of rescue drops to zero."

"Yes. That's correct."

A little bit of thrust goes a long way in space. So although the clock is ticking, it's basically a waiting game once you propel yourself toward the station.

Even with my headset, I hear the instructor typing on a keyboard, probably logging in my order of operations for record.

Great.

As a veteran astronaut with an upcoming lead for a high-profile spacewalk, having to use the SAFER in a standard VR spacewalk replication is bad enough. I don't want it to go on record that I also burned up in the atmosphere because I was too busy worried about my friends with benefits situation to get my ass back on the station.

After what seems like an hour, but is only three minutes, I reach out my Manus glove and grab onto the S-3 truss on the zenith side—the opposite side from where I'm supposed to be.

"Well done." The instructor seems pleased with my time and SAFER controlling. "I'll shut down the simulation."

Jackie says nothing, which is nice of her seeing as she knows that had that been during a real spacewalk, my mistake would not have been as easy to correct. I would still have to maneuver myself back to airlock, the countdown to low oxygen, the worry of solar rays and lighting issues due to the station's proximity to the sun all life-or-death factors that this particular VR simulation wasn't set up for.

The VR mask goes black.

When I slide off the headset, Jackie's gaze is penetrating. Like she's trying to find the deeper meaning behind my mistake.

I hand her the headset, knowing she'll want a closer look at the equipment.

But instead of studying the headset's mechanics, Jackie runs her finger along the inside, then holds it up to the light.

Glitter.

I've taken showers, I've done laundry, and yet still, the glitter remains.

The perfect metaphor for my relationship with Rose West.

Even when she's not here, she's here.

———

Rose

.   .   .

Vance is being weird.

My phone is dark and silent as it rests screen up on my favorite table at the coolest work café in Houston.

Brass Tacks serves coffee and breakfast tacos, so I'm winning at life every time I come. Add in the converted old brick building that gives it its millennial/hipster vibe (in all the good ways), and the atmosphere is legit amaze-balls. Top it all off with the plant lady, Gladys, the owner of a local garden shop, who keeps a steady rotation of oxygen cleansing plants arranged throughout the café, and I've died and gone to bougie heaven.

I'd seriously consider franchising this place after I graduate, but the hipsters would probably drive me out with pitchforks made of recycled tires if I mentioned the F word to them.

I tap my phone screen just to make sure I didn't miss any notifications.

I didn't.

After Vance and I set off the glitter bomb and successfully coated the kitchen mixer, I told him I'd be majorly swamped during exams this week. And I am. Graduation is imminent.

But I also needed a break from my warring emotions.

At the start, I told Vance I wasn't looking for a boyfriend. We said friends with benefits. I probably should've said sex buddies instead. Booty calls only. Stranger danger pals. Because all these extra 'benefits' that aren't sex are starting to confuse me.

And then he went and threw lotus in the mix.

So distance. Distance is good.

I tap my pen on the flea market found table, wondering why I am so annoyed if distance is good.

Vance is giving me exactly what I asked for. Space. Quiet. Breathing room.

All the things a Business Fellow in their last week of college needs.

I've got shit to do. Shit that doesn't include having an emotional breakdown over a man.

I nod to myself for emphasis and settle back into my work, the clacks and clinks of the café soothing me.

For about five minutes.

Giving up, I close out my screen before I do something stupid to my completed thesis presentation.

Over the past few days, I've turned in all my papers, taken my exams, and said good-bye to my fellow Fellows. All that's left is the presentation on Monday. A presentation I'm already prepared for but came to Brass Tacks to fiddle with so I wouldn't sit in my apartment and obsess over my phone.

Hashtag feminist fail.

You'd think I'd be excited or nervous or *something* about this presentation. It marks the culmination of all my hard work. The end of co-ed life and the beginning of... adulthood? Becoming a contributing member of society?

Ugh. I rub my face with my hands, disgusted that I still have no idea what comes next.

I've always known I was born lucky. Aside from selfish parents and a lonely boarding school upbringing, I was born with a silver spoon I had no hand in forging.

Like I told Vance, technically, I don't *have* to do anything. I can live the Richie Rich lifestyle and spend my days in a mansion with a butler and a pool boy.

And true, I did party it up with Houston's young socialites for a while. The same crowd that took Flynn down the wrong path when he was younger.

Hashtag troubled youth.

But after a while it all seemed so... meh. I saw it for what it was—a cop-out. A life devoid of all meaning. And I do know one thing I want for the future—I want my life to *mean* something.

And when I met Jackie, Jules, and Trish and saw their drive

and determination, it simply solidified my decision to be better. Do more.

Yet here I am, the world at my fingertips, not sure what it is that I should do more of.

Gladys comes by, nearly taking out my head with her potted Boston fern. "Sorry!"

I drum up a smile for her. "No problem."

She places the fern on a nearby windowsill and moves on to water a ficus, humming happily as she goes.

Maybe I should be a plant lady.

I tap my phone screen. Nothing.

I'm probably just missing Vance right now because when he's around, I don't so much worry about my next step or fixating on all the things I should be doing or becoming. When he ran me to ground at the Whiskey River saloon, I thought he'd make for a brief distraction. But now, with him going AWOL on me, I realize he's more than that.

Vance calms something inside me. Makes me feel like it's okay to just be me. That I can stop and take a breath. That I don't have to do everything at one hundred miles an hour to prove my worth to everyone—including myself.

And I *like* hanging out with him. Even, dare I say, without the sex. Though the sex is good.

Praise Jesus, the sex is good.

He's fun and unassuming. Sweet to his nephews and kind to his sister, though it's obvious she knows how to push a few buttons (said as a fellow button pusher).

"Ugh." I slide my computer to the side and drop my head onto my folded arms next to my lemonade. Brass Tacks' butterfly lemonade is topped with antioxidant pea powder that turns the drink blue. It is as delicious as it is ridiculous.

I stifle a yawn. As delicious as it is, though, I probably should've sprung for the dirty chai latte. My energy of late is *flagging.* I didn't realize how much the end of the semester was taking out of me. And my current emotional roller coaster.

My phone dings, and in my mad scramble to pick it up, I knock over my lemonade. Blue, sticky liquid runs over my keyboard, and the screen goes black.

Well, shit. Good thing I have everything backed up in the cloud.

Throwing a napkin at the dead machine, I light up my phone with a touch, expecting a text notification from 'Old Man.'

Nope.

Group text from the girls. Which is just as good. Better even.

I ignore the bite of disappointment.

Trish: *What time should we be at the ranch this Saturday?*

Jules: *Laser tag! Laser tag!*

Me: *10 a.m.*

Jules: *Laser tag! Laser tag!*

Trish: **eyeroll emoji*

Me: *Y'all told the boys to fuck off, right?*

Jackie: *Work phone.*

Me: *You told the boys to bang off, right?*

Jules: *I told Holt to go do manly stuff with Flynn and Ian.*

Me: *So what, they're going to bake cookies?*

Trish: *Probably *laughing emoji*

Jules: **middle finger emoji*

Jackie: *Work phone!*

Jules: *You're just jealous that my man bakes orgasmic cookies.*

Me: *Dude. Brother, remember? *vomit emoji*

Jules: **gif of Britney Spears rolling her eyes*

Me: **gif of woman riding a cow like a bronco*

Jules: **gif of a stripper falling off her pole*

Me: *gif of a woman falling off her motorcycle

Trish: *Are you two done yet?*

Jules: *gif of Alan Rickman as Professor Snape yelling 'Silence'*

Jackie: WORK PHONE!

Jules: *Hooker, please. This is also my work phone. And as I haven't been picked up by the NSA, I'm pretty sure we're good.*

Trish: *Anyhoo... West Ranch at* 10.

Me: *Leave your heels at home, Shortstack.*

Jules: *gif of people dressed in camo Army crawling under barbed wire through mud*

Jackie: *I'm pretty sure laser tag isn't that involved.*

Me: *Then you don't know laser tag.*

Trish: *gif of Ryan Reynolds sighing*

Me: *gif of Ryan Reynolds as Deadpool air banging*

Notification that Jackie has left the group text

Jules: *gif of The Simpsons' Mr. Burns evil laugh*

As usual, the girls put me in a good mood. My pre-graduation laser tag girls' day is going to be fabulous. My brothers insisted on throwing a party at the ranch next Saturday, but *this* Saturday will be all about the girls and me. I make a mental note to stock up on Baileys, edible glitter, and shoe polish.

Smile on my face, I slide my sticky laptop and notebooks in my backpack and head out.

It's time to see a brother about automotive clear-coating a glitterized KitchenAid mixer.

EIGHTEEN

LIFE SUPPORT SYSTEM

Vance

I MISS HER.

I tap my pen over the Bartolomeo procedure plan, a spec of glitter on my finger catching in the florescent overhead lights above my cubical.

My phone, face up on my desk, buzzes.

Rose. For her first text since she asked for space, she's sent me a picture of the blinged-out KitchenAid mixer hanging from her self-made contraption at her brother's car shop. Texting me that Flynn's going to epoxy the finish for her to keep it "legit awesome for life."

Another vibration, another text. This time a picture of Rose, tongue out, her pinky and pointer fingers making rock and roll hand signs as she stands in front of Flynn, who's decked out in what looks like a white hazmat suit and holding a paint sprayer. To say Flynn looks less than enthused is an understatement.

Without responding to Rose's texts, I straighten in my chair and pick up the stack of papers in front of me. The Bartolomeo spacewalk plan. The project I've been waiting for since I accepted the small American flag pin that marks me as one of the NASA elites. I'm in charge. I'm leading NASA into the future by building a payload platform that will bridge the gap between government and commercial cooperation in space.

This spacewalk is the moment I've been waiting for. What I've been working for. What I've given up so much for.

I should be reading this plan over and over again. Memorizing it now so that when I'm moving five miles per second in space, my movements are second nature.

So I don't let go of the ISS handrails when the memory of Rose joking about being pregnant crosses my mind at seventeen thousand plus miles per hour.

The papers in my hand, the work that I do, they all prove that I'm trained to handle any situation. To figure out the unknown. With my engineering background, I'm supposed to be able to MacGyver my way out of anything. On Earth and in space. Yet when it comes to Rose West, there's no instruction manual to memorize and follow. The lack of one has me feeling lost. Untethered.

And as my recent VR simulation fail taught me—that's not safe.

I should've been more careful, kept my guard up longer. Maybe then her throwaway joke about being pregnant wouldn't have spooked me so much.

I grab another pen from my father's Army mug that my mom gave me when I was twenty. It's become a talisman, a reminder of the deal I made with myself to do the work I do. That decision, made by the fissures of my mother's grief, is so engrained it's become a part of me. One I've forgotten about since Rose West introduced me to barnyard masturbation.

The smart thing would be to walk away from Rose now. But even I know that shuttle has long since flown.

The thought of her smiling at someone else, laughing with someone else, *being* with someone else, stabs at my chest.

Our agreement may not include love, marriage, and a baby carriage, but maybe I can propose something else. Something that won't change her life for the worst, hold her back, or set her up for heartache. Something more than friends with benefits but less than happily ever after. Something where everyone wins.

When my phone rings and I see my sister's name, for once I don't cringe. I take it as an opportunity.

An opportunity to get Rose and me back on track.

"Hey, Brit."

"Wow, you actually picked up. I was all ready to leave a message." Seeing as she isn't being sarcastic, I must have really surprised her.

"Well, you got me." I sound more upbeat than I feel.

"Okay, well, I just wanted you to ask Rose if she has any allergies." Still no sarcasm, just excitement. "I didn't know she was coming to Thanksgiving, and she didn't seem particularly picky about her food, but I thought it would be best to ask her before Christmas dinner."

A man announces a sale on Granny Smith apples. My sister is back at the grocery store.

I take a deep breath. "Sorry, I misspoke when we talked last week. Rose won't be coming to Christmas dinner."

There's a beat of silence before Brit asks, "You misspoke?"

"Yes." I've crossed the line too many times recently. With Rose and with my family. Now I need to fix it. "Actually, I might have to work, so I'm not sure when or if I'll be there either."

"You're kidding me, right?" There's an edge to her voice. "But you messaged the boys over that stupid game that you'd come. That both you and Rose would come."

I cringe, the video gaming one more thing I need to stop. "Sorry, but you know how it is."

"I know how *you* are."

I let the barb hit. I deserve it.

"I gotta go, Brit. Talk to you later." I hang up before she can reply, dropping my phone back on my desk.

It doesn't take a master's degree in engineering to know my sister is pissed. Probably ramming her cart into some grocery food pyramid and buying junk food she'll binge eat later while cursing me,

But her being mad is better than... well, it's just better.

Picking up my office landline, I make a call. Not to Rose, but to someone who can help make sure I don't lose track of the promise I made to myself.

While it rings, I wipe the glitter off my hands.

———

Rose

"Oh. My. God." Trish's mouth drops open as she takes in the scene before her. She climbs off one of the four-wheelers that she and the other girls drove out to the far north field to reach my laser tag extravaganza.

I saunter out from my hiding space behind one of the *many* enormous, rolled stacks of hay. "You bitches ready for this?" I shoot my laser gun in the air, the tinny *pew pew* sound reminiscent of *Star Wars*.

Although I don't remember any of the *Star Wars* characters wearing full camouflage jumpsuits and tactical vests.

Jules leans forward on her four-wheeler, laughing. "I should've known you'd go all out." She pushes up, looking around at the field I had prepped with six-foot hay bales, wooden fencing, an old tractor, and two kid playsets, complete with monkey bars and an elevated clubhouse. I had each spray-painted camouflage and set on opposites sides of the battlefield. I even had a narrow, shallow trench dug across the middle of the area and filled with enough water to create a murky, muddy mess.

Hashtag mud wrestling with friends.

The West Ranch workers who volunteered to help with "one of Rose West's crazy ideas" are probably busy right now spending their extra overtime cash.

Hashtag everybody wins.

Jackie swings her leg off her four-wheeler. "Happy graduation." She crunches across the hay and slides out a slim wrapped box from her pocket. "From all of us."

"Aw, you guys," I sing-song, taking the glitter-wrapped present from Jackie. "You shouldn't have."

"Yes, we should." Trish squats down and scoops up a few pieces of the congratulations confetti I had sprinkled over the battle ground.

Biodegradable, of course.

"We probably should've held off and given it to you next week at your actual graduation party, but we couldn't wait." Jackie, looking more like a little kid at Christmas than a bona fide aerospace genius, bounces on her toes, waiting for me to open it.

Jules smirks. "Open it before Jackie passes out, will you?"

Jackie blushes, lowering her heels.

Smiling at my friends' excitement, I peel off the paper and lift the lid. The smell of cement glue from inside the box hits my nose. I take out a piece of folded card stock. "What's this?"

"Read it, sugar," Trish says, all of them sharing the same eager smile.

I drop the box and open the accordion folded paper. On the top of each folded section a different day is written. Under *Day 1* there are cut-out pictures of a clear blue water beach and one of tropical drinks with cocktail umbrellas. Under *Day 2*, a picture of people dancing, one of fireworks over the beach and another of different tropical drinks with cocktail umbrellas. *Day 3*'s column includes a woman para-sailing, a picture of Bloody Marys with cocktail umbrellas lined up on a bar, and one of sunburned people passed out on the beach.

Flipping the paper over, *Rose's Epic Graduation Trip* is written in marker at the top with pictures of a resort and an airplane underneath.

"Girls' trip!" Jackie, unable to hold back anymore, jumps up and down.

Jules smirks, shaking her head at our friend. "For New Years. Figured we'd make the most out of the built-in vacation time."

"Just you and us," Trish adds, making me think that maybe my carefully hidden resentment about them being in relation-ships wasn't all that hidden.

"This is great, guys." I clear my throat. All this hay must be affecting my allergies.

"I know, right?" Jules saunters over to the hay bale where I have all their matching camouflage jumpsuits, vests, and guns. "We rule."

"And are so humble about it," Trish mumbles.

"What's that, Shortstack?" Jules picks up a jumpsuit, pausing when she sees the back of it.

"Nothing." Trish blinks her eyelashes innocently at Jules.

Jules snorts. "Check this out." She tosses the jumpsuit in her hand to Jackie.

Jackie doesn't so much catch as gets slapped in the face with it. Pulling it off her head, she adjusts her glasses and reads the back. "Hooker." She giggles.

Jules grabs another one, this time hers. "Commando." She cocks an eyebrow. "Isn't that supposed to be commander?"

"Nah." I smirk. "I got it right."

"Smartass." But she laughs and tosses the last jumpsuit at Trish.

"Let me guess," Trish starts, straightening the jumpsuit so she can read it. "It says Shor—" She blinks. "Kimble?"

All of them frown.

I can't help but chuckle. "You know, Dr. Richard Kimble?"

Deeper frowns.

"Harrison Ford's character?" I prod.

Jackie's eyes widen. I knew the genius would put it together first.

I stare at Trish. "From the movie *The Fugitive*?"

Jules chokes on a laugh, looking at Trish, who's still frowning. Probably wondering if Trish is ready to joke about her recent brush with the law yet or not.

"Too soon?" I ask, feeling very much like the smartass I am.

Trish's lips twitch.

"It was the one-armed man!" I yell, and Trish gives in, laughing.

"You're such a bitch." Trish wipes under her eye.

"I know, I know." I help her step into her jumpsuit.

"What does yours say?" Jackie leans to the side, trying to read my back.

I make a dramatic turn so everyone can see.

"G.I. Juggs," Jackie reads.

Jules snorts. "And the letters are bedazzled."

"Well, I do have bedazzling boobs." I reach into my jumpsuit to situate my girls better in my sports bra.

I look over my shoulder and see Trish rolling her eyes. "You're too much."

"That's what she said," I deadpan.

Jules, finished with her jumpsuit, sticks out her fist. "Nice one."

We bump.

"You two think you're so funny." Trish shakes her head at us. "We'll just see who's laughing once I light up your vest."

"That's big talk for such a little lady," I drawl.

A herd of cows moo as they amble across the next field.

"I feel like I'm back in basic training, but with a farm theme." Jules picks up one of the guns, *pew-pewing* it in the air.

"How does it work, exactly?" Jackie inspects her gun.

"For the next forty-five minutes we'll shoot at each other." I tap my chest. "At the end of the round we'll check the monitor in your vest that keeps track of how many times you got hit."

When we're all covered, vested, and ready to shoot, I get out my selfie stick and take a picture. "This is going to be awesome."

———

"THIS SUCKS." I rest my forehead on my arm, which is resting on the windowsill of one of the treehouse forts. My stomach muscles contract again, and I shove my head out the window once more. "*Huah.*"

Thankfully I stopped upchucking a few heaves ago. Now I'm just gagging on air.

Jules reaches out with her leg from her seat on the opposite side of the fort and taps my shoe with hers. "There, there."

"You're a real caregiver, Jules." Trish's sarcasm makes me smile until—

"*Huah.*"

"I'm a regular Mother Teresa," Jules sarcasms right back,

then catches my eye. "Um, not to make this any weirder than it already is, but why are you rubbing your boob?"

I glance down to see my arm that's not holding my head up is massaging lefty. "Huh. I guess it's still sore from the Black Friday tit punch."

Jules snorts. "Damn, I would've paid money to see the great Rose West taken down by a Croc-wearing Godzilla."

"Har, har." I pause, thinking I might heave again, but manage to head it off with a calming breath through my nose.

"I thought you were punched in your right breast?" Jackie asks.

I pause mid-rub. "Croc-zilla hit so hard my left one hurts now too." I sit back, leaning against the fort wall, taking another deep breath through my nose, the nausea abating.

We sit in silence for a bit, enjoying the rare breeze cutting through the tree fort's windows and the distant sounds of farm animals and equipment.

"When was your last menstrual cycle?" Jackie looks oddly serious.

Jules snorts. "We really have to work on your girl talk, hooker."

Trish's eyes go wide. "You're not thinking..."

"What?" Jules sits up straighter. "What am I missing?"

"Nausea and sore boobs?" Trish prompts.

Jules' mouth drops open. "Holy shit." She turns to me. "You pregnant?"

I'd laugh at their expressions, but I'm worried that would set me off again. "Listen, guys." I swallow some saliva, testing my stomach. "It's like I told Vance"—I wipe the sweat off my fore-head with the back of my hand—"I have an IUD and he used a condom. The chances of pregnancy are like..." I wave my hand around, trying to think of some minuscule number.

"One point three to one point seven percent," Jackie says, tugging at her laser tag vest.

"Exactly!" I point at Jackie. "What she said."

"So you're saying there's a chance." Jules' *Dumb and Dumber* impersonation is not amusing.

"Correct," Jackie says, not picking up on the comedic undertones.

"Bullshit." But I don't sound as sure as I'd like. Before, I could explain the sore breasts and nausea—Thanksgiving overload and Croc Woman spinning—but why am I sick now? And if *Jackie* says there's a chance...

"Listen." Trish shifts forward in her cross-legged position between us. "Why don't we just get a pregnancy test?" Her voice is unnaturally bright. "You'll pee on a stick, prove you're not pregnant, and then we can move on to planning our girls' trip."

I take a minute to mourn the end of my epic laser tag battle.

"Fine." I slide my gun out from my pocket and point it at Jules' vest. "But first"—I hold down the trigger until her entire vest lights up red—"I win."

Open mouthed, Jules looks down at her vest. "What the fuck?"

I smirk. "Don't be a sore loser."

Jules fires at me with her gun until my vest glows blue. "There."

"Dead people can't shoot, Jules," I say, enjoying her defeat. "Doesn't count."

Narrowing her eyes, she aims her gun at my head. "Just be glad these aren't real bullets, G.I. Juggs."

"Come on, now." Trish takes Jules' gun away from her. "We've got a drugstore to get to."

"Fine." I rip open the Velcro of my vest and turn off the power.

"But when I prove you worry warts wrong, y'all have to promise to take me out for sushi tonight." I narrow my eyes at Jules. "And none of this 'I know a place' where it turns out all the men are waiting."

"Yeah, I've been meaning to say sorry about that," Jules says, not looking very sorry. "Kind of a dickish move on my part."

"Kind of?" I toss my vest down and crawl over to the edge of the platform where the ladder is. "Try *very*."

"To be fair, though, it wasn't really for me. It was more for Holt." Jules crawls after me. "He rarely goes out, so when he does, I like him to be surrounded by his favorite people."

"Aw, we're his favorite people?" Trish asks, waiting for her turn to get down.

"No. Me." Jules looks at Trish like she's dumb. "*I'm* his favorite people."

Jackie and Trish laugh.

I try to but end up gagging.

———

"Holy Mercury." Jackie's voice echoes in the small half-bath off the kitchen.

After a race to the nearest drugstore in our camouflage jumpsuits, we're back at the ranch, piled into the four-by-four tiled space, staring at the white wand of fate siting on the bathroom vanity.

The wand I peed on.

And even though we haven't waited the recommended three minutes, there's no mistaking the blue plus sign that's getting darker and darker by the second.

"Does this mean we're going to be aunts?" Trish's surprising excitement is tempered by the what-the-fuck nature of this moment.

"We should first ask if she wants to keep it." Jules' cool logic makes me flinch.

Their eyes move from the plus sign to me.

I'm sitting on the closed toilet, my hand hovering over my stomach. "Am I going to keep it?"

It's a rhetorical question, aimed more at myself than my three friends who are wearing a mixture of emotions. Of course, that doesn't stop them from answering and reassuring me all at once.

"It's your choice."

"We'll support you no matter what."

"Legally, you have options."

I don't know who is saying what; my brain is busy repeating the question over and over again.

Am I going to keep it?

There are a thousand reasons not to.

I'm only twenty-one.

I'm unemployed.

I have a history of causing drama that ends with official badges being waved and lawyer fees.

I drive like a maniac.

"Maybe you should talk this over with Vance," Jules ventures, the seriousness of her words underscored by using Vance's real name.

Vance. The man I'm only friends with bennies with. The man I'm in love with. It only took a week of silence and a fried laptop to figure that out.

I settle my hand against my abdomen, the weight and warmth reassuring.

One by one I dismiss the reasons for why I shouldn't have it and think about *it*. What's growing under my hand.

A baby. *My* baby.

The elusive feeling I've been chasing these past few months

settles over me, radiating inside my chest. The feeling of purpose and certainty I was missing in my life.

This. This is what I've been waiting for. This is what I was meant to do.

"I'm keeping it." My voice is soft but strong and met with a beat of silence. Until Trish claps her hands and squeals while Jules and Jackie share a look I can't decipher.

Clearing her throat, Jules leans against the door frame, crossing her arms and motorcycle boots. "How you gonna tell Flashlight?"

I pull my phone out of my jumpsuit pocket. When the screen lights up, it tells me what I already know. Three outgoing texts to 'Old Man,' no responses. "I have no idea."

NINETEEN

SURFACE OPERATIONS

Vance

"Dr. Sato?"

Dr. Rebecca Sato, NASA flight surgeon, glances up from her phone. "Oh, hey, Vance."

I step out of the elevator and into the white polished tile medical lobby. "You're back from maternity leave?"

"Just." She slides her phone into the pocket of her lab coat. "Today's my first day back."

I run a hand through my hair, stalling. "Congratulations, by the way." When I called earlier, I was told I'd have to see the interim doctor, since Dr. Sato was on maternity leave, which was A-OK with me. Even though I know that everything on my medical record is available to all NASA doctors and Rebecca will see it anyway, it would've been nice to *not* have to have the conversation I'm about to have with a brand-new mother.

"Thanks." Her smile dims as I shuffle from foot to foot in front of her. "Did you need something?"

"Yeah." I sigh, giving in to the inevitable. "I have an appointment to get a referral. But I think it's with the interim doctor." I can't keep the hope out of my voice.

"Referral?" Her professional mask drops into place in an instant. "I was just going to go through paperwork today, but I have time to see you." She glances at her watch. "I think Dr. Zamir is still at lunch."

"Oh, that's okay." I curse myself for coming early. "I don't want to bother you."

"No bother at all." She grabs the iPad resting on the lobby front desk and starts tapping on it. "Let's talk in my office."

I follow her down the brightly lit hallway and into her new office with a wall of windows. A marked difference from the old medical building that was retrofitted with modern conveniences and cluttered with furniture past vintage and heading into antique territory.

"So," Dr. Sato says once we're seated on opposite sides of her large, glass-topped desk. "What can I help you with, Vance?"

————

TEN MINUTES later a frowning Dr. Sato guides me out of her office, and I have the referral appointment reminder card in my pocket.

"Just do me a favor and think about this a bit longer, Vance." She closes her office door behind us. "As much as soap operas like to say otherwise, this really isn't reversible. Once you do it, there's no going back."

I nod. "Sounds good to me."

The V between Rebecca's brows deepens. "I—"

"There you are."

We both look up to see Ryan, Rebecca's husband, pushing a

double stroller into the lobby. "I was wondering what was taking so long."

"Didn't you get my text?" Rebecca pulls her phone back out and checks the screen. She sighs. "Sorry babe, I forgot to hit send."

"No problem, the kids and I just took a stroll." He looks down at the twins, sleeping soundly in their seats. "Knocked Emma right out." The baby in blue waves and smacks his lips, drool sliding toward his chin. "As usual, Charlie doesn't want to nap."

Rebecca's eyes light up as she leans down to unbuckle Charlie from his stroller seat, picking him up.

I'm not one for babies, as the piece of paper burning a hole in my pocket can attest to, but even I must admit that these two are damn adorable. The mix of Rebecca's Japanese heritage and Ryan's classic all-American looks made for two cute kids.

Guilt over my reason for being here hits me, and I cover my pocket with my hand.

Rebecca sees my move and assesses me. "I need one more minute." Dr. Sato shifts Charlie in her arms and kisses her husband's cheek. "I forgot to sign off on something."

"Sure thing, babe." He reaches for his son, but Rebecca turns to me.

"Here." She holds out her son, and my arms lift by instinct.

Before my brain can register the soft weight in my arms, she walks back down the hallway to her office.

As Charlie settles in against my chest, my initial spike of panic fades.

Ryan grins. "You're a natural."

"I have two nephews." Though I don't remember holding them as babies very often. I don't believe I let myself, come to think of it.

Ryan's wearing his Houston Fire Department shirt. The

sight of that and the reason for the appointment card in my pocket converge. "Aren't you worried?" The words shoot out of my mouth before I can think them through.

"Worried about what?" Ryan's Thor-like muscles in his arm flex as he pushes the stroller back and forth, rocking his sleeping daughter.

"About dying?"

Ryan pauses, looking at me with wide eyes. "Isn't everyone?"

I only just register his comical expression. "No. I mean, because of your job."

"My job?" He's looking at me like maybe I need more than just a physical doctor.

"Firefighting is dangerous." I say this as if he doesn't already know.

Ryan just laughs. "So says the astronaut."

Gently, my thumb traces the bridge of Charlie's nose. He closes his eyes from the soft touch. "But I don't have a family."

When Charlie's breath evens out, I look up to see Ryan staring at me as if all my fears are written across my face.

"Yeah." He nods, his voice resigned. "Fighting fires *is* dangerous. And unfortunately, I know of quite a few families who lost a fireman parent in the line of duty." Ryan's eyes suddenly look much older than his twenty-something years. "But—"

"Okay, ready." Rebecca, lab coat gone, walks over to me, holding her arms out. "I'll take him now."

I frown at Ryan, wanting him to finish his thought. Thinking maybe what he says will make me understand why he's so willing to risk hurting the ones he loves. But he's focused on his wife now, his normal grin sliding back into place.

"Okay." I shift the now-sleeping Charlie from my chest and

hand him over, the loss of his tiny warm body leaving me with an unfamiliar longing in my chest.

At the same time, the appointment card in my pocket lies heavy against my leg.

———

Rose

"I HEARD YOUR PRESENTATION WAS PERFECT." For once, John is not tapping his fingers on the desk. He's leaning back in his high back rolling chair, legs crossed, his tapping hand still on the shiny mahogany wood.

"That's what they tell me." I shift in my seat, my khaki pants sliding across the hard wood. It *was* perfect, but boring. Afterwards, one of the professors asked if I was feeling okay. I think she'd been expecting a laser light show and streamers, and was disappointed with my well-designed, but standard, PowerPoint.

"Have you given any more thought to what we discussed last time? About what you want to do next?" His stillness is more unnerving than his habitual tick. Or is it because I'm dressed like a young professional, having taken the time to de-Rose myself? No glitter, no stripper shoes. I even tamed my hair into a low chignon, sans sequined clips. My usual extra-ness dimmed by the rogue stowaway in my uterus.

I didn't realize how much I cared about John's opinion until I woke up this morning, our final meeting reminder glaring at me from my phone's calendar app. I tug at my shirt collar.

Crossing my legs, I lay my hands on top of my knee and clear my throat. "I decided *not* to enroll in the master's program." My voice is level and clear, ready to defend myself if needed. Just as I practiced.

"Okay."

There's a beat of silence.

"Okay?" I ask when he doesn't say anything else. "Is that all?" His right hand is still not moving.

Both bushy, steel-gray caterpillar eyebrows arch. "You seem surprised. What did you think was going to happen?"

Smoothing out my khaki material on my top leg, I speak to my knee. "I thought you'd be disappointed."

"Why?"

Exasperated at his calm tone, I sigh, my arms flying out to the side. "*Because* whenever I come in, you tell me about the program. You're always saying how it will help me take over West Oil Industries." I catch myself making wild hand gestures and still.

Meanwhile, John stays calm and collected, looking completely unfazed by this turn of events. "I mostly gave that speech because I knew it annoyed you."

My mouth falls open.

John's lips twitch. He leans forward in his chair conspiratorially. "It was my small form of payback for all the antics you enjoy bringing to my door."

I snap my mouth closed.

John chuckles.

"Well played, John. Well played." Then I laugh with him.

He smiles. "Thank you."

Forgetting my pre-planned professional stature, I scoot my chair forward and lean both elbows on his desk. "You know, I might have given you a raft of shit the past few years, but you are, by far, the best counselor I could've asked for, Johnny-boy."

"Again, thank you." He nods. "For both acknowledging the, um, *raft*, and for the compliment."

We bask in mutual admiration for a moment before he sits up, donning a more professional air. "Honestly, though, what can I help you with?" The right side of his smile lifts. "What's next for the great Rose West?"

Swallowing, I remember my plan. I'm going to tell him that I'm still thinking about it. That I'll be in touch. Then go home, send him a gift basket that includes a raffle ticket to a large sum of money that he'll "win."

"I'm pregnant." Whelp. There goes that plan.

At first, John's expression seems nonplussed. But I notice a small rise to his eyebrows. Not much, but enough for me to know I've surprised him. "I see."

I try to laugh, but I just sound awkward.

"Can I congratulate you or..." He trails off, probably not wanting to ask the question that first comes to mind when a young, unwed woman finds out she's pregnant.

"You can congratulate me. I'm keeping it." That is the only thing I've been sure about since I peed on the stick.

His smile grows. "Well then, congratulations."

I feel stupid by how happy his congratulations make me. "Thanks."

John's expression turns carefully blank. "And may I ask about the father?"

"He's my boyfriend." Sort of. "And we were careful, but..." I shrug.

"These things happen. I just hope he took the news well."

"I'm on my way to tell him." I stare at the floor, remembering both my relief and nervousness when Vance finally responded to my texts after my presentation yesterday.

"Well, I hope this boyfriend of yours knows how lucky he is."

I look up. "Lucky?"

"Yes, of course." He looks bewildered by my surprise. "He not only has you in his life, but now you're the mother of his child. He is *very* lucky." John's smile is softer and more real than any I've seen from him before. "Because you, Rose West, are going to be an amazing mother."

I swallow through the sudden tightness in my throat. "You think?"

"I know."

"But, I mean, you always seem so exasperated with me."

He thinks for a moment. "Did you know I was going to retire three and a half years ago?"

The semester I enrolled. "Uh, no, I didn't."

John's eyes move to the side to where a gold picture frame rests.

On one of my previous visits, I snuck a peek. In the picture John has his arm around a woman with short, dark hair, both smiling. It had to have been taken earlier, as John's hair is darker in the photo, and he's more salt than pepper now. I figured it was his wife.

"Diane passed away from breast cancer just before you enrolled."

"Oh." My mind blanks on anything else to say.

"I was having trouble getting up in the morning." John's voice is flat, as if reading from a script. "Getting to and doing work was even harder."

I flash back to all the antics I put him through right from the start of my college career. The inappropriate jokes, the stripper clothes, that one time with the roller skates. "John. I am *so* sorry."

He blinks a few times, coming back to the present. "Don't be." He smiles. "I'm telling you this to thank you."

I point to myself. "Thank *me*?" My incredulous tone makes him chuckle.

"Yes, you. Because it wasn't until you came bounding in, trailing glitter, popping bubble gum, and throwing out terms like

YOLO, which I had to look up later, that I found myself looking forward to something again."

"Ugh." I drop my head in my hands. "Don't remind me of my YOLO phase."

John laughs and reaches out to take my hands.

I give them to him, still looking down.

"Rose." He waits for me to lift my head. "You not only have a knack for lighting up the room, but you also do it while managing to make deadlines, write publish-worthy papers, and ace exams. You think you're being covert, but I know all the times you've helped pay for a student's tuition or their living expenses through fake scholarships that you made up on the spot." He squeezes my hands when I start to look away. "Only you would name scholarships The Oliver Clothesoff Foundation or The Drew P. Weiner Fund."

I snicker. "Drew P. Weiner. Classic."

"Yes. Classic Rose West." He stares intently at me. "I could never be disappointed in you."

I am not crying.

"And you are going to be a *fantastic* mom."

I may be crying.

When the first tear falls, we both mutually pull back, me mumbling about hormones, him straightening his desk blotter.

Though I've always cared about John and knew he cared about my academic career, this is the first time we've gotten personal.

I clear my throat. "So what you're saying is it only took three and a half years for me to drive you to retirement?"

The joke falls flat, but he smiles nonetheless. "That's right. You're my swan song." He clears his own throat, both of us pretending we aren't emotional idiots. "And I couldn't be prouder."

"I'm glad you're not disappointed that I'm not doing something noteworthy or monumental." I put on a snooty accent. "Something deserving of the West name and status."

"But you *are* doing something worthy and monumental." He gestures to my stomach. "And I really couldn't care less about the West name and status." His eyes narrow, assessing my expression. "And neither should you."

That earns him a watery smile. "You're one cool dude, John."

He raises his hands, accepting my compliment with a smile. "That's what they tell me."

As the tension of the emotionally charged moment dissipates, I lean back in my chair, my legs falling open into a full-on man-spread. I'm lighter now that all my pre-meeting anxiousness is gone. That's when I notice his non tapping hand. His wedding ring hand. Which, for the first time since I've known him, is bare.

"John, John, John." Pulling my hairband out, I use both hands to give my hair a good shake, bringing back its volume and crazy. Feeling more like myself than I have since I found out Vance slipped one past the goalie. "I've got a great retirement gift for you."

TWENTY
#YOUREADICK

Rose

I'm fine. This is fine. Everything is fine.

From my seat in the back of Brass Tacks, I repeat the mantra I've been replaying in my mind as I watch Vance scan the room for me. As always, he looks sexy as hell in a sapphire blue, long-sleeve pocket tee, well-worn jeans, and laced boots.

I'm wedged between two ficus plants. But maybe I should've chosen the seat under the air vent because I'm sweating like a pig at a barbecue.

Vance sees me and smiles. Damn those sexy eye crinkles.

I pull my polo shirt away from my chest, trying to generate some air circulation. After leaving John's office, I didn't have time to go back home and change into something more me before meeting with Vance. I also didn't trust myself not to cancel if I didn't head straight here from campus.

Vance finds his way to me. "Rosie-girl."

Ugh, he's trying to kill me before I even start. "Vance." Just as with my presentation, I keep my tone even and professional.

Vance frowns. I wonder if he notices I look more like a member of the LPGA than I do myself.

Palm extended, I gesture to the chair across from me. "Take a seat."

He sits, his eyes never leaving mine.

I take a fortifying deep breath. "So—"

"I'm sorry." Vance reaches out, taking one of my hands in both of his, looking mildly panicked. "I didn't mean to ghost you this past week. I just needed to do some thinking."

"I see." Not only is he derailing my pre-planned speech, but he just confirmed that he had indeed been ghosting me and not just giving me the space I asked for.

Whelp. That feels awesome.

"I should've responded to your texts." His chin dips toward his chest. "That was a dick move on my part."

His choice of words has my lips breaking into a small smile.

We sit like this for a beat, the hum and buzz of the café picking up as the lunch crowd filters in.

It's nice sitting here, holding hands, occupying the same space. But it isn't why I agreed to meet him today.

"Vance, I—"

"I don't want this to end when I fly up to the Space Station." His words rush together, his hands tightening on mine.

It takes a second for my brain to register what he said. "You don't?" Hope rears its fickle head.

"No, I don't." His eye crinkles deepen, and my heart quickens. "You and me, we're good, right?" His thumb sweeps back and forth on the back of my hand.

Babump. Babump. Not only is my heart beating faster, but it's also louder, hope making it want to burst from my chest. For the past three days I prepared myself for disappointment and awkwardness. I steeled myself for what I'd decided was inevitable—being left.

But maybe my worst-case scenario won't happen. Maybe he won't think my news is bad. Maybe he'll have room for me and the baby in his future. Maybe he loves me too.

But it's all the maybes that have me wary of showing just how hopeful I am.

"I think so." My words are slow.

"From the start, we've understood each other." Vance shifts forward in his seat. "And I hope you'd like to continue it."

I fight to swallow back my emotions. I want to say yes. *Hell* yes. I want *all* the things to continue. The family holidays, the glitter projects, the late-night talks, and the cuddles. I want it all.

But it isn't just me on the line anymore.

I need to be clear. I put my free hand over my stomach. *We* need to be clear.

Squeezing the hands still holding mine, I take a deep breath. "You want to keep being together?" I can't help my growing smile.

"Yes."

My heart is out of control, as is the smile on my face. "Like in a regular, serious relationship?"

His smile wavers. "Well, sort of."

It's like the air has been sucked from my lungs. I try to pull my hand back.

"Don't get me wrong." Vance's hands tighten on mine. "I really do want to be together. But I think maybe, well, haven't we blurred the lines lately?" He laughs, sounding stiff.

I'm frozen in my seat.

When I don't say anything, he continues, "Thanksgiving was fun, but part of my thinking this week was that maybe Christmas isn't such a good idea."

I swallow.

"That day at NASA, I think you were right when you said friends with benefits don't do holiday stuff."

I could kick myself.

"Holidays aren't casual."

"Casual." My voice is monotone, my brain slow to register his words.

"But even so, this past week not seeing you... I didn't like it." He does that awkward laugh again. "What I mean is I like you, and what we started, and I don't want that to end." He lifts my hand, kissing the back of it. "Let's just continue to have fun without a timeline."

"Fun." My heart is still pounding, now in rhythm to the headache brewing at my temples. "Until when?"

He shrugs like the theoretical end of us isn't a big deal. Like our parting is inevitable somewhere down the line. Like it won't hurt him to leave. "I mean, it's not like either one of us is looking to settle down, right?"

I feel like he's testing me. But I can't get a grasp on the onslaught of emotions rushing through my chest to figure out what he's testing me on.

Sarah, one of the baristas, walks up to the table. "Here you go, Rose." She puts the butterfly lemonade that I'd forgotten I'd ordered down between us, giving me an excuse to lean back and retract my hand from Vance's.

"Thanks." I can't meet anyone's eyes. Instead, I follow the stream of condensation running slowly down the made-from-one-hundred-percent-recyclable-materials cup.

"Anything I can get you?" Sarah asks Vance.

"Ah, no." His eyes don't leave me. "I'm good."

There's a pause, and Sarah must pick up on the awkward-ness between Vance and me. "Uh, okay. Just let me know if you change your mind." She backs up a step then fast-walks herself over to the counter.

I really want to follow her.

"Rose." He tries reaching for my hand again, but I move it to my lap. "I thought you'd be happy about this." He sounds confused.

My nostrils flare with a big inhalation as I try to manage all the hope dying in my heart. "So you just want to change the timeline of our arrangement. You don't want anything... *more?*" I try to firm up my voice, but I sound weak even to myself.

"Why would we?" The surprise in his voice stabs at me. "I mean, I know we might've crossed the line a few times, but you and I, we're both not looking for more." His eyes try to probe mine.

I glance away.

"You're a Business Fellow and a West." He says this like it's the explanation I need, the answer to all my problems. His tone implies all the things I hate about being both a West and a Business Fellow. The expectations. The pressure. The assumptions. The things I know now don't matter.

Things that I didn't think mattered to him and our relationship.

"And I should mention that during this past week I also did some thinking about the pregnancy comment."

My heart flutters. A wisp of hope rising from the ashes?

"It got me thinking."

"About?" My voice cracks.

"How that would be such a worst-case scenario. For you and for me."

"Really." I reach out with shaking hands to grab my lemonade.

He nods, not noticing my distress. "I would hate myself if I did that to you." For the first time since he sat down, Vance's gaze leaves me, focusing on the ficus to my left.

He almost looks angry. But at me or at himself, I'm not sure.

"I never want kids. It's something I decided when I was accepted into the astronaut program."

"Never?" I can barely get the word out. I take a sip of my drink; the sweet liquid cools my throat but sits heavy in my stomach.

"Never." He takes advantage of my shock and grabs my hand again. "But that's what makes us an even better match, don't you think?" He squeezes, probably to reassure me, but it only feels like a vise. "You're too young to worry about all this stuff."

The nausea churning in my gut has nothing to do with morning sickness.

Misinterpreting my silence, just as he's misinterpreted a lot of things, Vance frowns. "And just to make sure this doesn't become a worry again I've seen my doctor."

My eyes snap to his. "What?"

The crinkles deepen, his expression self-satisfied. For once, his sexy laugh lines don't make me swoon. Instead, I yearn to slap them off his face. "I scheduled a vasectomy for after the holidays. I even cleared the procedure with NASA to make sure it doesn't mess with the upcoming flight plan."

This... this isn't right. *Can't* be right.

Vance. Normally sweet and considerate Vance wouldn't do this.

Not the guy who tickle-wrestled his nephews. Not the guy who held my hair back as I threw up. The guy who came by every night to make sure I was eating properly during exams without a thought to getting any of his sex benefits.

He wouldn't go so far as clearing a vasectomy with NASA to ensure it wouldn't derail his flight schedule but not mention it to me until now.

Right?

But as I continue to stare at him, to study his hopeful and unrepentant face, the truth of it all sinks in.

I concentrate on breathing in and out through my nose in an effort not to vomit all over him and his stupid eye crinkles.

I pull my hand back, jerking it out of his grasp.

Vance's smile falls. "Rose?"

In and out. In and out.

"Absolutely not." I tighten my hands into fists under the table. "No."

"No?" Vance can't hide his hurt. But what he's feeling is nothing compared to the pain he's carved in my chest, though I fight not to show it.

I've always been a fantastic emotional poker player.

I've had to be. All my life. When my father left. All the times my mother left. When my grandparents died. When my brothers shipped me off. When one by one, all my friends fell in love.

I nod once, short and fast. "I need more than that." *We* need more than that.

"What do you mean more?" He leans back, frowning.

That small distance helps me breath. Helps me find the courage. "I love you."

Vance's mouth drops open.

"And I want all those things you seem so sure I don't want. Like a serious relationship, kids, and happily ever after."

His ass slides back in the seat, as if trying to get as far away from me as possible. "We said... *you* said..."

I shrug, pretending his lack of reciprocation doesn't hurt. "Things change."

One of the hands that was holding mine so tightly just a moment ago rubs down his face. "I didn't believe your brother when he said—"

"*What* did my brother say?" Anger, only one of many emotions swirling inside me, surfaces.

His eyes widen at my tone. "At dinner the other night, he mentioned how you go all out for the people you love." He shifts in his seat, looking down. "And I"—his empty hands begin to fidget—"didn't believe him. I mean, you said you weren't looking for a boyfriend. So why would you—"

"Love you?" I'm questioning it as well.

In the back of my mind, I recognize the truth of his words. I *did* say I wasn't looking for a boyfriend. And until this moment I never said differently. But seeing him shell-shocked instead of elated over my confession hits me hard. Subdues any grace I may have felt obliged to offer. And any desire to tell him about being pregnant.

About the baby whose surprise existence has made me feel complete and resolved.

I close my eyes for a beat, letting my newfound sense of purpose settle over me. Give me strength for what I need to do next. "I'm ending this."

"Ending it?" He looks younger and more insecure than I've ever seen him.

Too fucking bad.

I straighten in my seat, one more deep breath clearing the churning nausea. "Yes." I grab my purse off the seat next to me, pulling the strap over my shoulder. "Now. No need to wait until your flight."

It's his turn to be verbally bitch-slapped into silence. But when I move to stand up, he rallies.

"I thought we were having fun."

"Fun?" I snort, covering the hitch in my breathing. "Is that all I am?"

He shakes his head, as if trying to figure out how he misstepped. It seems I'm not the only one whose plans for today got derailed.

"No, it's just I..." He pauses, unclear on what to say next.

Before I cry or puke, I stand. Looking down at him, I make sure to be very clear. To him, and myself. "I'm a lot more than a good time, Vance. And the fact that you don't seem to think so only solidifies my decision to end this now." Deep breath. "You don't deserve me." I press my hand to my stomach. He doesn't deserve *us*.

I have a hard time swallowing, my tears choking me, but I manage. "You know, people have been underestimating me my whole life. I usually find it amusing." Another hard swallow. "Funny how I'm not laughing now."

With that, I grab my lemonade and sidestep our table, bobbing and weaving through the small crowd, careful not to trip on any laptop cords, and leave.

Leave before he can leave me.

When I make it to the counter, and he hasn't called after me, I regret not throwing my stupidly delicious butterfly lemonade over his head. But I'm going to be a mother. I should start acting more mature.

Hashtag fuck that.

Spinning on my heel, I dart back to the table, popping the top off my drink as I go. I find Vance frowning at one of the ficus trees, looking sad and confused.

Well, that makes both of us, buddy.

When he sees me, he smiles, hope lighting up his eyes. "Rose, I—"

I overturn the cup, sticky blue liquid running in rivulets down his silky hair and over his eye crinkles. Dousing him like he did my hopes.

The café goes quiet. I drop the cup on the table and stalk

away from him, promising myself to tip extra big the next time I come here.

I keep my head held high and refuse to make eye contact with anyone. Until I catch my own gaze in the glass doors as I exit. A mixture of determination, satisfaction, and loss stares back at me.

The tears start as soon as I step outside.

Hashtag motherfucking hormones.

TWENTY-ONE
ADAPTING SUPPORT PINS

Vance

"Hey, man, you looking forward to the next mission?" Luke Bisbee, chief astronaut and the tallest astronaut to ever fly, claps me on the back as we get on the elevator.

"Yeah." My tone belies the word. It's been four days, and my mind is still reeling from Rose's confession and good-bye.

Luke's paw-like hand squeezes my shoulder. "You okay?"

"Hmm?" I shake off my mental fog. Since being doused with blue liquid, I haven't been myself. I say the things I need to say, and I do the things I need to do, but it's like I'm not all the way here. Like I left part of myself back at that artsy coffee house next to the ficus trees. "Yeah, yeah. I'm good."

"You better be. Don't think for a minute that I won't boot your butt off that flight." He pushes the button for the astronaut floor. "Building Bartolomeo sounds fun."

"You looking to get back up there?" It's a throw-away question, as what astronaut doesn't want to get back in space?

Luke's position as chief astronaut is rotational. For the past year he's had the responsibility of assigning flights to all the other astronauts. Everyone takes their turn manning the flight schedule then hands it off to someone else. If it were me, I'd be antsy as hell to get back up there.

"You know it." Luke confirms my thoughts, his smile getting bigger. He leans into me. "And the next time I go up, I've got something exciting planned." Another cool thing about being chief astronaut is that you can assign yourself the best mission when you finally give up the managerial post and return to flight ops.

"Oh yeah? What's that?"

He looks me up and down, his evident excitement probably making him unable to see the lack of mine. "Can you keep a secret?"

I hold up three fingers on my right hand. "Scout's honor."

Picking up on my sarcasm, Luke shoves my shoulder. "Smartass. You're spending too much time with Jules."

I snort. In reality I haven't seen Jules all week. And the last time I saw Jackie was in the VR room. It makes me wonder if Rose had given them a heads-up. Maybe they knew I was a single man walking before I did.

Ding. The elevator doors open, and Luke sticks his head out, glancing left then right around the cube farm. Finding the coast clear, he waves me out. "I'm going to be the first astronaut to propose from space."

For some reason, his words feel like a shot to my chest. "You're going to propose to Em?"

Luke's been dating the public relations director, Emily Durant. She's as short as he is tall.

"Hopefully." He chuckles. "Not sure I can wait until I get a flight, but that's the plan right now."

I frown, his words not making sense. "Marriage?"

Luke frowns back at me. "Yeah, that's what proposing

usually means." Both his hands drop on my shoulders. "You sure you're okay?"

"Yeah man." I shrug off his heavy mitts. "I'm just surprised is all. I thought you and I were the perpetual bachelors at NASA." Which, now that I've said it out loud, sounds juvenile and sad.

Luke shrugs. "Hey, when you know, you know." His smile turns smirk. "*And*"—he nudges me with his elbow—"from what I hear you've been getting serious with a special someone as well."

I swallow. Unable to say the words *she ended it*, I deflect. "Now who's been spending too much time with Jules?"

His laugh echoes across the quiet floor. "Touché."

Reaching his office door, Luke turns, blocking me from continuing to my cube. "It is surprising, though, I'll give you that."

"What is?" I ask, though I'm pretty sure I don't want to hear the answer.

He takes out a ring box, flips it open, and flashes me a large teardrop white diamond set in yellow gold. "Finding the person who changes everything for you."

I want to argue, but I can't, because I know what he means. Rose changed everything for me. My life, which before I'd thought full and important, now seems empty and pathetic compared to the time I've spent with Rose. Her laugh, her energy, her thirst for life.

Luke snaps the ring box closed. "But I guess that's what love does, huh?" His smile is almost as blinding as the diamond.

"Love?" The word seems to echo in my head.

"Yeah." He chuckles, pocketing the box. "Isn't it great?"

"Yeah." My voice is faint. But Luke doesn't notice. He's too hopped up on...*love*.

I manage to listen through Luke's detailed outer space

proposal plans until his office phone rings, allowing me to escape to my cubicle, my mind still spinning.

Luke's laughter booms across the floor once more, and I wonder if he's talking to Emily.

Love.

I didn't believe Rose when she said she loved me. Part of it was shock. I hadn't thought love was in the scope of possibilities. Not with the concrete parameters we set at the start of our relationship.

All Rose said in explaining her sentimental one-eighty was 'things change.'

The engineer in me couldn't grasp such a subjective, abstract explanation. I may have even chalked it up to woman's prerogative.

God help me if my nephews heard me admit that. They'd rake me over the coals of a thousand burning bras.

And rightly so.

Because it isn't *things* that change.

It's *love* that changes *things*.

Love changes everything.

―――――

An hour later, I massage my temples, trying to ease the headache brewing and take a deep breath of stale office air.

I love Rose.

And to make matters worse, she loves me back.

Fuck.

And now I'm facing another, lesser problem. The problem that comes from distancing yourself from others out of concern for their well-being. Because now, as I'm drowning in self-pity and reflection, there's no one around to get shit-faced with.

Not that I'm getting shit-faced. I *want* to, but as much as

NASA prescribes to the work hard play hard mantra, I'm pretty sure they'd draw a line at cubicle drinking.

"Earth to Bodaway. Hello?"

Coming out of my reverie, I find Ian behind me, leaning against the half-wall of my cubical.

"I've said your name three times." He angles forward, glancing at the notebook I'm hunched over. "What were you doing?"

Too late I try and cover the graph paper with its straight lines and perfect angles of the Bartolomeo blueprints—now marred by my absent-minded doodling of Rose's name.

Ian snickers. "What are you, twelve?"

I toss my pen on the desk. "Fuck off, Kincaid."

"Nah, man. We need to talk." He pushes my shoulder, rolling me back from my desk. "I've been voted in as the mediator."

"Voted in?" I swivel my chair to face him. "What are you talking about?"

"Rose won't take Holt's or Flynn's calls." He sighs and rubs his hand over his face. "And to make matters worse, Jackie and Jules are acting weird as hell, dodging them when they ask about her."

"What does Trish say?"

If looks could kill, I'd be dead.

"I wouldn't know as she suddenly got the idea to take her trailer somewhere for a 'writing retreat.'"

I try not to laugh when he air quotes.

"So the guys cast straws to see who had to come talk to you about it."

I shoot him a sardonic smile. "Let me guess, you lost."

"Nope. I won." He raises an eyebrow at my dubious expression. "And trust me, you should be on your knees thanking whatever god you believe in that it's me and not one of the West brothers. Because even though Holt is the more levelheaded of the two, after Rose cancelled tomorrow's graduation party, which according to him he's been planning for months, I got the feeling both he and Flynn weren't going to talk so much as beat your ass."

I wince, the guilt in my stomach getting heavier.

"So it *does* have to do with you."

I run a hand through my hair, trying to figure out what to say.

"What exactly did you do to the girl who can usually steam-roll her way through life's problems using just the power of glitter that upset her enough to cancel a party?"

"Hey." I stand, poking my finger in his chest. "Don't talk about her like that. Don't underestimate Rose just because she's fun to be around." I think of the devastated expression she made when I, like an idiot, did just that. "She's more than a good time. She works hard at everything she does, and she *cares*. She cares deeply."

Ian lifts his hands in surrender. "Yes, I do know that, actually."

I lower the finger digging into his sternum. "Oh, ah, good."

"I was just making sure *you* did." He rubs his chest. "And I think I can say with certainty that you do."

"Sorry about that," I mumble, nodding at his chest but too disgruntled over him testing me to sound sincere.

"Yeah, yeah. I know." He waves away my apology. "Come on." He taps the hard plastic of the cubicle wall frame. "If we're going to get any more awkward, we might as well do it over drinks."

———

Ten minutes later, over a pint of True Anomaly at Boon-doggles Pub, I tell Ian how Rose ended things.

"Wait." Ian looks at me like I just confessed I think the Earth is flat. "You're telling me that *after* you told Rose that the very thought of her having your baby scared you so much that you scheduled a vasectomy you asked her to keep banging you until she finds someone she wants to have kids with?"

I shift in my seat, thankful my Native American heritage keeps me from blushing. "Yeah, I know. It wasn't my finest hour." I take another sip. "But I'd like to think it didn't sound that bad when I said it."

Ian whistles low. "Man, no matter how you say it, it sounds bad."

I drop my head in my hands. "Fuck, I know."

"So is that why she ended things?"

"Maybe."

"Maybe? Don't tell me there's more?"

"She may have told me she loves me."

"And..."

"And I may have not believed her."

Ian rubs his eyes, looking dumbfounded. "I guess now it makes sense that Rose is MIA. The guy she loves just sucker punched her in the heart."

I thought I knew, but to hear someone else say it pinches at my heart even more. "I was just... shocked."

"Why?" Ian frowns. "Everyone else knows."

I tighten my grip on the pint glass, once again angry at myself for being so emotionally blind.

"No kids is a pretty big deal breaker for any relationship, though." He takes a sip of his beer as he thinks that over. "Are you *sure* that's what you want?"

I remember my dad's mug. "It's the right thing to do."

Ian lowers his beer to the table with a thunk. "How is not having kids the right thing to do?"

"It's not just about not having kids. It's about not being irresponsible by loving people you could end up leaving." Staring into my glass, I see my eyes reflecting in the amber liquid. "I'm an astronaut. It's dangerous. It wouldn't be right if something happened to me and I left behind people who loved me." As I put into words the rationale I've been so certain of for years, I expect Ian, another rational thinking engineer, to see the logic behind it.

Instead, when I look up, his expression is incredulous. "But there are a lot of astronauts with families. In fact, most astronauts have kids." He frowns harder. "Isn't there some statistic about driving a car being more dangerous than space flight?"

"Statistics can be skewed."

Ian talks right over me. "And plus, there are a lot more dangerous jobs than astronauts. First responders, loggers, steel work—"

"They're all idiots." I think about Dr. Sato's husband Ryan, the firefighter pushing around their twins. Twins who are just one fire, one backdraft away from losing their dad. I shake my head in disgust. "They don't know what could happen. They don't get it." I look intensely into Ian's eyes, trying to convey without words how right I am, how important my decision is. "You think *my* idea to not want to be in love is selfish?" I scoff. "The *truly* selfish people are the ones who know there's a good chance they'll die but have wives and kids anyway. Families and significant others they'll leave behind to wallow in grief." When I'm finished, I need to take a deep breath, surprised to find myself panting.

"Okay, wow." Ian's eyebrows are practically touching his hairline. "So...that's quite a lot to unpack." The normally strait-laced senator's son cocks his head to the side and exhales a long breath. "But before we try delving into all *that*, I'm going to do three things for you."

Before he can explain, the waiter stops by with our next round of beers.

When I reach for mine, Ian pushes my hand away. Addressing the server, he says, "We're gonna need two shots of Jameson for these."

The waiter nods, like two men doing boilermakers before noon is a common occurrence, then walks away.

Ian focuses on me and holds up a finger. "One, I'm going to get you drunk."

"Yes." That sounds like a great idea.

"Two." He shifts in his seat and pulls out his wallet. Flipping it open, he slides out a business card and hands it to me. "I'm going to give you this."

I take the card and read, "Dr. Betty Brown, psychologist." I frown harder, not understanding. "A shrink?"

"Yes." Ian nods. "And a damn fine one."

"Huh." I look at Ian with new eyes, processing this information. "I didn't know you were in therapy."

Ian shrugs like it's no big deal, which only makes me respect him more. "But that's not going to help you right now." He points at me. "You owe Rose an apology. For the sake of your co-workers and friends, but mostly for her own sake."

I swallow, the heavy feelings of regret settling over me once more. "Yeah, I know."

"And the sooner the better. Because not only do you have two West brothers to deal with, but also a crazy astronaut who I wouldn't put past killing you and making it look like an accident and another astronaut who's smart enough to help her get away with it."

"Fuck." I forgot that on top of a broken heart, I also have to deal with a normally instructive, but now probably psychotic Julie Starr.

The waiter comes with our shots.

"You might as well bring another set," Ian says to him while sliding me my beer.

"What's the third thing?" I ask when the waiter leaves.

"I'm going to tell you something, and you're not going to like it, but I promise you it's one hundred percent true."

"That sounds great."

Ian looks me dead in the eye. "You didn't believe Rose because if you accepted that she loved you, with your skewed, emotionally damaged logic, you'd be forced to let her go."

I flinch.

Still holding my eyes, Ian tilts his head, as if assessing my reaction. "And you don't want to let her go because you love her."

It's hard to swallow. Both his words and the lump in my throat.

Ian hands me my shot.

Silently, I take it.

When I can finally breathe evenly again, I level Ian with a look. "You're brutal."

He nods. "I was raised on politics."

"I thought maybe that insight might've come from therapy."

"Oh, it did, but politics drove me to therapy, so—" He shrugs.

"So what do I do about it?"

"Fuck if I know."

I laugh despite the sudden need to blink back my emotions.

Ian holds the ounce of Jameson over his beer. "Let's drink and see if we can't figure it out."

I grab my shot. "Sounds like a plan."

We drop the shots and chug.

TWENTY-TWO

#RIDEORDIE

Rose

I MAY HAVE GONE OVERBOARD.

Emerging from my new minivan, I push the button for one of the two side doors to slide open.

Doug, the valet, hustles over, pausing when he sees a few of my purchases tumble out of the van. "Hey, Marty!" Doug calls over his shoulder, eyes still on the plethora of baby items piled inside. "We're gonna need the dolly cart."

"Good thinking, Doug." I pop up on my tiptoes, looking over the bags and boxes in the one hundred and forty cubic feet of storage that my new seventeen by six-and-a-half-foot vehicle allowed me to haul. "I want to—"

"What. In God's name. Did you do?"

Startled, I pivot on my sandals toward the front of my building where Jules, Trish and Jackie stand, mouths agape. Trish and Jackie look confused while Jules' shock takes on a more personally affronted vibe.

"It's one kid," Jules says, like I don't know how many babies are in my belly. "Why the hell do you need a minivan?"

"And why is it covered in glitter?" Jackie asks.

"Are those spinning rims?" Trish squints at my newly jacked-up, twenty-five-inchers. That do, indeed, spin.

"I'm pretty sure that isn't a standard factory color," Jackie remarks.

I shrug as they come closer. "I'm not going to be your standard mom." The Texas sun glints off the surface of my newly refinished holographic rose gold glitter car paint, making me smile. "Plus, it's one kid now. Who knows what will happen?"

That stops all of them in their tracks.

"And a minivan is like, super safe." In case they didn't know. Because they're looking at me like I'm crazy instead of a responsible thinking adult about to have a child.

"So is a tank," Jules deadpans. "Which would also be less embarrassing to drive."

"It's so...blinding." There's a hint of wonder in Trish's voice.

I grin wider. "I know, right?"

"What do you mean by one kid *now*?" Jackie asks.

I decide *not* to tell them about my newfound plans for becoming the old lady who lived in a shoe with her immense number of children. Except, you know, make it the young woman who lived in a penthouse.

After I left Brass Tacks, I promised myself that with or without Vance, my kid was going to have a large family. Brothers, sisters, aunts, and uncles. The whole shebang. Whether that means I need to become Houston's Angelina Jolie and adopt a hoard of orphans or visit a sperm bank to make withdrawals, I'll ensure *all* my kids are surrounded by nothing but love.

I'm saved from answering Jackie when Martin rolls up with the dolly cart.

"Thanks, Marty."

"No problem, Miss West." He stands next to Doug, both frowning at my van's packed interior. "We'll have this sorted in no time."

I reach out to help, but Martin shoos me away. "Doug and I will bring your purchases up to you and park the car in the garage."

"You sure?" I feel bad, but also, I've been doing retail therapy all week. I thought it would help, but my heart is still as sore as my feet are from my marathon of shopping.

"Yes." Martin isn't even looking at me now, completely absorbed with Tetris-ing my boxes and bags onto the cart.

"Okay, thanks guys." And even though I'm not supposed to, I slip them both a fifty in their pockets when their hands are full.

When I turn to head into the building, I'm barricaded by my friends.

"We need to talk, sugar." Trish, ever the diplomat, smiles. It's a smile you give a wounded animal when you're not sure if they're going to bite your head off or not.

"Yeah, this week has fucking sucked." Jules, ever *not* the diplomat, crosses her arms over her chest.

"Because it's all about you," I reply straight-faced.

Not looking at us, Jackie reaches out and touches the van, as if trying to analyze each glitter particle. "I think what Jules means is that avoiding Vance has become a logistical problem at work. Not to mention the moral and emotional implications of keeping a secret from a colleague and friend."

"I was afraid I'd let something slip, so I drove the Airstream to Myra's trailer park and parked it, telling Ian I was going on a writing retreat," Trish adds. "I mean, it kind of is since I'm just holed up in there writing all day, but still, I'd rather be home."

"Oh," I say, chastised. I'd been so busy in my own world I

hadn't thought about how my friends were dealing with my baby news.

Jackie turns to me, looking annoyed at my lack of forethought. "You also stopped taking our calls, so we didn't know when or how the talk with Vance went about the fetus development." She pushes up her glasses. "Which bring us back to the avoidance issue."

Jules pinches the bridge of her nose. "Fetus, Jackie? Really?"

Seeing as Martin and Doug are hefting a cow print car seat and boxes of diapers out of the van, I'm sure the fact that I'm pregnant is not going to shock them. However, I don't necessarily want to discuss my baby daddy drama out in the middle of the street. "Come on, bitches." I push between them. "Let's go upstairs."

The elevator ride is quiet. Mostly because Jules and I are trying hard not to laugh at Mrs. Smalls, my elderly neighbor on the sixteenth floor with the flatulence problem that she likes to blame on her equally ancient dog, Gilda. I don't know whether to be glad or disgusted for the small reprieve.

When my neighbor and her dog get off on their floor, Mrs. Smalls crop dusting with each step, the stench remains as the elevator doors close again. Trish is almost blue from holding her breath.

Finally, we reach the top floor, stumbling out into the small security foyer and gasping for clean air.

Unlocking the front door, I walk inside and kick off my sandals.

"Gol-*ly*. That poor woman." Trish, one step behind me, freezes in the doorway when she notices the changes to my apartment.

"Poor woman my ass." Jules pushes past Trish, still waving her hand in front of her nose. "It's the dog I feel sorry—" She also freezes. "What the hell happened here?"

Jackie peers between them, rocking forward on her toes. "Are you moving?"

I set my purse down on the automatic baby food masticator. "No." I look around at all the stuff I bought in two days, my twenty-five hundred square foot penthouse looking cramped. "Well, maybe." Vance's mother's house, in the family friendly neighborhood with a fenced-in backyard, comes to mind. Me, instead of Helen, sitting at the head of the table filled with family.

I take a deep breath through my nose.

"Are you moving in with Vance?" Jackie asks, probably thinking that is the next logical step.

Trish claps her hands in front of her, looking hopeful.

"No." My voice is monotone. "We broke up."

This is met with silence until Jules cracks her knuckles. "Did that asshole call it off after you told him about the baby?"

All three sets of eyes bore into me as I rub my foot back and forth over the soft fibers my rug.

"Rose." Trish says it like a warning. "What aren't you telling us?"

Sighing, I push the three Louis Vuitton tote bags I bought to use as diaper bags off the ottoman and sit down. "I didn't tell him."

"I don't understand." Jackie purses her lips. Not understanding something is Jackie's pet peeve.

"How could you not tell him?" Jules turns like she wants to pace but is stopped by packages. "You *have* to tell him. Not only is he the father, but he's also my friend."

I glance at Trish, but there's no help there. She looks like a mamma disappointed in her kid.

Feeling cornered, I go on the offense. "Well, none of this would've happened if I knew you were his friend to begin with,"

I say to Jules, my voice rising. "You never even mentioned his name before."

"What are you talking about?" Jules frowns. "I talk about Flashlight all the time."

"Yeah, *Flashlight*. Not Vance or Bodie." I throw my hands in the air. "I thought you were referring to some sort of newfangled Robonaut."

Jackie sucks in a deep breath, eyes wide. "You can't replace Robonaut." Any other time her mild look of horror would be funny, but right now I'm feeling all kinds of foolish and frustrated.

"Flashlight is his *nickname*," Jules explains, like I'm dumb.

"It's a horrible nickname," I retort.

Jules takes a step toward me. "Why, you—"

"That's enough." Trish's Southern accent whips across the room. "You both are just upset." She glances between Jules and me. "And you're about to say things you don't really mean."

I take a deep, calming breath. Finding my inner Zen, I look Trish dead in the eye. "Flashlight is a horrible nickname. And I mean that with every fiber of my being."

Jules opens her mouth, but I'm saved from her retort by my doorbell.

Good old Martin.

To the soundtrack of awkward silence, Martin and Doug haul my purchases into the master bedroom, seeing as both the soon-to-be-nursery and the living space are full. When they're finished, I walk them to the front door and slip them another fifty each.

"Rose," Trish says to me once I've shown them out. "You need to tell him." Her voice is gentle but firm.

I stay facing the front door, not wanting to see my friends' faces while I admit my biggest fear. "It won't change anything."

"You don't know that, sugar."

"Yes. I do." Taking a deep breath, I face them. "He doesn't want kids. He told me that before I got a chance to tell him I'm pregnant." I laugh, annoyed that my eyes are stinging. "He's even scheduled a vasectomy."

Jules drops onto the sofa, crushing the bag of baby clothes from Marc Jacobs.

"Yeah. He's *that* serious about not having kids with me." I swallow past the lump in my throat. "But he wouldn't mind staying casual. Just not anything serious." I can't disguise my hurt.

We sit in silence, all of us thinking over what I just said. Even though I've tried hard not to think about his words to me that day, now that I've admitted it, they spin round and round in my head and heart on replay. Killing me softly with each turn.

Jules breaks the silence. "I'm going to kill him." Her calm tone is scarier than if she sounded angry.

"You can't." I slump back down on the ottoman, feeling drained, but also emotionally appeased by Jules' declaration. "He's your friend."

"Yeah, but hoes before bros."

I laugh, some of my sadness ebbing. "I fucking love you too, Jules."

"Yeah, I know." Her eyes soften, and she smiles. "I love you too."

"We all love you," Trish manages before biting her lip, like she's trying to control her emotions.

Welcome to the club.

"Love." I laugh, but it sounds hollow to my own ears. "Yeah, I told him that too." Staring at my toes, my vision blurs, the heat behind my eyes growing. "Loving him didn't change anything, either." I bite my lip, the pain grounding me. "In fact, it made things worse."

Trish walks over to me, arms out. I lean forward, my arms

wrapping around her waist, my head resting against her stomach. As she runs her fingers through my hair, a few tears fall.

"So, you see, it's just better this way." I say into Trish's shirt. "Better he not know."

We're quiet for a bit. The only sound comes from the glitter room, where the white noise machine I bought for the nursery is. Turns out it was easy to turn on but not so easy to turn off.

"You know"—Jackie's rational tone has me smiling, my tongue tasting the salt of my tears—"I've done some research."

"Of course, you have." Jules sighs, and from the rustle of bags I can tell she's settled in for one of Jackie's oratorical speeches.

"Yes," Jackie intones. "And it turns out there have been quite a few psychological studies about how men and women conceptualize pregnancy and parenthood. The concept of becoming a mother for women begins at the idea of motherhood. For men, the idea of parenthood is too abstract; they generally don't accept being a father until conception, and even then, they only embrace their impending responsibilities *after* the birth of the child."

I get ahold of my tears and sit up. "So?"

Trish grabs me a tissue from the side table.

Jackie's eyes get big, like she's surprised we haven't made whatever forward leap her brain already concluded with that information. "So it would be logical to think that Vance's opinion on fatherhood is skewed due to lack of information. The simple fact of knowing he's going to be a father and then becoming one could alter his whole outlook."

"All those woulds and coulds sound a lot like maybes." I blow my nose. "I'm not the biggest fan of maybes."

"No one is." Jules sits wide legged on my coach, her motorcycle boots looking out of place next to the baby llama stuffed animals that I decided would be the nursery's theme piled on the floor. "But there is no maybe about this baby coming, is there?"

I look down, where my by no means toned but still flat tummy belies the existence of a baby growing inside. A baby already causing drama before it's even fully formed.

Hashtag totally my kid.

"Yeah, no maybe about this little guy. Or girl."

The state-of-the-art, five-star safety rated stroller parked in front of the glitter room has me imagining pushing around a sweet baby boy with big brown eyes and gorgeous dark hair. Or maybe a little girl dressed up as a unicorn just as all little girls should get a chance to do.

I swallow hard.

Trish shifts and sits next to me on the ottoman. It's a tight squeeze, but I appreciate her closeness. "Can you tell us what he said when you told him you loved him?"

"He didn't believe me."

Jules' head falls back against the sofa. "I'm seriously going to rip his nuts off."

"Jules," Jackie reprimands.

"What?" Jules shrugs, trying to look innocent rather than murderous. "It's not like he treasures them anyway if he's scheduled to get his tubes tied."

"Women get their tubes tied. Men get—"

"*Anyhoo.*" Trish rolls her eyes at them, making me smile. "Is that all he said? He didn't say that he didn't love you, right?"

I remember his wide eyes. His frown of confusion. "Well, no," I say slowly. "But he didn't say that he loved me either."

"Maybe he was just in shock." The hope in Trish's voice makes me feel nauseous.

Jackie pushes aside the portable bathing tub and sits by Jules on the couch. "Men are considerably less aware of emotional entanglements than women."

Jules smirks at her. "Isn't that the pot calling the kettle black?"

"What pot?" Jackie's glasses slide down her nose when she frowns. "What kettle?"

"Never mind, hooker." Jules chuckles. "Never mind."

Jackie continues frowning before sliding her phone out of her pocket, no doubt looking up what Jules just said.

Studying these three women, I'm hit with a sudden sense of gratitude. I'm so thankful I met them. That they're here with me now. That they'll be here for the baby.

I smile, feeling better with these girls around me than I did while buying thousands of dollars' worth of baby gear.

"Hey," I say, nodding at Jackie when everyone looks at me. "Look something up for me, will you?"

"Sure, what?" Jackie poises her thumbs over her screen.

"The role of a godmother." My smile grows when all three stare at me with wide eyes. "'Cause I expect all of you to take your new responsibilities very seriously."

Trish claps her hands together and bounces on the ottoman, almost dislodging me from my seat. "We're going to be godmothers!"

Jackie nods solemnly, her thumbs flying.

I glance at Jules, whose usual smirk is absent. Catching me looking, she blinks and rubs at her eye. "Yeah." She clears her throat. "That sounds pretty cool."

I couldn't agree more.

TWENTY-THREE

INTERNAL PAYLOAD

Vance

THERE's a marked difference between the first time I sat in Heartbreakers' parking lot and today.

Parked a few spots down, with high shine glitter paint that's giving me a headache, is a stripper van. It must be a stripper van, because why else would anyone take the time to make a soccer mom vehicle that flashy?

Which begs the question of why a stripper needs a van. For road trips? Is it some sort of strip club Uber? And if Heartbreakers was going to make it *that* noticeable, why not plaster the side with their logo?

In my 4Runner's driver seat, I angle myself away, trying to hide my eyes from the van's cornea-destructive glare. One look at that unbelievably conspicuous paint job and my headache from Friday's Boilermaker bonding session with Ian comes roaring back. It makes me want my space helmet, with the sunshield coated with a thin layer of gold to filter out harmful solar rays.

But as noticeable as the stripper van is, what's equally noticeable is the absence of Rose's gold sports car.

It's a half hour past the start of pole dancing class, and Rose isn't here.

I tried texting and calling her yesterday. Nothing. It went straight to voicemail.

I even drove to her apartment but was stopped in the building's foyer by the doorman. It seems Vance Bodaway is no longer on the approved visitor list.

In just days, Rose has affectively cut me out of her life.

Which should be fine. It was what I was hoping for, after all. That Rose's feelings would be casual enough that she'd be able to simply move on once we put an end to our friends-with-benefits relationship.

But instead of feeling gratified by it, I'm depressed. I hadn't needed the weight of the doorman's condemning stare to know I screwed up. Not just by misunderstanding Rose's feelings but misunderstanding my own.

A cloud shifts away from the sun, and the van's blinding reflection becomes a death ray.

"Screw this." I turn off the ignition then shove open my door. The van glares at me as I stalk past, and I glare right back. By the time I reach Heartbreakers' front doors, dots of light float across my vision.

The first thing I notice when I enter is the music. Instead of the usual hard rock and hip hop, Bing Crosby's *White Christmas* plays from the speakers. The second thing I notice are the rotating ceiling fixtures. Rather than the normal multi-color lights, they're a mixture of green and red.

"I'm telling you, Helen, he's a big ol' sweetheart. He's perfect for you."

I blink a few times, wondering if the van did more damage to my retinas than I thought. Because the third thing I notice is

Rose. Rose in a full length, metallic red, sleeveless spandex onesie, complete with black belt and fur-trimmed neckline. And if that wasn't enough, it's tucked into thigh-high, black stiletto boots.

I have never, not once, in all my life desired to dress up like Santa. But seeing Rose dressed as a sexy Mrs. Claus, looking like a Christmas morning wet dream, makes me want to rethink all my life-long fantasies.

"I appreciate it, Rosie, but I haven't dated, in well"—my mother, dressed in white leggings and matching sports bra and doused in what looks like a gallon of silver glitter, shrugs and laughs—"ever, really."

"Go on, girl!" Myra, in a hunter green track suit and elf ears, eggs on my mom. "Get yourself some."

"Yeah," Angela butts in, eyes down as she arranges her brown triangle bikini top more securely over her breasts. "Holiday nookie is the best." She sighs and reaches up to straighten her antler headband. "Or so I've heard. It's been so long I'd make a better Virgin Mary than reindeer."

"Sooooo." Rose cajoles my mother with her elbow. "You'll let me give John your number?" More elbows. "Eh? Eh?"

Mom flushes. Or I think she does. It could be the red spotlight. "I don't think so. I'm too old for all that nonsense."

"What?" Rose steps back, looking my mother up and down. "You're not old—you're hot."

My mother laughs again, appearing youthful. Enchanted. Almost like she really, really wants to say yes.

But Mom doesn't date. She never has. I always thought it was because she never stopped grieving Dad.

Mom opens her mouth to respond, and I'm suddenly very nervous about what she's going to say.

"Rose." I cut my mother off, my voice projecting over Bing's and sounding hoarse in comparison.

Rose's eyes snap to me, her smile vanishing. "What are you doing here?"

Four sets of eyes focus on me, their weight enough to tip the scales of judgment out of my favor.

"Is anyone else getting a sense of déjà vu?" Myra glances around. "At my age you have to be careful. One minute it's déjà vu, the next it's dementia."

"I didn't think you were here," I tell Rose. "I didn't see your car."

"Anyone?" Myra asks, ignoring me.

Angela pats Myra's shoulder. "You're fine, Myra. I feel it too."

"Oh, good." With that, Myra adjusts her fold-out chair to face me and sits down, looking ready to be entertained.

Rose's head tilts to one side. "If you didn't think I was here, then I take it you're not here to see me?"

One of the lights shoots across my face so I can't make out her expression. "No. I *am* here to see you." Holding up my hand to block the light, I walk closer to the stage. "I was going to apologize after class was over, but I got worried you weren't here."

"Well, I'm here." She chews on her red bottom lip a moment. "Now what?"

My mother's eyes have been moving back and forth between us. With each glance, her frown gets deeper and deeper. "Did you do something wrong? Is that why Brit said Rose isn't coming to Christmas dinner?" One of her white platform fur boots taps an impatient, angry rhythm, causing silver glitter to fall around her like a snowstorm. "Do we need to have another talk?"

"God, no more talks." I hold up my hands, warding her off. "It has nothing to do with the clitoris, Mom."

She crosses her arms over her sports bra that doesn't cover

near enough of what I would like it to. "But you did do *something*."

"Yes, I did." Looking at Rose, I let her watery eyes dig the pit in my chest deeper. "I am *so* sorry, Rose. Honestly."

Myra, looking like she wants a bag of popcorn, scoots forward on her chair.

Mom switches to Rose. "What happened?"

Rose lays a hand on my mom's shoulder. "I didn't tell you sooner because I didn't want our last class before the holidays to be awkward." She flicks her eyes to me, then back to my mother. "The truth is, Vance and I aren't seeing each other anymore."

"What did you *do*?" Mom didn't look this mad when I drove the car through the garage door when I was fifteen without a license.

"I—"

"It's not his fault." Rose surprises me by coming to my rescue. "Not really." Not even the glitter and disco lights can mask Rose's pain. "We just feel differently is all."

"No we don't." My voice is firm, echoing around the empty club.

Rose startles, facing me. "We don't?"

"We don't." I stride to the stage steps and bound up them, not stopping until Rose is just inches away, her sky-high-heeled boots bringing her eyes level with mine. "I love you." I've never heard a 'ring of truth' until now. It gives me confidence that I can make this right. Make Rose and me work. For *real*.

But I have to be honest. I *have to* make sure she understands the risks.

"You do?" The wonder in her eyes brings me so much satisfaction that I call myself ten times more an asshole for not discerning my feelings earlier. She tilts her head back, her gaze now skeptical. "Since when?"

"Maybe since I caught you getting drunk on bridal champagne at Jackie's wedding."

Rose snorts.

Out of the corner of my eye, I see Myra nudge Angela with her foot. "This is getting good."

I hold Rose's gaze. "Probably when you dared me to take Blow Jobs at the bar."

"What now?" Myra asks.

Angela waves her to be quiet.

Rose bites her lip, holding back a smile.

"And definitely when you bribed a butcher for a Thanksgiving turkey when my sister failed to defrost hers."

"I *knew* it," my mother mutters behind me.

"I'm sorry I didn't realize it as fast as you." I let my gaze meander over every inch of her, noting the chunky snowflake glitter in her hair and the peek of a cash roll between her breasts. "Because I do love you."

Myra sighs. "This is just like when my second husband proposed."

Angela covers Myra's mouth with her hand.

Rose reaches out a shaking hand to me but retreats before I can grab hold. "But you don't want kids."

Mom gasps.

Ignoring what I know without even looking is my mother's wounded expression of betrayal, I close the distance between Rose and me, holding her in my arms. "I know I said that, and I'm sorry." Unable to hold back longer, I kiss her forehead, inhaling her sweet scent and praying I can find the right words. "I was wrong to spring all that on you like that. I must be going senile in my old age."

Myra scoffs, and I lean back to catch Rose's eyes. Fingers crossed she'll mirror my smile.

She does.

Until she doesn't.

Rose's eyes narrow. "So... you're *not* getting a vasectomy then?"

"*Vasectomy!*"

I hunch my shoulders in preparation for the attack my mother wants to launch, but thankfully it doesn't come.

"I'm going to cancel it." My thumbs sweep across her shoulders, the feel of her skin calming me.

"You want kids then?" She's speaking in the same slow, careful way that a police officer would to someone on a ledge. Which may sound dramatic, but me imagining even the possibility of children feels pretty on par with jumping off a building.

Breathing deeply, I prepare myself for what I'm praying will be enough for her. "Maybe."

Her eyes blank. "Maybe."

Not enough then.

"The reasons I told you about not wanting kids still stand. I made that decision because having kids meant having a family. People who cared if something happened to me." I'm rushing my words, afraid she'll leave again before I can explain. "But if *you* can come to terms with that danger, I can't help but be selfish enough to want to be with you."

"Wait." Rose pulls back, shaking her head. "You're telling me that the only reason you didn't tell me you loved me and that you don't want to have kids is because you're worried something will happen to you in space?"

"Vance..." my mother's soft plea barely registers.

"Lots of people with dangerous jobs have kids, Vance," Rose says, sounding exactly like Ian. "My dad was a race car driver."

"Yeah, and he's dead."

Rose flinches.

"*Vance.*" The shocked, disappointed tone of my mother's voice whips across my back.

"Yes. He's dead." Rose takes another step back, the distance between us growing. "And so is my mother. But not from racing."

I frown. "You said they died in a car crash during a race."

"Yes, an *unsanctioned* race during which my mother had no business being in the passenger seat. And they were probably under the influence of something." Her neck juts out. "You can't honestly tell me that you work like that? That you'd take those kinds of chances?"

"No, of course not." But neither did my father.

"Then why do you think it's such a sure thing that something will happen?"

"Because it might." Because it did.

"Might and will are two different things." Her exasperation ignites my anger.

"I'm not taking that chance." I slice my hand across the air, like I'm drawing a line in the sand not to cross.

We're silent. There's no music, Bing Crosby having finished his song a few heartbeats ago.

"Rose." I raise my hand to her cheek, thankful when she doesn't dodge it. "We... we don't need to decide this now. We don't have to argue about what ifs." Taking a breath, I try to order my thoughts and emotions. Things, which around Rose, become scrambled. "If, in ten years, after you've settled into your career and I've completed more missions, you're still set on having kids, we can talk then. By that time, I could retire early."

One tear slips between the fingers cradling Rose's cheek. And just like that tear, I feel Rose slipping away from me as well.

"Don't you see how much I'm already bending? How much I'm already risking by loving you?" Shaking my head, I plead, "Don't ask me to risk more. Not now." I wipe away the second tear that falls. "We have plenty of time."

She covers my hand with hers, holding it tightly before letting both fall. "No, we don't."

A black hole opens in my chest. "What do you mean?"

With her head turned to the side, I watch tears drop like glitter onto the stage.

"Rose?" I reach out to hold her, but her hand moves between us, warding me back.

Finally, she looks at me, and I *know*. I know without her saying anything. I shake my head back and forth.

She nods in answer. "I'm pregnant."

Everything stops. Even my breath. Blackness creeps along the edges of my vision. It's hard to swallow the onrush of salvia in my mouth. The black hole in my chest grows, consuming me, leaving me exposed and vulnerable.

Rose apologizes and says something about the IUD failure rate. I don't really hear it. Her words are drowned out by the pulsating rush of blood through my veins, the echo of rapid heartbeats in my ears.

Her hands fall to her abdomen, a small smile lighting up her tear-streaked face. Her lips keep moving, but I can't make out the words.

A gathering hum starts. Probably more people talking. Something smacks against my back. It all sounds distant and otherworldly.

I'm drifting away, untethered from this moment in time, surrounded by the dark void of my emotions.

Fear and panic.

I'm hugging my father good-bye on the front steps, listening to him tell us he'd see us soon. Watching him walk away in his uniform.

I'm standing between his military portrait and his coffin at his funeral. Holding my sister's hand. Surrounded by white flowers.

White flowers very much like the ones on my mother's robe, that she wore for weeks after the funeral, walking around the house like a zombie, her eyes vacant and sad.

Except now it isn't my mother, it's Rose. Rose and a small child with wild blond hair, both of them crying.

The pain in my chest is excruciating.

I gasp, surprised to realize I'm in my SUV, driving north on the Gulf Freeway, my back throbbing from what I'm pretty sure was my mother's fist.

But it's not nearly as painful as the tear stains on my chest.

––––––––

Rose

I HAVE TEARS TO DRY.

My van's powerful air-conditioning blasts at me as I sit in Flynn's auto shop parking lot. It isn't necessarily that hot out right now with the mild December temperatures and all. But I'm hoping the A/C will cool the fire burning behind my eyes.

I thought I would've handled the fallout better than this. I mean, I called it. I said Vance knowing about the baby wouldn't matter. That he'd still leave.

I'd only stared after him for a moment before leaving myself. As I reached the doors, Helen called out, "He loves you, I know it." She said the words like they'd somehow ease my pain instead of gutting out the rest of my heart.

Because I know he loves me; I could tell he meant it when he said it.

Hashtag but not enough to stay.

Not knowing where to go, but realizing my tears were a driving safety hazard, I found my way to the shop.

Might as well tell Flynn now that I'm here. Pour salt into the heartbreak.

Though it would probably make more sense to tell Holt first, seeing as he's the oldest and the one usually in charge of West family affairs. But the ranch is a longer drive, one I'm not sure I can make right now.

I stick my face closer to the air vents and blink, trying to stem new tears. I'm not sure I can blame these on hormones.

Watching Vance leave hurt more than watching Flynn and Holt walk away from airport security after waving good-bye on my way to boarding school.

It hurt more than watching the dust cloud behind Dad's '68 Chevy Malibu as he hauled ass down the ranch's dirt lane drive. Off to find my mom, or to a race or to some dive bar to drown his regrets.

It hurt more than every single time Mom left. Whether she had a bag packed or not, she'd leave without a backward glance or farewell. And I never got used to it, right up until the day she never came back.

"Rose?"

I smack the back of my hand against the closed window. "Son of a bitch!"

Mike, my brother's right-hand man at the shop, tilts his head in amusement. "You all right, there?" But as he asks it, his smile fades, probably taking in the tears sliding down my cheeks.

I gasp, trying to both calm and lock down the pain. Wiping frantically at my right cheek, I put on a smile and lower the window with my left. "I'm fine. Everything's fine."

Mike arches one eyebrow, calling me on my bullshit. "Is that so?"

I nod, eyes wide, trying to keep any more tears from falling.

Mike snorts and walks around the front of my car. "Open up."

I manage to find and hit the unlock button before he pulls the handle.

He hops in, his blue coveralls sliding against the leather seats. He glances around the interior. "New ride?"

I wipe the other cheek. "Um, yeah."

Mike and I have never been very close. I know him, he knows me. Or rather he knows *of* me. I'm sure Flynn's told him enough *Rose* stories to give him an interesting impression. And there have been occasions like Flynn's wedding, random get-togethers, and times when I was bored and decided to cause a little mischief at my brother's shop where we've had a few conversations. And lord knows he's had to bang out a lot of bumpers and doors from minor accidents I may have caused over the years. I always had the impression he didn't like me very much.

"It suits you."

For some reason, this observation makes me laugh. Maybe it's the deadpan way in which he says it, or maybe I'm at the tipping point between sobbing and laughing and my heart just can't take any more tears. So I laugh.

Mike smiles. He's always had a nice smile. "You got car trouble already?"

"Um, no." I sniff. "I'm just here to talk to Flynn."

"It's Sunday."

Shit. I forgot. Pre-Jackie the shop was open seven days a week. Post-Jackie the shop is closed on Sundays except for special appointments. Flynn doesn't like anything getting in the way of him and Jackie spending time together.

Mike doesn't look like my distress bothers him. "You gonna tell me what's wrong?"

I'm tempted, but... "Nah, that's okay."

He nods. "That's cool."

We sit for a bit, neither of us saying anything, not a hint of pressure coming from him to talk.

Mike opens the glove box and checks out the console. "I'm seeing someone."

"Really?" The admission catches me off guard. Mike is one of those deceptively good-looking guys. He's handsome, very much so, but he is so under the radar that you don't much notice it. In the few years I've known him, I've never heard him talk about a girl. And the fact that's he's talking to *me* about her surprises me one step out of my current pit of emotional despair.

He reaches down the right side of his seat and messes with the controls. His seat slides back, allowing him to lower his legs out of their hunch. "Well, I'm trying to, at least."

I can't help but find his mellow demeanor amusing. "And how's that going for you?"

"It's hard." His eyes meet mine for a moment, a seriousness there I didn't expect. "Anything worth having is."

I hum in acknowledgement.

"She has trust issues, you know?" Seat adjusted, he drops a hand on the arm rest. "Doesn't think I'm serious about her."

"Really?" I give him the once-over, trying to see how reliable and laid-back Michael Falasco could be anything but serious and trustworthy. "But you're so..." I gesture at him, unable to think of the word I mean.

"Thanks." His face expressionless, he shifts forward to look over the hood. "Flynn didn't do this, did he?"

"God no." I laugh. "He'd have given me hell. Easier to have someone else do it."

This time Mike hums.

I tap the steering wheel, feeling guilty for not giving my brother's shop the work. "Less arguing and questions, y'know?"

Another nod.

"Anyway, what are you going to do about the girl you're dating?"

"Just keep trying." He shrugs. "What else is there to do?"

Sighing, I lean my head back against the leather. "But isn't that exhausting?"

"At times."

I close my eyes, the events of the day already catching up to me. "Doesn't it hurt?"

"Yeah."

I tilt my head toward him, looking up from under my brow. "You can be kind of annoying, you know that, right?"

"I can see that." He smiles.

I nudge him in the shoulder.

"She's older than me." He catches my frown. "The girl I like."

"Oh." I hesitate a moment before offering, "The, um, man I like is older too."

"Then you get it," Mike says, having more confidence in my intelligence than I do. "Everyone comes at life from varying paths, with unlimited opinions formed by our experiences. I've found that the older one gets and the more of the paths they've walked, they tend to be more set in those opinions."

"Yeah." I think about Vance scheduling a vasectomy. "Tell me about it."

"But"—Mike stabs his fingers at the touchscreen in the console looking over my pre-programed radio stations—"a pretty nice benefit of having all that experience is it hopefully won't take them long to set aside their emotions and recognize their mistakes."

I let that sink in.

Vance has a fear of dying and leaving loved ones behind, which I only found out about today. After which I sucker-punched him with the baby bombshell. Is it fair to expect him to sort through those emotions in an instant?

I was so hurt that he didn't feel like I did, that he wasn't overwhelmed by a sense of rightness over my pregnancy that I wrote off his reaction as concrete proof that when he left, he left for good.

Brittany Spear's "Baby One More Time" plays from my speakers.

Mike scoffs. "The pop station? Really?" His look of disgust is the most emotive I've seen him since he got in my vehicle.

I laugh. "Calm down, Eddie Vedder." Remembering what blares from the auto shop speakers on any given weekday, I push his hands away and switch the audio source. "I have satellite radio. All the nineties stations your little grunge soul can handle."

Brittany switches to Nirvana with the touch of a button.

"Well, that's something." Not pausing to enjoy Kurt Cobain's iconic laconic growls, Mike pushes a few more buttons. Instead of "Smells like Teen Spirit," nursery rhymes set to soft music play. "This is a good one, I'll set this in your top five."

My stomach drops.

Mike pushes more buttons. "Remember my date from the wedding?"

I nod, remembering the brunette.

"That was my sister. She just had a baby a few months ago, and this is the station that always puts my niece to sleep when all else fails. Especially in the car. Something about the purr of the engine and the rocking in the car seat." He gives me side-eye. "Remember that in case it comes in handy. Some babies are finicky sleepers."

I close my mouth and swallow. "How did you..."

He drops his head forward and levels me with a look. "Rose.

You're twenty-one and sitting in a newly purchased mini-van crying."

My face heats.

"And if that wasn't enough—" He thumbs behind us.

I glance in my rearview mirror at the reflection of the car seat I set up yesterday, having wanted to make sure I could do it properly.

"Oh."

"Yeah." He laughs. "Oh."

An Escalade pulls into the lot, parking a few spots down from mine.

Mike watches a tall, good-looking man hop out from the back. "Ah, that must be my customer." The man adjusts his jacket, then reaches into the SUV again to pull out what looks like a pet carrier.

"Is that a cat?" I look at Mike, trying not to laugh. "Your customer is a man who carries around a cat?"

"Says the girl with a glitter van and cow print car seat."

"Touché."

Mike opens the door. "He's in the market for a pink Cadillac. Nineteen fifty-five Fleetwood series, just like Elvis bought his mom."

My eyebrows jump. "He's a mama's boy?"

"Nah. It's for his girlfriend. Not only is she an Elvis fanatic, but she's also my girl's best friend." Mike slides out, catching the guy's eye and waving.

In the back of my mind, I remember the Elvises at the honky tonk downtown and someone saying something about a cat.

But before I can ask him if his customer had anything to do with it, Mike leans down in the open door. "You know that saying *It doesn't hurt to try?*"

"Yeah?" I'm wondering if this is the moment he morphs into

Wilson from the TV show *Home Improvement* and lays down his mad wisdom on me.

"It's a lie."

"Oh." Or maybe not.

"Trying can really fucking hurt."

"Uh, good to know." I don't know what else to say.

"But it doesn't mean it isn't worth it."

Ah. There it is.

"Plus"—Mike sighs heavily, like what he's about to say will cost him—"you deserve to be happy, Rose. Make sure you do all you can to make that happen." He nods at my stomach. "For you *and* the baby."

I'm too shocked to respond before he closes the door.

He walks over to his cat customer with the Elvis-obsessed girlfriend, then stops, turns, and jogs back to my window.

When it's lowered, he points at me, face serious. "And for the love of God if Flynn doesn't know about the baby go tell him now, 'cause I sure as shit don't want to get caught hiding that from him."

As he walks away, I know he's right. First, I need to tell my brothers. Second, I need to figure out how to try again with Vance. Even if it hurts.

TWENTY-FOUR

CHARLIEFOXTROT

Vance

By the time I went back to the strip club, everyone was gone. Even the stripper mobile.

"What the fuck did I do?" Dropping my head on the steering wheel, I let my frustration eat at me. In addition to the growing, self-directed anger, there's an icy feeling slithering beneath my skin, boring its way deep into my bones.

Fear.

I'm so fucking scared I can't think straight.

Me. A man who flies at breakneck speeds and has stared into the abyss of the unknown but instead of recoiling, jumped out into it, linked to safety only by a simple tether.

And I'm scared of a baby.

My phone vibrates in my pocket, my mother calling for the twentieth time. I roll my shoulders, her attack from earlier still smarting. From what she heard me say in the strip club, I'm sure she has some idea why I reacted the way I did, but I'm not sure Mom's the person I need to talk to right now.

I lean back and wipe cold sweat from my forehead. The more I think about it, the more I realize there's only one person who'd be able to understand me. And she's either going to help me or leave me to my own dumpster fire of emotions.

I never can tell with my sister.

———

TEN MINUTES later I ring my sister's doorbell. She lives in a newer neighborhood in League City, about fifteen minutes from Mom's house in Clear Lake. The lots are smaller, the houses bigger. Her house is the one with the rotating light projector casting the front of her house in dancing snowflakes.

From the long windows on either side of the solid wood front door that's more than half covered in a monstrous home-made Christmas wreath, my sister peeks out, surprise written all over her face.

I raise a hand in greeting, feeling as awkward as I probably look.

My sister pulls the door partway open, staring at me with a string of tangled Christmas lights. "Vance?"

"Hey, Brit."

She continues to frown at me. "What are you doing here?"

I tip my chin up, gesturing behind her. "Can I come in?"

"Oh." She pushes the door open all the way and stands back to let me pass. "Of course, yes."

I get that I'm unexpected. Not only did I not give her a heads-up, but I can count on one hand the number of times I've been to her house.

She's invited me plenty, but if it wasn't a birthday or holiday, I always had a reason not to go. And even then, I might not have shown up.

Stepping inside, I grin at the shiplap feature wall in the

dining room that Matt was complaining about at Thanksgiving. As the wall isn't flat but has an inset where Brit's put a china cabinet, I can see why Matt said it's a pain in the ass.

It looks good, though.

Her whole house does, especially decorated for the holidays. Two feet away from where I stand, a large, twelve-foot tree decorated in all shades of white and silver lights up the space.

Even devoid of color, I know Rose would love it for how it sparkles.

"What can I do you for?" Brit asks, closing the door.

I shove my hands in my pockets, rocking back on my heels. "Would you believe me if I said I just wanted to stop by and see my sister?"

"On a Sunday afternoon?" Her mouth flattens into a sardonic expression. "Nope."

"Yeah, didn't think so." I look across the foyer at the office. Or the room that realtors would list as an office, but which Brit has converted into a craft room devoted to all things Pinterest. In the middle of the space is yet another tree, this one a more manageable eight feet.

And pink.

The house is quiet. "Where are Matt and the boys?"

"Football game." Brit steps around me. "They always try and skip out when I start adding to my tree collection."

"Collection?"

She smirks. "I'm up to six, but I've got my eye on a multi-colored tinsel tree for the boys' game room."

I chuckle, feeling sorry for my nephews.

"So what's up? You okay?" She pauses in trying to untangle the cords in her hands, panic in her eyes. "Oh shit, is *Mom* okay?"

"Yes." I hold out my hands, taking the lights from her. "Everyone is fine."

Her shoulders slump in relief. "Thank God."

"Speaking of Mom." I redirect my gaze to a framed cross stitch hanging on the wall, displayed in the middle of family photos. The quote *That's what she said* is encircled by embroidered flowers. "Have you heard from her today?" When I look back at her, my sister narrows her eyes.

"Why?"

I shrug. "No reason."

When I don't say more, she walks into her craft room to the pink tree and picks up a sectioned ornament box on the floor.

I follow, surveying the open shelves topped with baskets and a pegboard filled with spools of thread on a wall above the sewing table. There's even a large drop-down table installed on another wall, currently folded up to make room for the tree. There's stuff everywhere, but all artfully organized.

My sister is *really* into DIY.

One shelf has rows and rows of jars of glitter. All lined up and gleaming in the morning light streaming through the front window, reminding me of Rose and why I'm here.

"Were you ever angry at Dad?" I hadn't realized the question that I needed to ask until now.

Brit freezes, eyes wide. "Are you *sure* you're okay?"

My breath comes out in a huff, embarrassment setting in. "Why would you think something's wrong?"

Her eyebrows rise. "Why?" She scoffs. "Maybe because you're doing things you never do." She waves her hand, now holding a large pink iced donut ornament. "Bringing someone to Thanksgiving dinner, playing video games with your nephews online, stopping by my house unannounced. Asking about *Dad*." She reaches out and hangs the donut at the top of the tree next to an ice cream decoration.

The whole tree is confectionary themed.

"When people start doing things like that, it usually means

they're sick." Brit leans back, checking the donut placement. "Or in love." Her mouth drops open as wide as her eyes. "Oh my God." Her head swivels slowly in my direction. "You're in love."

When I don't deny it, a large, Cheshire grin spreads over her face. "I *knew* you were more than just friends with Rose." She pumps her fist. "Yes. This is so great." Lost in her own thoughts, she tells me about how the boys each got notes from their teachers praising their newfound feminist terminology. And how Rose has been sharing her Fortnite treasure boxes with them when they play together online so they could all climb the ranks together.

All things that prove how good Rose is with kids. Prove how amazing she'll be with ours.

"Vance?"

I shake off my thoughts, still not ready to go there yet.

Brit leans in and squints at me. "You look like you're going to be sick."

I ignore her. "Do you remember when Dad died?"

She retreats into her own space and sighs, like she was hoping I'd forgotten about my earlier question. She might be right when she said I never talk about Dad, but neither does she.

"Yeah, I remember." Brit opens a large cabinet revealing a stunning display of organized chaos. Small tubes of paint, ribbon spools and jars of beads all color-coded and lined up in clear containers on shelves. It hits me that this is my sister's version of a glitter room. And, if given the chance, she and Rose would be great friends. Sisters.

Brit grabs a bag of light pink tinsel and hands it to me. "Here."

I frown but take it.

Then Brit picks up a cupcake ornament from the box. "We've never really talked about Dad, have we?" She assesses the tree, then squats down to place the white and blue ornament toward the bottom. "Come on." She gestures at the bag in my hand. "If we're going to get sad, you can at least help me tinsel."

I move carefully around the tree. "How do you tinsel?"

"Pinch a few strands then toss them artfully on the ends of the branches." She points to the top of the tree. "Start there."

"Okay." I elongate the word, having no idea how to artfully do anything. "But don't blame me if it looks bad."

"I make no promises." She waits for me to start. Once I do, she frowns and nods, like it isn't perfect, but she'll let me slide.

The next few minutes are quiet as we decorate. I'm concentrating so hard on not clumping the tinsel that I don't tense up when Brit breaks the silence.

"Why suddenly bring up Dad?" She's on her knees, repositioning an enamel bag of cookies.

I finish up a branch and pause for a beat. "I guess I just don't get it."

"Get what?"

I pull out a few more strands from the bag. "How could he sign up for such a dangerous job knowing that if he died we'd be left alone?"

I'm answered with silence. I glance down to catch Brit frowning at me.

"What?" It comes out more defensive than I meant it.

"I get what you mean, I do. But..." She sighs. "People in the military sacrifice so much already, you know?" Brit's usual sarcasm is gone, her inflection serious. "Their service requires their time, their bodies, and for some, like Dad, even their lives." She fiddles with the fake snow tree skirt, then stops and looks up at me. "Don't you think it's too much to ask them to sacrifice having a family as well?" From the look on her face, this isn't a rhetorical question. She wants an answer.

I don't have one. "But what about the people left behind? Like you and Mom." I swallow turning back to the tree. "Me."

Her lips twist like she's trying to control a rush of emotion. "Did you know I used to wish Dad wasn't in the military? That we had a normal nine-to-five dad just like most of the kids in school." She blinks a few times and clears her throat. "I used to think how much fun it would be to have him come home from work like the dads on the TV shows we used to watch. He'd put down his briefcase and then we'd all sit around the kitchen table and have dinner. Talk about our day."

"Yeah." It comes out more like a grunt. "Me too."

She gives me a sad smile. "But that's not the dad we had. Our dad was proud to serve his country. It was part of who he was. The Army was his calling. Not many people find that in life." She pokes me in the leg with her finger. "And *you're* just like him."

"Me?"

"Yes, you." Her condescending tone is back in action.

"How's that?"

She tilts her head, thinking. "Well first, you look just like him from the pictures still hanging on Mom's walls."

I shrug.

She grabs another ornament. "And second, it seems you both were born with the drive to pursue something bigger than yourselves. For Dad it was the military." She points a multicolored taffy stick at me. "For you, it's NASA."

"Huh." I never thought of it like that.

"And I tell you what." Brit shakes her head. "When you said you were going to be an astronaut, I nearly had a heart attack."

I frown, thinking back a few years. "I don't remember that."

"Yeah, 'cause I hid it from you, you dope." I have a feeling the only thing saving me from one of her dead leg attacks is the glass ornament. "Just ask Matt. Jacob had just turned two when you applied. I cried my eyes out every night for about a week while spending my days telling everyone how proud I was of you."

A shot of guilt hits me in the chest. "Damn, I'm sorry, Brit." I bend my knees, dropping down to her level. "I thought I'd distanced myself enough that you—" I stop myself, cursing myself for sharing too much.

"That I'd what?" I can *see* Brit putting the pieces together "You..." The taffy ornament drops to the ground, breaking. "You ignored me so I'd stop caring?" Her tone turns incredulous. "Are you seriously telling me that all the times you dodged my phone calls and skipped holiday dinners you actually thought you were doing me a favor?" She's gone from incredulous to screeching mad. "What kind of stupid-ass logic is that?" She shoves me with both hands, and I topple back onto the tangled string of lights.

"Ow." A few of the lights dig into my ass.

"I hope that hurt." Her eyes burn into mine for a few more moments until they close, and she lets out an exasperated groan. "I can't *believe* you're smart enough to be an astronaut with that kind of thinking." She shoves both hands into her hair, and I stop myself from pointing out that she has tinsel in it. "You not coming around as often as before didn't make me love you any less, you idiot." She drops her hands, looking me in the eyes again. "It just made me curse you a hell of a lot more." Moving her legs out from beneath her, she sits cross-legged. "Honestly," she mumbles, still not over it. "You're such a dick."

I know saying I'm sorry won't cut it, so I stay quiet, pull the lights out from under me, and start untangling, all the time under her silent, censorious stare.

When I finally have them straightened, Brit glances at her watch. "You're totally going to have to tell Mom all this too, you know." She gets to her feet and moves around the tree.

I rise, my knees popping. "Yeah, maybe—"

"Brittany?" Mom's voice echoes from somewhere in the house. "Vance?"

I freeze, mid-rise, probably looking like a combination of a hunch-back and a deer in headlights. "What did you do?"

Brit holds up her arm, flashing her smart watch at me. "I texted her while you were tinseling." There isn't an ounce of apology in her voice. "She called me earlier and asked me to tell her if you reached out or showed up."

I straighten to my full height, narrowing my eyes at her. "You said you hadn't talked to her."

Brit shrugs, completely unaffected by my posturing. "I lied."

My shoulders drop as I sigh. "I can't belie—"

A door closes somewhere in the house. "Where are you two?"

"Be right there!" Brit calls out, then reaches into the box, pulling out a tree topper. She turns and hands it to me.

I need two hands to hold the large, hollow cherry.

"Make sure it's straight."

I thread the top vertical branch through the bottom of the cherry, grumbling about untrustworthy sisters.

But when it's on, and straight, I step back, appreciating the cherry on top. "That actually looks pretty cool."

"Yep. Saw it on Pinterest." Then she strides out of the room, expecting me to follow.

———

Rose

"You're pregnant," Holt says for the third time.

Flynn hasn't said anything, which is worse.

I took Mike's advice and called my brothers to meet me at the ranch. It's a testament to how much Flynn and Holt must've been worried about me that they didn't even ask me why. They just showed up.

Hashtag brotherly love.

So now here we are. All three Wests, sitting in the ranch's living room that's decorated in rustic Christmas splendor, my brothers shell-shocked and me very thankful for the pitstop I made to my apartment after having the amazing forethought that the baby news might land better if I wasn't dressed like a slutty Mrs. Claus.

Hashtag ho-ho-no.

And although we're all older, and Holt and Flynn hopefully more mature and level-headed, I can't help but feel like I'm a kid again. Waiting for them to decide my fate, like they did all those years ago when our parents died.

"Yes. I'm pregnant," I answer, even though it wasn't a question. Maybe if I say it again it'll sink in.

Holt nods, staring straight ahead at the mantle wreath decorated with lights and shotgun shells, his body unmoving on the comfy, oversized linen-colored sofa Jules bought recently. Or rather, hired someone to buy as Jules couldn't care less about interior design as long as her ass was happy when she sat.

One thing in my favor is that Jules isn't here. She's staying over at her Clear Lake apartment due to an early morning flight simulation scheduled for tomorrow. Holt was there when I called and not at the ranch like I'd thought. But even though the weekends are when he gets to spend the most time with Jules due to their busy schedules, he still drove here when I said I wanted to talk.

My brothers mean a lot to me, and it's nice to know it's reciprocated.

A minute later, when both Holt and Flynn continue to stare

off in different directions, I decide I might as well lay it all out for them.

Clasping my hands together on my lap, I sit up straight on the loveseat. "Just so you know, I'm keeping the baby."

No reaction.

"Vance is the father."

Flynn grunts. I have no idea what that means, but just to be safe, I decide not to tell them how Vance took the news.

Palms sweating, I release them, rubbing them on the cushions beside me. "And I know this may sound crazy or naïve, but I'm actually happy." Well, mostly. "About being a mom, I mean." That's closer to the truth.

Holt swallows.

"Of course I'm nervous too," I rush to say. "I mean, I'm not stupid. Having a baby is a life-changing event."

Nothing.

"But I'm more than financially capable, so I'm already luckier than most." I scoot forward on the love seat, conjuring up the most pitiful puppy dog eyes I can muster. "And I'm even luckier because my baby will have two of the best uncles in the entire world."

Flynn grunts again. "Obviously."

The tension inside me eases a little, and I bite my lip, trying to hold back my smile. But when I glance at Holt, my mouth drops.

There are *tears* in my stoic brother's eyes.

"Holt?" I don't know whether to hug him or brace for impact.

"My baby sister is going to be a mother." Though he still isn't looking at me, he breaks out of his stare, looking down at the floor as he braces his arms on his thighs. "Holy shit."

Flynn and I both start in surprise over our brother's rarely used explicative. I'm tempted to remind Holt to be more lady-like, as he's told me countless times growing up, but, for once, I realize now might not be the time.

Expression still blank, Flynn turns to me. "Who else knows?"

"Um..." I bite my lip.

Flynn snorts. "Yeah, figures."

I let out a small breath when Flynn's lips twitch up and not down.

"Ian doesn't know. Unless Trish told him," I offer him with a grimace. "So there's that."

"Wait." Holt's head snaps up. "*Jules* knows?"

I nod, my pained expression deepening.

His eyes gain focus. "How long?"

Flynn leans back, seeming oddly relaxed about everything. "Probably since Rose started dodging our calls and Jackie and Jules started going into work early and coming home late. Basically dodging us." He rolls his head on the cushion to Holt. "When we sent Ian after Vance." Flynn cocks his head at me. "What was it, last week?"

Flynn is more astute than I give him credit for.

"Yeah."

And then the expression I came to the ranch fearing spreads across Holt's face. Anger. Disappointment. It's the reaction I was most worried about, delayed, but there now that the shock has worn off.

I lean back, my whole body tightening as if preparing for a storm about to hit.

Holt shakes his head in disgust. "That's the last time I bake her cookies for a while."

My jaw drops.

"And she can forget those Christmas butter cookies I've been bragging about."

A giggle erupts from my throat.

Holt and Flynn look at me like I've grown another head instead of a baby, but I can't help but find the fact Holt's anger is aimed at his girlfriend for knowing I was pregnant and not telling him rather than at me for being pregnant hilarious.

Another giggle escapes, and I try coughing to hide it.

Sighing at me, Holt slaps his hands on his thighs and pushes up and off the couch. Stepping around the coffee table, he reaches out his hand.

No sooner do I take it than I'm enveloped in a bear hug.

"You're going to be a great mama." Holt's hug would be glorious if only I could breathe.

I'm able to fill my lungs when Flynn pushes Holt aside and takes his turn. Thankfully, his hug is gentler.

"You need anything, you tell me, okay?" Flynn murmurs in my ear. "Even if it's a shovel and a shallow grave."

Yes, Flynn is definitely more astute than I give him credit for.

"Thanks, Flynn," I whisper, not trusting my voice to talk any louder.

He squeezes me tight before letting go. "Anytime."

———

Exhausted, I trudge up to my room. As much of a make-over as the house has been through since Jules hog-tied my brother's heart, my bedroom remains the same. Rodeo trophies, academic plaques, poorly done horse drawings made in crayon.

I pick up a shell-decorated picture frame off my bureau. Inside is one of the only pictures of my parents, brothers, and me together and smiling. It was my second birthday, and we took a day trip to Galveston beach. A trip I don't even remember but wanted the picture nearby all the same.

Hand on my abdomen, I sit on my twin bed, the pink and white comforter soft and fluffy.

I want my baby to have a lot more than one picture.

Try.

Staring at the picture frame, I think about what Mike said. Nothing worth having is easy.

I toss the picture frame aside and pull my phone out from my jeans pocket.

Try.

Seems like such an easy thing. Just try. Make an attempt. Take a shot. Give it some effort.

Except it's not easy. Just like Mike said, it's hard.

Staring at my phone, I think of all the worst-case scenarios. Vance could ignore me. He could not want our baby like my mother made obvious she didn't want me. He could say yes then change his mind. Show up only to leave again.

He could do a lot of things that would hurt. A lot of things I've felt before. But now, they'd be ten times worse because it wouldn't be done to just me.

Try.

I glance at the picture, face down, but I don't need to see it to recall every expression, every whisper of hair blowing in the sea breeze, every laugh line around my parents' eyes.

My hands tighten on my phone.

The easy thing is to not try. To tell myself that if Vance wants to be here for the baby, he will. And if he doesn't, he doesn't. It's up to him. His move. *His* try.

I fall back on my bed with a huff.

I've never been good at letting others have control.

Arms above my head, I bring the calendar up on my phone. I hover over tomorrow's appointment and copy and paste the information into a text to Vance. Then, just to make it easy, I send the address.

I stare at my text, unhappy. It's missing something. The calendar link and map impersonal. And considering I'm inviting him to a doctor appointment where a woman is going to stick her hand up my hoo-ha with him right next to me, maybe I should add something.

I write, delete, and rewrite several things.

Please come. No.

I want you to be there. No.

Hope you can make it. No.

I continue until my arms feel weak from losing blood.

Right before I lower them, I send one. *You're welcome to come if you want.*

An hour later with no response, I agree with Mike. Trying can really fucking hurt.

———

Vance

"WE NEED TO TALK." Mom, thankfully back to being dressed in normal clothes, drapes her jacket over a chair as Brit and I enter the kitchen. She must have come in through the side door.

When I don't say anything, Mom pulls out a chair and sits.

Brit does the same. "He was asking about Dad."

"Well that much was obvious from all the stuff you said to Rose today."

"Today?" Brit's interest peaks. "Pole dancing day?"

Mom proceeds to give Brit the lowdown on how I became the worst new baby daddy known to man. How I told Rose I loved her, then wouldn't commit to kids. How there mention of my getting a vasectomy or waiting ten years before I could start a family.

Brit's eyes get wider with each revelation.

"And then Rose said that she was pregnant with *my* grand-baby!" Mom covers her heart with her hands, eyes closed as if overcome with happiness.

Brit gasps. "Holy shit."

Mom opens her eyes, the happiness draining when she focuses them on me. "And you left." She spits the words at me.

Brit chokes on air. "Holy fucking shit."

Mom smacks her arm with the back of her hand, but Brit doesn't even register the hit. Instead, she backhands me, like we're playing a violent game of whisper down the lane. "How could you not tell me right when you got here?"

"I needed to ask you about something else."

"Oh." Brit's glare vanishes. "Oh yeah."

"What? What did he ask?" Mom straightens in her seat, indignant once more. "Because I'm telling you that if your father was here, he'd be *so* disappointed."

Rage slams into me, and I stand, my chair sliding back across the tile. "That would be pretty fucking hypocritical of him then, wouldn't it?"

Brit and Mom look up, mouths as wide as their eyes. I don't think I've ever yelled at them before. I don't think they've ever heard me yell period.

I take a deep breath, trying to get under control. "Do you even remember my last spacewalk this year? The emergency one Jules and I had to make to protect the ISS from impacting space junk? An impact that could've potentially killed everyone on board?" I smack my chest. "Including me."

Mom shudders. "How could I forget?"

"Exactly. I can't either." I run a shaky hand through my hair. "And I'm going back in just a few months." My laugh is hollow. "Hell, I *want* to go back up." I shake my head at myself in disgust. "What kind of man does that make me?"

Brit frowns. "What are you talking about? How does that—"

"How does that relate to Dad?" I ask, annoyed that she still doesn't get it. That *no one* gets it.

I look at Mom. "I think we all remember how Dad's death changed you."

She flinches.

"Wrecked you even," I add.

She swallows. "What do you—"

"I heard you cry yourself to sleep at night." I sit, the feelings I've kept tightly bottled inside draining me as they overflow.

"I... I didn't know." Mom's head drops forward. "I had no idea that you remembered any of that."

"Like you said, how could I forget?" I turn my gaze to the window, watching the swing of the playset I had delivered to my nephews for Christmas six years ago sway in the breeze. "And yet still, all these years later, you still live in a house that is basically a shrine to when he was alive. You never dated, you never moved on. Dad left you and never came back, and you still love him despite it."

"But he was in the military. It was his duty. He didn't have a choice."

"That's bullshit."

Mom jerks back at my vehemence.

"He had a choice. It's not like there was still a draft. He signed up. And he kept making that choice every year he chose not to get out."

Brit bites her lip.

"How could I take the chance on doing that to someone else? Someone I love." I swallow. "And I love Rose, Mom. I love her so much." I wipe angrily at my eyes. "I didn't want to. Because I didn't want to put her through what you went through when Dad died. But then, like a selfish jerk, I talked myself into thinking that if Rose still chooses to be with me despite the risks, it would be okay." My fingers dig into my thigh under the table. "But a baby? A baby doesn't get to make that choice. They don't sign up for the gamble of being raised by a grieving, single parent."

The swings move back and forth a few times before Mom speaks. "I loved your father. So much. And yes, I still love him. I always will." She takes a deep breath.

Brit, head down, sniffs.

"You were robbed of having a father at an early age. That's not fair. Death itself isn't fair after all, military or not. But I also like to think how *lucky* you were to have your father in your life, even for the briefest of times, than not have had him at all. He loved you so much. And he showed that love by being the best man he could be.

"It isn't fair, and maybe it isn't right, but that's how it went. And when you handled his death with far more maturity than a boy your age probably should've, I failed you when I didn't say anything. Because even though you never complained, and you never cried at the unfairness of it all like you heard me do at night when I thought you were asleep, I should've known better. When you didn't talk about your father, I thought I was respecting your feelings. I chose instead to keep the house as your father left it, thinking you would find comfort in its familiarity. I didn't know it felt more like a burden, or a cage I locked you into."

It seems absurd that such soft-spoken admissions from my mother could have such a profound effect on me, a grown man. That even now, I still needed to hear them.

"I'm so sorry, Vance." She reaches out and grabs Brit's hand. "And you too, Brittany."

"It's okay, Mom. I understand." Her voice cracks on the last words, and she stands. "Fuck." She marches over and grabs a box of tissues and tosses it back on the table before sitting back down. "What happens in the kitchen stays in the kitchen."

We all grab a tissue.

"And I want to tell you something, Vance, and I want you to look me in the eyes, so you know I'm telling the truth."

I have to blink a few times, but I do.

"Even knowing what happened. Even knowing that one day your father would fail to come home to me, to *us*, I'd still marry him all over again."

I swallow.

"Do you hear me?" She looks back and forth between Brit and me.

We both nod.

"I mean it." Mom lowers the tissue away from her eyes, her gaze serious and sure. "And I hope that you can feel the same. That even with all the pain you carry, you can both realize what a wonderful father Lonan Bodaway was to you. That you can remember the happiness past the sadness."

"I do, Mom. I remember." Brit gets up and bends down to hug her, each of them laughing a little, trying to break the tension.

And when they both look at me with the same question in their eyes, I feel the usual emotions I associate with my father—the anger, regret, and fear—shift inside me. Making room for more. For love. For possibilities.

My eyes sting, and my nostrils flare, but I take a deep breath and forge on. "Remember the time Dad stayed up all night trying to put together our Christmas presents, and we all raced downstairs in the morning to find him sleeping under the tree?"

Brit laughs. "Oh my God, yes. I'd almost forgotten about that." She blows out a happy but shaky breath.

I ball up the tissue in my hand, tossing it in the trashcan by the wall. "He said he was trying to catch Santa and we got mad that he didn't include us in his plan."

"Or what about the time he took us to Clear Lake Park and those geese started to chase him?" Brit asks, her smile growing. "I never saw him run so fast in my life."

I laugh, the act enough to release the rest of pressure bottled inside.

"Or the time he surprised us all, coming home a week early." Mom's eyes get misty again, but I can tell it's from happiness this time. She nods at me. "Just in time to welcome you back at the bus stop on your last day of kindergarten."

"My friends were so in awe of him in his fatigues." I recall the look of worship on their faces as they stared out the bus window at my dad, who was standing tall and proud in his camo and boots. "He looked like a giant."

"He did, didn't he?" Brit asks, mostly to herself. "He could hold his arm straight out, and I'd swing on it, my feet not touching the ground."

The side door swings open, and Matt files through with the boys.

"Hey, Uncle Vance!" Jacob's smile lights up the kitchen.

"Uncle Vance is here?" Jase's head pops around the side of his dad, his hands laden with a foam finger and a Big Gulp.

"Hey guys." I hug them a little tighter than normal.

Right before they can start giving us a play by play of the game, my phone vibrates.

Rose: *Dr. Barrios, tomorrow at 3:30pm*

She follows it with an address for an OBGYN office.

I stare at it, shocked as my nephews talk a mile a minute about the game and all the junk food their dad let them have.

"Thanks for that," Brit says to her husband.

My phone vibrates again.

Rose: *You're welcome to come if you want.*

I stand, this time the chair beneath me topples over. "I got to go."

"Yeah ya do." My sister's mocking tone is firmly reinstated.

"Yes, it's about time," Mom adds. "Don't forget to ask Rosie when my grandbaby is due."

"Aunt Rose?" Jacob asks. He and his brother perk up at the mention of their Fortnite cohort.

"Wait." Matt looks from his wife to his mother-in-law to me. "Rose is pregnant?"

"A cousin!" Jase's foam finger shoots in the air.

Jacob looks at me, confused. "But you're not married."

"Idiot." Jase nudges him. "Women don't need to get married if they don't want to, remember?" He straightens, tipping his chin up. "Marriage is an archaic form of ownership that was originally used to claim a woman as property."

The adults all stare wide-eyed.

Brit turns to me, all seriousness. "Please, for the love of God, go marry that woman."

TWENTY-FIVE

#COUPLESTATUS

Vance

I AM SERIOUSLY TOO old for this shit.

It's past sundown, and I'm peeking into the windows of the West Mansion from the porch while on the phone with my sister. I make out Flynn and Holt sitting on opposite ends of the couch, the lights from the television illuminating their faces. Are they... are they watching *It's a Wonderful Life?*

Jimmy Stewart as George Bailey is hugging his family in front of a Christmas tree.

Yes they are. I never would've pegged the West brothers as fans of such a sappy holiday classic.

"Well? Is she there?" Brit asks.

Nose pressed almost to the glass, I look left and right. "I don't see her," I whisper.

"You sure she's there?" Brit whispers back even though she's forty minutes away holed up in her Pinterest room like it's Mission Control and she's the flight controller for my spacewalk.

"Yes, according to my intel, she's here." Plus there's the fact that the holographic van is parked in the drive. I should've known that if it didn't belong to a stripper, the glitterized vehicle would belong to Rose.

I love that about her. But I'm also going to buy our kid polarized sunglasses to protect their eyes from its blinding reflections.

Our kid. The more time I've had to think about the baby and not about my irrational fears, the more excited I become about my impending fatherhood. I'm going to be a dad, and not just any dad, a dad to Rose's baby.

"How reliable is your intel?"

I sigh, coming back to the present. "How reliable is any bribable kid in his twenties?"

"Ten-four."

A headache knocks at my temples, and I ask myself why I felt the need to take my sister's advice.

In a weak, desperate moment, I showed Brit Rose's text about the doctor appointment, wanting to know how to decipher *You're welcome to come if you want*. Does her use of *you're welcome* mean she's willing to give me another chance? When she says I can come to the appointment if *I want*, does that mean *she* doesn't want me to but she's inviting me for the baby's sake?

Hoping female insight would help, I listened to Brittany.

"Don't text her back," she said. "Show up on her doorstep," she said. "Everyone likes a grand gesture," she said.

So I showed up. After an hour of relentless Houston traffic, I showed up at her condo.

Only to have Rose's doorman bar me from entering again.

Pacing the sidewalk outside her building, I called. And I called. Despite Brit's advice, I called.

Finally, after the fourth message where I pleaded for Rose to pick up, a young valet waved me over. For fifty bucks he informed me that Rose wasn't home. For a hundred more, and a promise that I'm not a murdering stalker, the valet admitted to hearing Rose on her phone as she walked out of the lobby, telling someone to meet her at the ranch.

Why I called Brit when I arrived at the West property, I have no idea. They say you're a fool in love. I think I'm taking that saying too much to heart.

I glance down the porch. "Tell me again why I can't just knock on the door?"

"If some asshole had knocked *me* up when I was twenty-one, then ran off like a coward only to come knocking on the door a few hours later, would *you* have let them in?"

Damn it. "Point made."

A minute later, I'm tiptoeing around the side of the house like a thief in the night, sticking to the grass to avoid noise, hoping not to get shot by any late-night workhands patrolling the area.

I've seen too many Westerns.

"So?" Brit asks after I've remained silent for too long.

"It's dark." Unlike the front of the house, which is lit from the nearby barn spotlights, the back is not. The only thing helping me make out where I am is the soft glow Christmas lights twenty yards away wrapped around a small, in-ground Christmas tree and outlining a one-stall barn.

"Any lights on upstairs that you can throw pebbles at?"

"Not a one."

"Hmm. Maybe she's sleeping."

A crunching sound has me pulling the phone away from my ear. "Are you eating?"

"What? We're hungry." More crunching. "The boys made popcorn."

"Wait. What do you mean '*we're*'? Am I on speaker?"

In answer, Jase shouts, "Climb up to her like Romeo, Uncle Vance!"

I pinch the bridge of my nose, the headache growing.

"She'll love it," Jacob pipes up, his voice garbled. Probably from popcorn.

"I thought this romantic stuff would go against your new feminist principles." I wonder if they can pick up on sarcasm yet.

Someone scoffs.

"Please," Jase says, sounding like he does, in fact, recognize sarcasm. "Everyone knows that romancing a woman is the most feminist thing you can do."

"Yeah, everyone knows that," Jacob adds.

I'm not sure what this says about my mental state, but I take my pre-teen nephews' advice and evaluate the area. "The porch doesn't wrap around to the back," I tell them, running my hands across the wood siding. "All I've got to work with is smooth board and batten planks." I step back and look up to the second-floor windows. "There's not a foot hold, trellis, or tall enough tree in sight."

"Climbing up Romeo-style would be an awesome grand gesture," Brit says, followed by more crunching.

"Jesus, Brit, it's not like I can fly—" My eyes catch on something leaning against the barn.

"What? What is it?" Brit sounds slightly panicked, which makes me mildly less annoyed with her.

"Did you get caught?" Jacob asks.

Squinting into the soft glow of the tiny white lights, I make out wooden rungs. "I'll be damned. There's a ladder."

"Yes!" I'm pretty sure all three of them fist-pumped when they shouted that chorus style.

With a promise to call them back as soon as Rose forgives me (they have way more confidence in both me and their Romeo plan than I do), I hang up, needing my phone's flashlight feature to guide me across the rail fenced enclosure.

If Jules could see me now, Flashlight with his flashlight, I'd never hear the end of it.

Surprisingly, I make it to the tiny barn and get back with the ladder without stepping in shit *or* running into Cookie the pet cow. She must be sleeping.

But whatever luck got me to this point ends when I set the ladder under the window I *think* belongs to the bedroom Rose took me to at the wedding. Upright and up close, the ladder is old, worn and *not* structurally sound. The engineer in me screams, *"Abort mission, abort."*

However, as it's all I've got to Romeo to Rose—up I go.

———

Rose

*T*AP, *tap, tap.*

Opening my eyes, I study the ceiling fan above me. Is it unbalanced?

Tap, tap, tap. Not the fan. It's coming from the hall.

Rolling on my side, I slide off my bed, walk to the open door-way, and stick my head out into the hall, my loosely secured top-knot wobbling.

Knock, knock.

Louder now. From the guest room. Maybe a bird flying into the window?

Shuffling in my fuzzy socks across the hall, I push open the guest room door and peek in. Where I'm blinded by a beam of light.

"What the—" Hand up to block it, I hit the light switch with the other. "Vance?"

His face lights up behind the glass, and he lowers his phone.

Fucking eye crinkles.

I may not look threatening at the moment in my oversized and threadbare Goofy T-shirt and florescent yellow panties, but my narrowed eyes and frown seem enough to dim the happiness in his eyes.

I should just flip him the bird and walk away. Walk away like he did to me.

Vance, either brave or stupid, points to the window lock. *Tap, tap.*

Sigh.

A second later I have the sash pushed up, and I'm looking down at him without any glass blocking my death glare. "What do you think you're doing knocking on the guest bedroom window?"

My question wipes the beginnings of a hopeful smile from his face. "Guest bedroom?" He peeks over my shoulder. "This isn't your room?"

"Nope."

"Oh."

When he doesn't say anything more, I cross my arms over my chest, hiding my favorite Disney character in the hope that'll make me more intimidating. "So?"

He shakes his head. "Sorry, yes. I ah..." His frown deepens. "Wow, I guess I spent so much time trying to track you down that I didn't think of what to say when I found you."

"Maybe that's a good thing." I pop my hip. "Seeing as the last two times you did stop and think before we talked it didn't go so well."

He cringes. "Yeah. About that." His breath blows out sharp and fast. "I know sorry won't cut it, but I *am* sorry. First for making assumptions about your feelings and ignoring my own. And also for leaving Heartbreakers after, well, after—"

"I said I was pregnant?"

"Yeah."

"If you can't even say it, I'm not sure what you're doing here. And just so you know, in case you didn't hear me at Heartbreakers, I'm keeping it."

"Good." He straightens on the ladder. "I *want* you to keep it."

"You do, huh?" He'd be an idiot to think I'd believe him.

"I know that's hard to believe."

Guess he's not an idiot.

"But I *am* happy about the baby. I just needed to sort through some stuff."

I lock down, the hope wanting to surface. Fool me once and all that.

"Words aren't going to cut it, I get it, but that's why I'm here." His expression is expectant, like he's waiting for me to grasp the obvious.

Whatever it is, I don't get it. "On a ladder?"

His smile is as awkward as it is annoyingly adorable. "I'm Romeo-ing you."

That surprises a laugh out of me. "That can't have been your idea."

"Brit's." He considers. "Well, Jacob and Jase's idea really. Brit was the one who told me not to text you back but to show up." He follows this with an eye roll, showing me that we're both on the same page about how that turned out.

"Word of advice to you and Brit, texting back is important if you're going to take longer than an hour to show up."

"I did." Vance pushes his palms into the sill, his vehemence making me jump.

"Not at first," he concedes with a shrug. "But when your doorman wouldn't let me in, I called and I called."

"Huh." I guess that's what I get for turning my phone off an hour after I sent the text so I didn't obsessively stare at it.

Vance crosses his arms on the ledge. "It's lucky there was an ATM next to your building, otherwise Doug's lips would've remained sealed on your location."

"Doug sold me out?" I pout. "That bastard."

Vance raises one hand. "Yes, but only *after* he made me swear I wasn't a murdering stalker."

That appeases me somewhat, especially when I think of Doug working extra shifts to get his sister the new iPhone she wants for Christmas. "I guess that's okay, then."

Vance adjusts his position, the small movement making the ladder sway. "Jesus." His fingers dig into the ledge. "This ladder takes more balance and core strength than spacewalk maneuvering." He takes a breath once he feels steady. "I'd hate if my epitaph read *He died in a field of cow patties.*"

"I'm surprised you let your nephews talk you into this." My voice is snider than I'd like to admit. "If you're so afraid of dying and all."

The dig hits hard, and he winces.

"I deserve that." He looks down, as if ashamed. "And I know that what I said probably sounded ludicrous to you, but those feelings... those feelings were *real* for me." One of his hands clenches into a fist. "I spent thirty years being mad at my dad. Blaming him for leaving us, for dying." He lets out a long, low breath. "I blamed Mom too."

"Helen?" Despite myself, I lower to the floor, settling on my knees. "Did you talk to her after Heartbreakers?"

He nods, holding eye contact. Easier now that we're at the same eye level. "Her and Brittany."

My lips twist thinking about how *that* conversation must've gone. "I bet that was a fun talk."

He snorts, but after a moment, the amused glint in his eyes turns to beseeching. "Give me another chance, Rose. Please."

Caught off guard, I rock back.

"And it's not just because of the baby."

"Vance, I—"

"I love you."

Biting my lip, my eyes drift past him toward the glow of Cookie's barn.

"I loved you before you told me about the baby, and I still love you." He shifts his weight, moving into my line of sight. "I love how you go all in, no safety net, just live life to the fullest. I love how you care about those around you, not only in big ways but in smaller, sometimes overlooked ways. I love how you push me out of my comfort zone, and not gently. You showed me how dark I'd made my life by lighting everything up around me."

"I love you too," I can't help but say. I don't have it in me to lie or omit it. "And not just because you have super sperm."

One side of his lips twitches.

"I love the drive and perseverance inside you that got you where you are today at NASA. I love how you might not be outgoing, but you actually enjoy being around people." I glance down, taking an interest in the freckle on my knee. "And I love how you never once tried to change me, but like me just as I am." I tilt my head, the corner of my lips curving. "Even when I'm riding a racist bully in blue Crocs like a prize bull at a rodeo in aisle five."

"*Especially* when you're riding a racist bully in blue Crocs like a prize bull in aisle five."

That earns him a smile, but it fades when I continue. "But you *hurt* me when you left today."

His mouth flattens. "I know."

"And even now, after understanding why you freaked out the way you did, though I can empathize with it, the fact that running away was your first reaction really fucking stings. Especially when I was so happy. Like I finally found what I was meant to do."

"Rose..." He looks lost like he doesn't know what to say.

"You know my parents died, but I never told you about how they left me long before the car crash." I slide to my side, my hip resting on the carpet in front of the window. "I grew up watching my parents leave. My dad, being on the racing circuit, mostly left for work."

Vance opens his mouth, but I hold up a hand, knowing what he's going to ask.

"This isn't about you being an astronaut and flying into space for months at a time. I know the difference between leaving for work and leaving for other, more selfish reasons."

Vance's shoulders drop, and he lets out a sigh of relief.

"But my dad leaving to chase my mother, that was selfish. Mom made it very obvious she wanted to be anywhere else than with me. No matter how large the mansion or spending account. She was gone more than she was here, and instead of staying beside me, my father ran after her. I was always left."

My body, heart, and soul feel deflated after confessing that, but instead of hiding it behind my usual sarcasm, I stare Vance directly in the eyes, letting him see all my pain. "You need to know that I *refuse* to live the rest of my life worried about that happening with someone else I love. And I definitely won't have my kid feel that way either."

"*Our* kid." Vance grabs my hand. "And they won't feel unwanted because they aren't. Promise."

Whisps of hair that have fallen out of my top-knot swish back and forth as I shake off his words. "I'm not sure you get it.

I'm not settling for less than everything. And if you can't give me everything then I don't want anything."

"Okay." Neck muscles tighten as he sets his jaw. "Then tell me what everything is."

I drop my other hand over the one of his holding mine. "I want a *family*." I press down, trying to imbue the word with everything it means to me.

"I want that too."

I snort and pull my hands back, waving him away. "See, you say that *now*, but if we do this, you need to know I'm going to go *all* in." Better to know now than later, I decide to let him in on my dreams, see if he can handle everything.

Vance frowns. "What's all in?"

I sigh, running a hand through my hair, stopping when I remember it's tied up. "For starters, I'm buying a house. A house in a good school district with a big yard, and maybe even a white picket fence."

"I'll call a realtor tomorrow."

I narrow my eyes at his quick response. "It needs to be two story, with room to grow into but not a new build. Something with projects. Something Pinterest worthy."

His nostrils flare, but he nods.

Thinking I have him on the ropes, I add to it. "And a big tree out back for a swing and a spot where you'll barbecue every Sunday."

This time the nod comes more easily. "I'm Texan. I love barbecue."

I shift up on my knees, warming up to the topic. "And room for a pool, but not actually have a pool because pools are dangerous for little kids."

"Agreed."

"And when we *do* have a pool, you'll have to host lots of

neighbor get-togethers so we can vet all our kids' friends to make sure they aren't assholes."

His eyebrows jump. "Kids?" he asks, elongating the s.

"Yes." I slap my hand down on the sill. "Plural. As in more than one." I eye him, waiting for a fight. "I'm not having an only child."

Instead of rising to the bait, Vance smiles. "Sounds great. More cousins for Jase and Jacob."

I sink back on my heels, my heart melting a little, thinking of my two feminist warriors holding my child's hands while they toddle around Helen's dining table at next year's Thanksgiving.

"And the house needs an attached garage so you won't get caught in the Texas weather while unpacking groceries from your new minivan."

I start, needing a moment to recognize he's adding to my dream. "Perfect. I love it." My hands clap together.

I barely notice his chest puffing out, our future taking on a life of its own in my mind's eye. "I want a Labrador."

He considers this. "Labradors are smart. We should probably get two."

I drop my hands, which have been gesticulating wildly, to my waist, considering him and if he's being serious or not.

But his expression remains level, so I change the image in my mind to two dogs. "Yeah, two dogs would be better."

He smiles.

"And I'm going to be super extra about this mom thing." I get serious again, poking myself in the chest, nearly taking out a nipple. "I'm going to join all the mom groups, facilitate multiple play dates, volunteer at all the schools, and be a contributing member of the PTA." I raise my hand to strike that last thought. "No, fuck that. I'm going to *run* the goddamn PTA."

"You'll be a phenomenal president."

My chest feels fit to burst. "And every night we're going to sit down and eat dinner as a family."

His eyes get soft. "I like that idea."

Carefully, I slide my hand over his hand on the sill, trying to calm down my excitement so I can choose my words wisely. "And you are going to do *amazing* things in space and be a father whose kids will not only love but be so freaking proud of."

His lips press tight like he's trying to hold back his emotions.

Pressing in closer, I touch my palm to his cheek, my fingertips grazing the hair curved around his ear. "And our kids will tell everyone how their dad's an astronaut then make you call down from the space station so they can show you off to their friends."

He clears his throat. "The friends we previously vetted to make sure they're not assholes."

I close my eyes, his words music to my ears. "Exactly."

When I open them, we stare at each other, smiling, all the reasons why we love each other crystal clear in this moment.

But beneath the surface, not quite yet water under the bridge, are reasons for not letting him in.

At least not through the window. Not tonight.

As if reading my thoughts, Vance lets go of my hand. "You better get some rest, okay?" He sniffs. "I'll see you at the doctor's tomorrow."

Though I know that's the smart thing to do, I'm still reluctant for him to go.

"Maybe..." I bite my lip. "Maybe you should come in?"

I can see his internal debate, the desire to say yes, but, stronger than me, Vance shakes his head. "Thank you, but no." He rises, kissing my cheek, lowering back to his perch when the ladder creaks. "Let me work on giving you and the baby everything first, okay?"

He's off to a good start with that answer.

"Okay."

He gives me one last eye-crinkling grin before dropping a foot one rung down on the ladder.

Reaching up to grab the window sash, I pause. Before Vance gets any lower, I lean out the window, angling my neck to kiss him. It's quick. Just a peck that touches the upper right side of his mouth. More stubble than lip. But it does wonderful things to my hoo ha.

And my heart.

TWENTY-SIX

JOINT OPERATIONS PLANNING

Vance

"SHALL WE TAKE A LOOK?"

My eyes remain on the perforated ceiling tile, only dropping down every few seconds to make sure Rose is okay. Up, down. That's it.

I don't know why, but it's like a house of mirrors in here, with one hanging across from me and another behind, making every angle of the room visually accessible.

And after seeing Rose slide her naked butt down to the edge of an exam table *inches* from the gynecologist's face, then put her feet in stirrups with her knees splayed with only a thin paper sheet to cover her all so the doctor can stick a large metal speculum that actually *cranks* into her vagina so that she can *then* insert a pair of scissor forceps to remove a shifted, and therefore ineffective, birth control device, I've learned the only safe place is up.

If I ever complain about my yearly turn-and-cough exam again, I won't consider myself any kind of man.

"This shouldn't hurt." Dr. Barrios rolls her stool over to the side and grabs what looks like a long white dildo attached to a computer on wheels. "But it might be a bit uncomfortable since I just removed the IUD." The thing is at least twelve inches long with a slightly bulbous head.

I'm vaguely threatened.

Rose must think the same 'cause she snickers.

The dildo, which is some sort of sonogram tool, gets covered with a plastic sleeve and coated in lube.

No joke.

Rose shifts on the paper when the doctor probes her while I hold her hand, which is all I've been able to do since we entered the room. I get it why women always joke about men being useless.

Whomp, whomp, whomp sounds from the machine.

Rose gasps.

Whomp, whomp, whomp.

I chance a glance at the doctor. "Is that...?"

"The heartbeat?" Dr. Barrios nods with a small grin at our expressions. "Yes, it is." She holds up her watch arm, probably counting the beats per second.

Pinpricks of light twinkle at the edge of my vision. I've been holding my breath, waiting for the verdict.

"One hundred and twelve." The doctor's smile grows wider. "Perfect."

Rose and I both slump forward. I squeeze her hand, sharing a look of relief.

The computer screen divides into four quadrants as the doctor clicks the dildo still inside Rose. "There it is." Dr. Barrios points with her non-dildo holding hand to the screen.

Rose frowns at the dark circles in each of the four photos. "That blob?" Her disappointment is cute.

"Yes, it's too early for what you're probably thinking—the

head, arms, and legs aren't discernible yet." She pulls her arm back, the sonogram wand sliding out and glistening in the light.

My eyes snap to the ceiling again.

"However"—out of the corner of my eye, I see the doctor point to the white static surrounding the darker shape—"this is the uterus, and that 'blob' is in the perfect position to grow into a healthy baby."

I lower my eyes down to Rose, who's beaming.

"But then again, not much of a surprise seeing as it would take a real fighter to get past a condom *and* IUD. Even if the IUD had partially slipped into the cervix."

I squeeze Rose's hand, feeling a ridiculous sense of pride at the doctor's words. Rose must pick up on it because she rolls her eyes at me. But she's still smiling when she does it.

When Dr. Barrios unsheathes the sonogram wand and puts it back in place by the monitor, I feel more confident about looking directly at the screen. After washing her hands, she pulls herself up to the sonogram machine again. "Let's get a few measurements, shall we?" A few clicks, this time with a mouse and keyboard, and small white cross hatches surround the smaller circle on the screen. Our baby.

"Twenty-one millimeters puts you at about seven weeks." With a press of a button, the four pictures print out as if from a large, slightly pornographic, Polaroid camera.

She hands the pictures to Rose, who gazes at them unblinkingly.

Dr. Barrios rolls back and grabs her iPhone off the counter. "So according to my good old pregnancy calculator"—she holds up the phone and wiggles it before tapping on it—"that puts your due date at August eighth."

August eighth. Fuck.

I try for nonchalance. "How accurate is that?"

"Well, seeing as we don't know when the IUD shifted or

because of her IUD the last true menstrual cycle, it isn't exact." She shrugs. "And, of course, some babies like to come early and some like to come late, but at this point, and with an intravaginal sonogram, August eighth should be accurate give or take two weeks on either end." She scrolls on her phone. "August twenty-second if the baby is running late and July—"

"Twentieth," I finish for her. The date engrained in my head and circled on my calendar.

Rose looks up from the sonogram pictures. Sensing something's wrong from my expression, she frowns. "What's wrong?"

"Ah..." I stall, trying to figure out how to word this without making her upset. But I must take too much time to think because Rose goes into full panic mode.

"Is it the conception date?" Her voice rapid fire. "Because that would put it around the time of the wedding. We were together then." Throwing a leg out of a stirrup, she nearly karate kicks Dr. Barrios across the face as she swings it over, spinning her butt on the exam table to face me. "This is your kid, Vance. I swear it."

"Rose." Placing both hands on her shoulders, I pull us together, our foreheads almost touching. "I am *one hundred* and fifty percent positive this is my baby. I have never, not once, doubted that."

She nods fast, swallowing. "Okay, yeah, good."

Even though I'm worried about her reaction, I continue to hold her eyes. "It's just that July twentieth is the day of my flight."

Understanding dawns, her eyes and mouth expanding. "Oh."

"Which means I'm scheduled to be in Moscow *at least* two weeks beforehand, if not more."

"Oh," she says again, and this time her nod's slow. "I see."

"In another six or seven weeks, I should be able to

doublecheck the due date for more accuracy," the doctor offers, rolling her chair back and standing. "Maybe the baby is measuring small today but—"

"No." I don't want to give Rose false hope. "The first time we had sex was the first Saturday of November. So the due date makes sense. If anything, it would be later, not earlier."

"Ah." She pauses, letting that sink in, then looks at Rose. "In that case your next appointment won't be for another four weeks, and you can schedule it today when you check out or call when you're ready."

"Thank you," Rose says softly, staring at my chest.

"Yes, thank you, Doctor." My hands still rest on Rose's shoulders.

She washes her hands again and leaves us to discuss things.

"I've always hated math," Rose finally says, raising her head. She's smiling, but it doesn't quite reach her eyes. "I always get it wrong."

"This is my fault. I don't think I told you when the flight date was, but *I* knew. I just..." I drop my hands expelling a large breath. "I just didn't put two and two together." I fist my hair and pull, angry at my brain. "I *should've*, though."

Rose takes a smaller breath and sits up, looking completely composed. "It's okay." She pats my shoulder and slides off the table. "I'm not mad."

I back up so she can retrieve her clothes.

Stepping into her panties, she catches my dubious look. "Your flight was scheduled long before this pregnancy happened. So really, it's okay. *I'll* be okay."

"Well, *I'm* not okay." I drop my head to the exam table. "Day one of giving you everything and I've already let you down."

"Aw."

Still resting on the table, I turn my head at her sympathetic tone, catching a glimpse of her black and white checked panties as she pulls up her denim shorts.

"Remember. I know the difference between leaving for yourself and leaving for work." Buttoning her jeans, she slides her bare feet into her sandals. Her toenails are painted blue.

I wonder if she's hoping our blob is a boy.

"And besides," Rose continues, "neither Jules nor Jackie are going with you on that flight, so they'll be here. And Trish." She snorts. "And let's not forget my brothers."

I do not look forward to telling Holt and Flynn I won't be here when their little sister goes into labor.

She bends down to me, still hunched over and depressed, and rubs my back. "I'm going to have plenty of people to choose from to be in the delivery room with me."

Rose is taking the news better than I thought. Much better than me. Which should be a good thing, but it's not.

I've always known going into space was a tradeoff. I get to see and experience wonders that very few in the world get to see and do. I've already missed birthdays, weddings, and a lot of my nephews' milestones. But I knew the people I wasn't there for had others around them to fill the void I left.

But this is Rose. The woman I love. Giving birth to our baby. Sure, one or all of her friends and family can fill in for me, help make sure Rose isn't alone during delivery—but who's going to fill my void?

"I'm not sure if this helps"—Rose continues to rub my back —"but just knowing you're upset about not being here for the birth makes *me* feel better."

I snort, my cheek sliding off the leather cushioned table. "I'm so happy my pain gives you pleasure."

When I lean back, Rose sits on my lap. "I'm helpful like that."

I hug her, each of us resting our chins on the other's shoulder.

And just when I think I'm going to have to just suck it up and convince myself that if Rose is okay with me missing the delivery, then I need to find a way to be okay with it too, I catch sight of her eyes in the mirror behind the table.

And the one tear that falls.

TWENTY-SEVEN

#SCHNAPPSANDDIAMONDS

Rose

"It's between the house in Trish and Ian's neighborhood and the one in Taylor Lake Village."

Vance shuffles the printouts of all the realtor listings he's compiled over the past five days to show his sister while I continue to kick butt in Fortnite.

"This is the one in Trish's neighborhood. It's a large two-story in an established neighborhood. It's priced to sell. They could be trying to drum up multiple offers, though."

Brit squints at the picture. "What's that?"

Vance turns the page to face him. "That's the house from an aerial view."

"I get it's a bird's eye view, but what is *that* in the picture?" She taps the page.

"The neighbor's fountain." He sighs. "For some reason, the house two doors down put in this ugly, ornate Italian fountain in front of their red brick colonial house." He shakes his head, already sounding like a disgruntled suburbanite concerned with degrading house prices.

Brit's eyes look a little heavy from her spiked hot chocolate. "Yeah, I don't even think Pinterest has anything that could make that look less ugly."

Vance snorts and flips the page. "And this is the one in Taylor Lakes."

I listen to Vance talk location and price while sitting on the floor between his legs as he sits behind me on the couch.

Brittany's house in nearby League City is wonderful. In the living room, the more family oriented of her six trees is full of hand-made ornaments the kids made over the years. Lots of googly eyes, pipe cleaners, and popsicle sticks.

I'd look for a house nearby, but League City is on the other side of Clear Lake, a tad farther than I'd like to be from the ranch, NASA, and my friends.

We've been here since noon, after Vance and I had our own Christmas morning together. The first of many.

Elvis Presley's Christmas album is playing in the background, reminding me of the horde of impersonators from Whiskey River that I never found out more about. I really should ask Mike about it and his new client. See if there's a connection.

"You know Mom's vote will be Taylor Lake Village." Brit takes a sip of her drink, smacking her lips. "It's only two minutes away from her."

"Yeah, but she's already talking about selling this place and downsizing, so I'm not sure that matters." He doesn't sound the least bit sad about Helen wanting to sell their old family home. I thought maybe he'd be sad about it, but he seems more upset about Helen's upcoming date with John. "But it is close to Flynn and Jackie."

I love how he wouldn't mind living close to my Neanderthal brother.

Tilting my head back, I read all the notes Vance made on each listing. And all the lists of possible baby names doodled in the margins.

He doesn't know yet, but I'm totally saving those no matter which house we choose.

Hashtag adorable.

"Aunt Rose, you're not paying attention!" Jacob shouts to hear himself over his new headphones. The ones I got him. He's stabbing at the buttons on his controller in a panic.

"Dang, sorry, kid." But I'm not fast enough, and both our characters die.

"Aw, man." Jacob's pout face is cute.

"My turn!" Jase slides down off the recliner and snatches his brother's controller.

Jacob opens his mouth, probably to argue, but I rush in with the save. "Here, have mine." I hold my controller to him. "I'm taking a break."

Jase's shoulder's slump. "Crap. Now we're really going to lose."

I ruffle his hair. "Gotta learn sometime, kid."

I'm suddenly grabbed from behind and lifted into the air by my armpits. "Wh—!"

"There." Vance settles me on his lap.

Brit crinkles her nose. "Ew, gross. Get a room." Her whine is ruined when she breaks into a large smile.

"We're trying to get a house," Vance reminds her, tapping the page on her lap. "So help me figure out which one is more Pinterest worthy." He gives me side-eye. "It's an important factor in the decision process."

I try, and fail, to hold back my smirk.

Vance settles me against him, resting his chin on my

shoulder and wrapping his right arm around me. His hand curves around his new favorite place to touch—my stomach.

I shimmy into him, sighing happily. And I'm not just happy with my newfound love of PDA. I'm just really fucking happy.

And have been every day since our doctor appointment.

Vance and I are together. Like, legit together.

After the doctor appointment, we hung the sonogram pictures on my fridge. Then went grocery shopping. And that evening, and every evening since, we've eaten dinner together at my kitchen table.

At bedtime, we stand next to each other in front of the bathroom vanity and brush our teeth.

And every morning he kisses me good-bye before leaving for work.

I'm living the dream.

"Shouldn't you be planning a wedding first?" Brit nods to Vance's hand on my abdomen while turning her new diamond studs Matt got her. "I thought that would be a priority."

"We'll get there." I shrug, unconcerned. And, surprisingly, I'm not.

Vance wasn't joking when he told me he was going all in with me. He's already moved into my penthouse even though it's a much longer commute for him. When he wasn't helping me decorate the new twelve-foot, multi-colored Christmas tree he bought for us as a cohabitation present, he's been helping sort through the massive amounts of baby stuff still piled everywhere.

Some purchases we're keeping, others we're donating. Because, according to Vance, the whole point of a pack 'n play is that you can pack it and take it with you wherever you go. So not every person I know needs to have one stocked in their closet for when the baby and I visit.

Which is fine. Because it means the women's shelter I

usually donate to gets even more goodies this year *and* all this sorting enables Vance to "shop" for baby stuff with me by picking out his favorites from what's already there.

Hashtag win win.

On top of that, he's seen the therapist at NASA twice this week. And even though he says it was the talk with his mom and sister that really helped him see straight, he decided to keep going just to make sure he's the best he can be for both me and the baby.

I may have blamed hormones on the tears I cried after he told me that. And Vance may have pretended he believed me.

I wiggle my fingers, enjoying how the Christmas lights from the tree by the TV play off the cushion cut diamond and all its surrounding pink pave ones. It's classic, with a twist.

Hashtag just like me.

Brit grabs my hand and smiles over my ring with me. "Just as long as you get hitched before my niece is born."

Vance rubs my stomach. "We won't know if it's a boy or a girl for a few more weeks."

"No, it's *definitely* a girl." Brit takes another big sip of her drink, and I wonder just how much peppermint schnapps she poured in to be this tipsy after one mug. "If God gave me boys, it's only fair you get girls."

I smile when Brit hiccups. "Not exactly sure that's how it works."

"Boy or girl, doesn't matter to me." Vance kisses my neck, causing more goosebumps to pop. "As long as the baby is healthy, then everything is good."

Raising my arm, I wrap it around his neck in a hug.

Yes, everything *is* good. Vance has given or has plans to give me everything I told him I wanted.

"I can't believe you're going to be in space though." Brit

downs the rest of her drink, a chocolate mustache on her lip. "Can I call dibs on being in the delivery room?"

Well, almost everything I wanted.

I catch myself frowning and shake it off with a large smile. "You'll have to put your name in the hat with everyone else."

Helen walks in from the kitchen, having spent most of the afternoon oooh-ing and aah-ing over the mixer I glitter-bombed for Brittany. Looks like I have another DIY project in the future. "I can't believe you're actually having a lottery drawing to see who's going to help you deliver my grandbaby."

I shrug, not knowing what else to say.

When I pulled up my panties in the doctor's office after finding out the due date coincided with Vance's flight, I made myself pull up my metaphoric big girl panties too.

So what if the father of my baby won't even be on Earth during delivery?

So what if, as a first time mom, I'll have to figure out breast-feeding, sleep training and deal with newborn vaccinations all on my own?

I'm Rose West. I got this.

"I like this one." Brit's speech slurs. "Very Pinterest worthy." She hands me the house in Trish's neighborhood. The one with the fountain neighbor.

It's larger than I originally wanted. But Vance convinced me that if I wanted more than two kids and a glitter room, we should probably increase our square footage. It's situated on the north side of NASA, almost in the middle of Flynn and Holt.

Plus, it's right across the road from Trish. And out of all the girls, I'm pretty sure she's going to be the first to get knocked up. Our kids could grow up together. Ride the bus together.

I study the white brick house, imagining all the personal touches I could make to this house to make it a home. *Our* home.

In just a few short days, I've gone from sleeping alone in my childhood bedroom to being in a committed relationship with a man who loves me and whom I love. A man who, now that he's put a ring on it, will be my dinner companion for life. Plus, I'm about to purchase a place where we will raise our baby —*together*. A place where we will all feel loved and wanted.

A place I can make special with help from Pinterest.

It might not be everything, but it's enough.

I drop my ring hand over Vance's, thinking about how love changes things. Because now, confident in Vance's love, of our commitment, the importance of getting everything I want quickly turned into wanting to get everything *he* wants too.

This upcoming mission means a lot to Vance. His whole career has been focused on getting to this moment. It's what he's always wanted.

So I'll take one for the team, as it were. A team is like a family, after all. And that's exactly what Vance, the blob in my uterus, and I are—a family.

"I'll tell the realtor to put an offer on it." I hold up the listing in my hand. "Cash. That should stop the bidding war."

"Whoa." Vance shifts me on his lap, half turning me so he can see my face. "I can't let you do that."

"Let me?" The tone and my one raised eyebrow has him backtracking.

Immediately he holds up his hands. "That's not what I meant."

"Uh-huh." I glance at the boys still absorbed in their game. "Just be glad I successfully wrestled for and won those headphones, otherwise if the boys had heard what you said, you'd be done for."

The back door slams, and Matt walks in, pulling off an oven mitt. Pinterest had a recipe for smoked brisket that Brit thought would go great with her mother's tamales, so the poor guy has been up even before his sons, stoking the fire, trying to maintain an even temperature all in the name of love and Pinterest.

"Oooh, Vance is in trouble," Brit sings, then giggles.

"What did Vance do now?" Matt leans over and kisses his wife. His eyebrows jump when he gets a whiff of schnapps.

I pretend to be mad. "He said he won't *let* me buy a house."

"Hey, man." Matt glances at his sons. "Let's not get the feminist parade started again, okay?"

"I just meant"—Vance dips his head forward—"I'd feel bad you doing that by yourself. I don't have that kind of cash. But if we put in a down payment and got a mortgage, we could split the cost, no problem."

"Then we might not get the house." I shake the listing in his face. "I want this house."

He frowns, and I can tell he wants to argue, but he also doesn't want to take the chance of me not getting what I want. He's so cute.

I drop the paper and lean into him, lifting my shoulders to bring my boobs, now slightly bigger from pregnancy, to his attention. "Just think of it as my Christmas present to you."

He talks to my chest. "You already got me a car."

I did. A gold one. Jackie is already jealous of the C7 Corvette.

I shrug, the move also doing good things for boobs. "It's a perk of having knocked up a billionaire."

Brit blows a raspberry at us, distracting Vance from my ta-tas. "Damn it, I knew I should've gotten you to elope with me. I could use a sugar mama."

"Again." Matt's resigned voice matches his expression. "Thanks."

Brit pats Matt's hand. Or tries to—she ends up patting the oven mitt he's holding instead. "There, there."

"Okay." Vance lifts me again, this time setting me beside

him. "I'll agree to you buying the house as a Christmas present for me if *you* agree not to argue about *my* Christmas present."

"My ring?" I hold up my hand. "I'd never argue about this. I love it."

He kisses my cheek. "I'm glad, Rosie-girl, but I was talking about the second Christmas present I got you." Vance pulls something out from behind him and hands it to me.

It looks like one of those envelopes you get when you purchase a gift card. "What's this?"

"It's not a house, but I'm hoping you like it."

Tilting my head, I study him. "So you're telling me that if I accept this"—I hold up the envelope—"you won't complain if I buy the house for us?"

Vance nods. "Correct."

This seems too easy. But thinking it's probably a gift card to some sex shop or some other store he thinks will embarrass me, I nod. "Deal."

"All right then." He gestures at my hand. "Have at it."

Not a gracious gift opener, I tear the flap of the envelope off instead of lifting it, revealing a three by two piece of white card stock with the NASA logo on it. "A business card?"

Vance's knee bounces. "Read it."

"Vance Lonan Bodaway, chief astronaut." Chief? Where have I—

"Chief astronaut?" Matt asks. "What's that?"

"My new job title," Vance answers, eyes still on me. "Took over from Luke. Effective immediately."

A rush of emotion hits me when I remember where I've heard that title before, and I fall back against the couch. My heart thumps, remembering what Jules said about her friend Luke, the tall guy at the wedding. How he wasn't going on any missions right now because he's in charge of all the flight rotations for the other astronauts. How she'd rather be caught dead than take that desk job, even if it was temporary. "What did you do?" I choke out the words, it suddenly hard for me to talk.

"Now remember," Vance says, leaning away from me as if bracing for impact, "you said you wouldn't argue."

"But—but your flight." I look at him, then the card, then at Helen, the boys, then back at the card. "You..."

"There will be other flights. And I'll be on them. Just not right now."

My eyes land on his, and I see his conviction. His commitment to me and our new family.

He taps the card in my hand. "This isn't about me being afraid to fly up while you're here with our child. It's about me wanting to be here so I don't miss out on helping you bring our child into the world." His fingers wrap around my hand. "Though, honestly, even after one doctor's visit, it's pretty apparent that the sum of all my help is me just holding your hand."

"Useless," Brit mutters.

"But—"

"No arguing. That was the deal, remember." And with a quick peck on my cheek, he stands, grabbing the oven mitt from Matt. "Come on, let's go check on the brisket. I have barbecue skills to practice." He takes a step to leave but stops, turning back to me. "Oh, here." He pulls his phone out of his pocket and tosses it to me. "You might want to call the realtor. Even with it being Christmas, I don't think they'll mind taking a call if it means a cash commission." He winks. "A deal's a deal, right?"

With that, he finger guns me and leaves.

The bastard stole my move.

Hashtag best Christmas ever.

EPILOGUE

SINGULARITY

Rose

I'M WEARING WHITE.

Tradition might demand that I wear color, or ivory at the very least, since my uterus blob is now a discernible baby bump, but I look good in white.

Plus, the deep-V neckline of my white jumpsuit makes my pregnancy-enhanced boobs look legit amaze-balls.

And since my soon-to-be nephews say that having a bride wear white on her wedding days is an archaic tradition that glorifies defining a woman's worth based on her level of chastity and not her person—I had *all* the women wear white today.

Hashtag stick it to the man.

"I can't believe my sister is getting married in a barn." Holt glares through the front window of the ranch house at the structure in question, shaking his head in dismay.

"Hey." I elbow him in the ribs. "Our *brother* got married in that barn not all that long ago."

"Yeah, what's wrong with a barn?" Flynn, sitting on the steps, frowns at our older, grumpy brother. We're waiting for Jules to text Holt and give the three of us the all-clear to enter.

Holt rubs his side. "That was different. You and Jackie had a professional wedding planner who directed a team of fifty to transform the barn into a glamorous venue." He continues to stare out the window, watching the last guests go inside. "All Rose had us do was sweep."

"And let Brittany decorate," I add, wondering how many Pinterest boards she made in preparation. "You haven't seen what that woman can do. I bet it looks freaking majestic."

"Why did you choose the back storage area and not the larger area where the stalls are, anyway?" Flynn stands, straightening his tux. "Did you not want us to have to move the horses again?"

The memory of Vance kissing my hoo-ha behind the reception curtains makes me shiver. "Think real hard about whether or not you two want to know the answer to that last question. Because as your sister, I'm thinking this might be a case of ignorance is bliss."

"Jesus." Flynn rubs a hand down his face.

Holt's phone buzzes. "Everyone's seated." He pockets it and smooths down the lapels of his tux.

I clap my hands. "Time to go."

Holt holds out his arm. "You ready?"

"You betcha." I thread my arm through his.

"'Cause you don't have to get married, you know. We can—"

"Holt." I lower my head, staring him in the eyes. "I'm getting married. Right now."

He holds my gaze for a second, then sighs. "Fine."

Flynn snickers. As well as he's been able to adapt to all the changes in my life these past few months, Holt... has not.

He's afraid I'm being pressured into marriage. After Vance and I got engaged on Christmas, I was so busy buying a house, adopting two dogs, and enjoying the horrified glances I get every Sunday after pole dancing class when I run errands to Home Depot and Lowes for all my new house projects still dressed up in my finest stripper apparel and glitter, the multicolored spandex showcasing my baby bump, that I didn't have time to plan a wedding.

Honestly, I never dreamed of a wedding when I was a little girl. I dreamed of family.

Then Vance sat me down after one of his therapy sessions, asking if I still didn't trust him. Apparently, he had taken my lack of wedding interest as a sign I hadn't forgiven him for leaving me on the stripper stage after I told him I was preggers.

Could've knocked me down with a feather. I mean, I accepted his ring. We cohabitate. We have *dogs*.

But it turns out Vance was sensitive to the fact that I wasn't in a hurry to get hitched.

Took me promising to get married ASAP and a round of lotus to get him to stop pouting.

Flynn opens the front door. "Stop getting your tux in a bunch, Holt. We have a bride to give away." He takes my other arm, and together, all three of us walk down the porch steps and across the drive to the barn.

Even with every guest in the barn and no one around to see them, Holt and Flynn strut with their chests puffed out. They were pretty touched when I asked them to walk me down the aisle. Or, you know, the barn hallway.

Holt had teared up again. He's such a softie.

I can't wait to see what he does when he holds his niece for the first time.

Much to Brit's amusement, her drunken Christmas prediction was right. Vance and I are having a girl.

Citali (Kit-tah-lee). It means star.

The music wafts out of the barn—instrumental and soothing.

We step inside, but instead of going left, we go right, toward the back storage room.

From this angle, I see Myra next to Angela, sitting behind Helen and John—my old counselor and her new boyfriend.

Another step and Jackie, Trish, and Jules are front row, each wearing whatever they wanted as long as it's white. How Jules found white leather pants and motorcycle boots is beyond me, but she manages to make them look badass and elegant. Jackie's white Converse clad foot bounces like a jack rabbit in the aisle, her eyes lighting up behind her glasses when she sees me. (Or, most likely, Flynn.) Trish, the most traditionally dressed in a white cocktail dress, breaks the dress code with scarlet platform heels.

At the threshold, the full impact of the magical fairyland Brit created with thousands of tiny lights on thin wires that she tacked on nearly every inch of wall and ceiling surface hits me.

And then I meet Vance's eyes. His dark, gorgeous eyes with the crinkles that catapulted us to where we are now. Full circle from the barnyard tryst to our wedding vows. Spoken right where he's standing now. In the exact spot he first put his lips on mine. After first kissing my hoo-ha.

As one, Holt and Flynn step forward, only to be jerked back when my feet remain planted.

"Are we running?" Holt asks out the corner of his mouth.

I pull my arm out of his and roll my eyes. "No, we aren't running."

There's a bit of a murmur as I reach my hand into my cleavage and pull out a small remote. With a click, the music changes. I thread my arm back through Holt's as a recognizable guitar intro starts.

Vance's eyes widen.

When Paul McCartney sings about a blackbird, I step toward him.

He knew where we were getting married. He knew about my brothers walking me down the aisle. He even knew about Brit's plans to decorate.

He didn't know about the song.

Tears form in the eyes I love so much as I get closer. One falling as I reach him.

My brothers take turns to buss a kiss on my cheeks, but my eyes never leave Vance's.

"Blackbird," he whispers when it's just us and Ian, our Internet-ordained officiant.

Reaching up, I cradle Vance's cheek, wiping his tear away with my thumb. "Thought it would be nice if your father could join us today."

"Yeah." Vance kisses my palm. "He's here."

Ian steps forward. "We are gathered here..."

We pledge to love and honor each other in front of our family and friends. All of them family, really. Family we were born to, family we chose.

We exchange rings, our hands resting on my baby bump when we're finished.

Family we made.

"I now pronounce you husband and wife." Ian gives us a self-satisfied smile as he looks at Vance and then me. "You may kiss the bride."

"Come on, old man." I lift both arms, wrapping them around his neck. "Pucker up." His eyes move from my eyes to my boobs and then to my lips.

"Sure thing, Rosie-girl."

We kiss.

Everyone cheers.
I press the remote again.
Glitter bombs explode.
Hashtag happily ever after.

BONUS EPILOGUE

Want to see how Rose and Vance settle into married life six year down the road? Get a glimpse to what the other girls are up to?

Go to www.SaraLHudson.com for the Bonus Epilogue!
You'll also be signed up for my newsletter, Sara's Sheet, and get access to updates, bonus content, sweet deals on romance novels and more!

KEEP READING to see a sneak peak into my brand new Moore to Love series— *All Little Moore Action.*

An Elvis loving red head, a gold-hearted playboy and a hairless cat walk into a luxury department store...

Chapter One

Chase

My pussy is anti-social.

Don't be crass. I mean my pussy cat.

He's a sphynx, so basically a hairless pussy. Yeah, I know. There are a lot of jokes there. They're all funny. But that isn't the point.

Right now, the point is I'm sitting on a bench in Central Park watching all these beard-growing, man-bun douchebags score with the ladies all thanks to their playful puppies jogging up to everything with boobs. Boobs encased in wonderfully tight and revealing spandex. And I'm stuck with a hairless cat that refuses to budge from under my hoodie.

Yes, I put my cat under my hoodie. What would you do with a hairless cat on a cool spring morning? Let him freeze his hairless balls off? You're heartless.

Anyway.

You might be wondering what a thirty-five-year-old heterosexual man is doing with a hairless cat. I wonder that every morning when I wake up to his wrinkly butt in my face at the crack of dawn.

Pun intended.

Truthfully, he's my ex-girlfriend's cat. Well, I got him for her 'cause she was crazy allergic to everything. Ownership had been iffy until she gave me an ultimatum—marriage or it's over. I chose over.

She tried to backpedal real quick, but I'd also just found out she'd been banging my business partner. When confronted, she broke down, saying I'd forced her to cheat on me. That I had commitment issues. Commitment issues? Hello? I bought you a cat. Also, I hadn't been the one with a side piece. And my business partner? When you stoop that low, you better sure as shit know that I'm taking said cat. Hairless or not.

So now here I am, trying my hand at rebounding with Mike Hunt, the sphynx.

See what I did there? Yeah, I know. Not very mature. But considering my ex had named him Fluffy, which I thought demeaning rather than ironic, I think Mike Hunt is an excellent upgrade.

I hunch over and talk to the bulge under my hoodie. This causes a few passersby to give me the side-eye. Whatever, keep jogging, man-buns.

"Listen, Mikey. You're not doing either of us any favors right now." The wrinkly ball of skin burrows deeper. "Okay, you asked for it." I fish my phone out of my back pocket and start an online search for cat sweaters. This is what my life has come to. Buying sweaters for hairless pussies.

God, that's depressing.

But just as I'm about to PayPal an entire wardrobe for Mr. Hunt here, my phone vibrates and my father's name flashes on the screen.

Not "Dad" or "Father", but his legit, legal name, Stanley W. Moore. That should give you some clue as to how close we are. Or aren't, as it were.

Since my outing today seems to be a lost cause for all types of pussy, I slide my thumb right and answer. "Stan."

"Chase."

"To what do I owe the pleasure of your cheerfulness on this fine spring morning?"

"Jesus."

I love riling the old man. It's the only thing he's ever let me know I'm truly good at. Gifted even.

"Shareholders' meeting at noon today," he barks into my ear. It's the same tone he's used with me since I was a kid. Since I accidentally (on purpose) blew up my science fair project by mixing too much vinegar and baking soda. Since the police brought me home for toilet papering the principal's house. Since I got caught in tenth grade with my hand up Megan Dumphrey's blouse in the janitor's closet. It's even the same tone he used when I graduated high school with a 4.0 GPA, was voted valedictorian, made varsity soccer all four years of high school and went on to graduate at the top of my class at University of Pennsylvania on academic scholarships.

Growing up, I'd quickly learned that no matter the situation, I'd be thought of as the flunky, the spare, the good-time kid. So why not act like it? Way more fun than trying to please the perpetually disgruntled Stanley Winston Moore.

"So, a family lunch?" I muse into the phone. "Considering all the shareholders are family members. Right, Pops?"

I could almost hear his teeth grinding. "You are required to be there."

He says it like if it were up to him I wouldn't be there. Which is probably true. Color me surprised when at eighteen I'd inherited shares in the family company, Moore's, a luxury retailer world-renowned and based in New York. Think Harrods, but American. I love the damn store, even though it was drilled into my head from a young age that it wasn't my destiny. I was the second son. The spare. The just-in-case. They let my younger sister Bess and me know, repeatedly, that our older brother would be given the reins. Bess, because she's a girl. Me, because... well, I'm me. My parents had no choice but to divvy up the shares. My grandfather made sure of that. But control? Hell to the no.

I blow out a quick breath and force a smile into my voice. "I'll be there, Daddy-O."

"Thomas has some information he wants to go over. Try to at least act professional."

Professional like having created a multi-million-dollar app? Like successfully investing in start-ups since I was twenty, without a dime of family money?

But I refuse to take the bait. Instead, I reply cheerfully, "Will do, Stanley."

Dead air. No goodbye.

Nice.

I wish I could say that this type of passive aggressive conversation is unusual between the old man and me. That Stan is normally a friendly, loving father, proud of my accomplishments and always inviting me over for family lunches and golf outings with his cronies.

But if wishes were real, I wouldn't be sitting on a park bench ordering argyle sweaters for Mike Hunt.

———

Bell

Momma had always said there's an Elvis lyric for every situation. And right now, sitting in my lawyer's office, in front of the man representing a thief and my former employee, I can surely feel my temperature rising. Well, *temper* is more like it. And he for sure isn't a hunk of burning love.

Not with more hair on his upper lip than a '70s porn star.

"Listen here, little lady…"

Annnnnd, I zone out. It's either that or strangle the bastard.

Look, I live in Texas. The odds are stacked against me that at some point I'll be referred to as "little lady." If I was lucky, it would have been by a cute, wizened old man playing chess in a rocking chair who means it with dignity and respect. However, luck does not seem to be my friend today.

Reminding myself that lawsuits are serious, even if his has no real foundation, I try to refocus on what the pompous, beer-bellied lawyer across the table is saying. But all I see is his '70s porn 'stache and fake gold Rolex. John, my former employee, is underestimating me if he thinks he'll win his ridiculous countersuit with this ambulance chaser.

"So, if you drop the suit my client will—"

"No."

Porn 'stache blinks. "Excuse me, missy?"

"My name isn't missy and it sure as hell isn't little lady. It's Campbell

King. Ms. King to you. I'm not dropping the lawsuit. And frankly, your client's countersuit is laughable at best. Your client, my ex-employee, is guilty of corporate subterfuge. There are records, emails and security footage." I glance over at my lawyer, Leslie Peterson, who is trying to hide her smirk by looking down and shuffling the stack of evidence in front of her.

"This is simply a misunderstanding. My client assures me that you just didn't know the system in which he was—"

"Trying to take credit for my work and poach clients? Yes, Porn 'stache, I one hundred percent understand the system he was using."

A laugh bursts from Leslie and she tries to hide it with a cough. Shoot, I'd said Porn 'stache out loud. Not very professional. When provoked, I have a tendency to say what's on my mind without much thought. It's a habit I developed after staying quiet one too many times in the past.

But seeing as Porn 'stache isn't a client, has called me little lady *and* missy, and works for my asshole ex-employee, I don't have one fuck to give.

Leslie clears her throat and addresses the 'stache. "On top of which, your client, Mr. John Dudley, who, I may add, didn't even bother to show up at this meeting *he* requested, signed an ironclad agreement not to compete during his two-year contract with King Marketing." Leslie's crisp east coast accent cuts through the room. A clear contradiction to 'stache's and my southern drawls. "So Ms. King's lawsuit will stand. Mr. Dudley will cease his unlawful marketing start-up with King Marketing's client information, which was taken illegally, and he will pay the penalty for his subterfuge against my client's company."

Porn 'stache narrows his eyes. "This is what happens when you let women in business. They make a play for a guy and then get all emotional when he doesn't feel the same way." His cheeks get bigger, his eyes smaller, so I can only assume he's smiling under that overgrown caterpillar on his lip. "Oh yes," he says, looking at me, "Mr.

Dudley told me all about your little crush on him, *Ms. King*." He looks at Leslie, who is no longer smiling. "We could always add sexual harassment to this suit if this is how your client wants to play it."

I choke down a surge of outrage at Porn 'stache's blatant lie, but remain visibly calm. John had been hired as an intern. When my former assistant left on maternity leave, then fell in love with being a stay-at-home mom to her sweet little girl, John applied for her job. As he'd just barely had the necessary qualifications and I'd been in need of an assistant ASAP, I gave him the job. Much to my current dismay. Though he'd always given off a skeevy vibe, it hadn't been until IT made me aware of his illegal activities that I'd fired him.

I take a deep breath through my nose, not wanting to appear *emotional*, as accused. Although, I do have a pretty big emotional need to stab Porn 'stache in his turkey neck with his gold fountain pen.

I stand up and turn to my attorney, whose narrow-eyed expression makes even me want to pee my pants a little. I figure it's time to let her earn her salary. "Leslie, you want to finish this up?"

"With pleasure." She doesn't look at me, keeping her gaze on Porn 'stache, who now squirms in his seat, much to my satisfaction. He has no idea the whoop-ass he just rained down on himself and his client. I was being nice. Leslie doesn't do nice. Best thing I ever did was hire her. Stupidest thing I did was hire John Dudley.

No, I take that back. Stupidest thing I ever did was eight years ago.

Elvis Presley once said, "Those people in New York are not gonna change me none." Even now, with all my current success, I wish I'd had more of the King's wisdom with me in my youth.

Fifteen years ago, I'd trekked clear across the country to the Big Apple, to one of the best business schools in the country. In my six years there I made my parents proud, earning scholarships, winning competitive internships and graduating at the top of my class. I'd foolishly thought all of that had prepared me for the real world.

It took only a few months at my first real job in a major marketing firm to prove me wrong.

I'd felt a lot of things at the time—shame, humiliation, disbelief, hurt. But the one that got me through it, that got me to my current level of success, was anger. I like to think I hadn't come home to Houston with my tail between my legs, but rather with a fire under my ass.

Throwing Porn 'stache a withering look, I gather my briefcase and stride out of the room. Once I clear the conference area, I spot my weasel of an ex-employee flirting with one of 'stache's secretaries. Guy would rather chase tail than show up to his own lawsuit mediation.

I slow my steps as I pass her desk, drawing a questioning glance from the secretary and an arrogant sneer from him. I lean in toward her and say in a whisper that's loud enough for the whole room to hear, "Make sure you're stocked up on penicillin. Otherwise it takes *forever* for it to go away."

Both of their mouths drop open in unison as I continue on to the elevator, humming a happy Elvis tune.

ABOUT ME AND THANKS

Sara L. Hudson is an author and mother driven by anxiety and a perverse sense of humor all while being fueled by coffee and newly acquired ADHD medication.

It's a wonderful, wild ride of a life made possible by her supportive (but cheap) husband and her incredible (but too far away) parents.

The Space Series was my first series and after four full-length novels, one short story and a novella, it's hard to say good-bye.

So I won't.

I still have a lot fun ideas and scenes in my head about all the Space Series couples and the craziness they get into in the future.

I'll make sure to write them and pop them in my newsletter from time to time.

xxx, Sara

www.SaraLHudson.com